NORTHFIELD

This Large Print Book carries the
Seal of Approval of N.A.V.H.

NORTHFIELD

A WESTERN STORY

JOHNNY D. BOGGS

THORNDIKE PRESS

An imprint of Thomson Gale, a part of The Thomson Corporation

Detroit • New York • San Francisco • New Haven, Conn. • Waterville, Maine • London

LIBRARY OF CONGRESS CATALOGING-IN-PUBLICATION DATA

Boggs, Johnny D.
  Northfield : a western story / by Johnny D. Boggs.
    p. cm. — (Thorndike Press large print western)
  ISBN-13: 978-0-7862-9790-0 (alk. paper)
  ISBN-10: 0-7862-9790-5 (alk. paper)
  1. Large type books. I. Title.
PS3552.O4375N67 2007b
813'.54—dc22   2007017969

Published in 2007 by arrangement with Golden West Literary Agency.

Printed in the United States of America on permanent paper
10 9 8 7 6 5 4 3 2 1

For Tyrone Power and Henry Fonda;
Ron Hansen and Max McCoy;
John Newman Edwards
and Jack Koblas;
Red Shuttleworth and W.C. Jameson;
the people of Northfield and Madelia;
and The Friends of the James Farm

PROLOGUE

COLE YOUNGER

Seven minutes . . . seems like seven lifetimes.

"For God's sake, boys, hurry up! They're shooting us all to pieces!"

The words still ring in my head, over the deafening roar of musketry. Over the bullets singing past our heads. Over the hoofs of our horses. Over all of Northfield.

Those words came from my mouth only minutes earlier. Long minutes, though. Think about it — seven minutes ain't nothing. Time it takes a train to cover a little better than two miles. Time it takes me to deal an interesting hand of stud. But those seven minutes that just passed. . . .

Biting back pain, I still picture myself banging on the door of the First National Bank, snapping off shots with my .44 Russian at city folk we figured would have no gumption to stick with a fight.

"For God's sake, come out! It's getting too hot for us!"

By then, I figured it was too late. Knowed it was too late for poor Clell Miller and Bill Chadwell, or whatever his name was, dead on the streets, their souls meeting up with St. Peter. Knowed it was too late for me. And my brothers. That's what I was regretting then, what I still regret now. Bob and Jim have always looked up to me, most times, anyway.

What strikes me, what shames me, what terrifies me ain't the thought of dying, but I see Brother Dick, shaking his head, more than disappointed. Behind him, I can just make out Pa's face. And Ma's. Both of 'em crying. The image humbles this old soul.

I ain't the oldest of us Jackson County Youngers. Brother Dick, he was the good one, the best of us all, the first son of fourteen children, him entering this world six years before me. Three girls come before him, and two after him and before me. Had God been merciful, things might have turned out different for my family. Dick got a gut ailment, though, pained his side something fierce — quick it was, though, so there's some blessing — calling him to Glory when I was but fifteen. Dick's death killed Pa, really. Or would have. But the war come, bringing with it every freebooter who spit on a Missouri man's rights, and I followed my heart, same, me thinks, as Dick would have. Then them murdering sons-of-bitches put three slugs in my daddy in June of '62, tossed his body in a ditch, like trash.

The war — that killed Mama, only there was no blessing to that. Pa and Dick, they didn't suffer none, but Ma, she just wore out, and with cut-throats chasing me because of my loyalties during the war, and all the torment, she just give up. We had moved her to Texas, but I reckon she knowed she was dying, maybe she wanted to die, so she asked for us to take her back to Jackson County, to be near our pa. She joined Pa, been six years now, and how I miss her. I see her crying. I feel shamed, for all the misery I caused her on earth, and now up on those streets of gold.

"Thomas 'Bud' Coleman Younger is a killer," they say. A bushwhacker. A murderer. A robber and black-heart. A soulless guerilla. A man who ain't fit to breathe. Well, let he who is without sin cast the first stone.

Yankees made me an outlaw, a bush-whacker, but I'm just a simple farmer fighting for my family, my home, my honor, my brothers.

I should have looked after 'em.

Thoughts like that haunt me as I ride. My

brother's arm tightens across my stomach, then slips.

"Hold on, Bob!" I cry.

"For God's . . . sake . . . don't . . . leave me." His words come out as he chokes, coughs. He's bad hurt, but he ain't dead . . . yet.

"I ain't leaving you, Bob!" My horse stumbles. No Missouri horse, but I sure can't fault his spirit. Horse has gotten us this far. Bob, riding behind me, almost lets go. He's whimpering now, like he was on the streets back yonder. I ain't got no reins. Ain't got a horn left on the saddle to hold on to. Got nothing but Missouri mettle, and a strong desire to get my brother out of here alive. Somehow.

"For God's . . . sake . . . don't . . . leave me!"

Seven minutes . . . and everything had gone to hell.

"Which way?" Charlie Pitts screams.

"Just ride, damn it!" Dingus shouts back. "Ride or get buried!"

We ride. Six men on five horses. I don't know how long we can hold out.

Now, I've made some mistakes in my thirty-two years. Always owned up to 'em, most of 'em, anyway. What happened at Lawrence back in '63 never should have happened, though nobody — not Rebel, not Yankee, not Redleg or Jayhawker, not Quaker nor freethinker — can ever say I did anything during that raid that should cause me to hang my head. Not in my book, by grab. I wisht it never happened, but the Lord can't damn me for anything I did on that horrible day all them years ago.

That was Kansas, though, and this ain't, not by a damned sight.

We never should have come to Yankeedom. Not now, no matter how bad things kept getting in Missouri. Certainly never should have tried to steal that carpetbagging son-of-a-bitch Silver Spoons Butler's money.

Biggest mistake of my life, coming here. Northfield, Minnesota. Our trail's end, could be, and there ain't nobody to blame but me. I should have known better. Only reason I come along is because of Brother Bob. Stubborn, he is, wouldn't listen to me. Wouldn't hear nothing Jim said, either.

Should have made Bob listen, only he thinks Dingus is cut from the same cloth as Pa, or Captain Quantrill. Should have pounded sense into Bob's head, or just pounded him. He never could whip me. And, Buck, my old pal, I don't know what he was thinking.

That damned Dingus.

He's the one who should have been left dead on the street in Northfield. Not Chadwell. Especially not Clell, as true a friend as they come.

If Dingus wasn't Buck's brother, maybe I would have killed him.

Still, I don't reckon I can fault him. Dingus and me may have our differences, but, like I said, it's me to blame. It's a cross I'll carry to my grave. I'm just praying I ain't buried in a land of Yankees.

CHAPTER ONE:

BILL STILES

Sounded like a damned tent revival meeting. People'll tell you that Bill Stiles ain't a man accustomed to fear. Hell, up in St. Paul just a few years back, on a bet I fought a bulldog in the street. Dog ripped me up pretty good, but I killed that shit-eating cur with my bare hands, won me $10 and a jug of applejack. But the time I tell about, I got me one damned bad feeling.

'Twas Jesse's idea to rob the Missouri Pacific that July night, though Frank done all the figuring. Those who knew Jesse longer called him Dingus, but I always called him Jesse or Jess. Likewise, Frank's pards called him Buck, but I never called him nothing. Just didn't care for him none is all. He was too highfalutin for my ways, quoting Shakespeare and the Bible all the time, or getting into them dumb debates about religion and war with Cole. Cole, they called Bud, while I called him a self-righteous bastard, only not to his damned face. Cole or Bud, Frank or Buck, Jesse or Dingus. Names don't mean much when you're an outlaw. Fact is several of the boys all knew me as Bill Chadwell. It's the handle I use when I'm down South.

Like I said, Frank done the figuring and, I'll give him this, he figured things pretty good. The No. 4 Express left Kansas City for St. Louis with a big payload, and Frank knew the spot to hit it was at Rocky Cut. Railroaders was building a bridge over the Laramie River, and trains had to slow down real safe-like to get through this gash. Dangersome it was, so damned wicked the Missouri Pacific put a night watchman along the cut with a red lantern so he could help guide the engineer through.

Perfect place for a robbery, Frank said, and it turned out to be exactly that, but even Frank couldn't figure on some damned preacher.

First thing we done was capture the watchman, him begging for his worthless life, then Clell Miller and Charlie Pitts began piling railroad ties on the track, just to make sure the train would stop, while Bob Younger tied and gagged the sobbing watchman.

Cole, Frank, and Jesse stayed on the banks

of the cut, watching for the train and any laws or Pinkertons, while me and Hobbs Kerry hung out a ways back. Once the train come past us, me and Hobbs hurriedly dragged ties and timbers on the tracks and had that train snared like a rabbit. Didn't have nowheres to go.

Once the train stopped, things got noisy, us filling the night sky with lead and cusses, firing our six-shooters in the air like the bushwhackers we was. Rebel yells and bullets put the fear of God in everyone in railroad coaches and express cars, especial down in Missouri in 1876. Went off pretty damned good. Not like that first robbery I pulled with the boys back in '73 when we just derailed the damned train in Iowa. Killed the son-of-a-bitching engineer, and almost left a passel of others dead or bad maimed, and got away with $2,000 from the strongbox, plus about half as much from the pickings of the passengers. What a disaster that was. Christ! Oh, the money was fine, and the killing didn't bother me none, but we just couldn't find the bullion aboard — three and a half tons. Had we made that score, I guarantee you we wouldn't have been at Rocky Cut. Least, I wouldn't have been there.

But this was all right, the Rocky Cut robbery, till we went through the passenger cars, and that preacher started praying. Not no brimstone. No, he was too damned scared to sound like some hard-shell Baptist. Kept praying for God's mercy, that their lives would all be spared, but me and Clell figured he was only interested in saving his own sorry-ass life.

Now, the boys and me don't go about killing no innocent people, so they didn't have a damned thing to fear. We wasn't scared, neither. Only person aboard with any backbone was a boy — some green pea who tried to pull this little pocket pistol on us when Clell robbed his concession chest. That struck me as damned funny, especially when Clell took the gun from the kid, who started yelling at us, tears in his eyes but showing grit.

"Hear that little son-of-a-bitch bark," said Clell, laughing as he went to the next car to relieve them damned passengers of their money and things.

But, Jesus, this preacher! Once he finished praying, he started leading them travelers in singing. Hymn after hymn they sang, in the dead of night, while Frank and Cole worked on the express boxes and Jesse stood guard.

I went to the horses, to spell Hobbs Kerry, half a mind to mount up and ride away, forsaking my damned share. Glad I didn't now, but damned if I wasn't spooked by that God-blasted singing. " 'Lock of ages, cleft for me.' "

It troubled me, I tell you. Pitch black night but for the lights from the train. Hardly a noise except the hissing locomotive. Horses even kept quiet. But the singing. Frightened voices, singing to God.

Hell, I shivered, and that got Hobbs Kerry to cackling.

"Someone step on your grave, Bill?" he says.

"Why don't you just go back to your damned coal mine!" I barked back at him, and that shut up his damned fool mouth.

Cole and the James boys jumped down from the express car, Jesse having his fun. "Good night, gentleman. Thanks for the business. We'll see y'all again sometime soon." And Cole, always trying to be so damned respectful, calling out to the baggage master: "Watch yourself, Mister Conkling! Tell the engineer the tracks are blocked fore and aft. Best clear them before y'all go on your way."

I untied the night watchman's gag and binds, then mounted up. Easy as you please, we rode out, laughing, while that congregation in the middle coach just kept singing them damned hymns. Wasn't quite mid-night.

Around dawn, we reined up to give our horses a rest, and pass out the shares.

"Mighty fine haul, Buck," Cole said to Frank as he emptied the wheat sacks.

" 'A feast is made for laughter,' " Frank replied, " 'and wine maketh merry . . . but money answereth all things.' "

That's why I wasn't on friendly terms with Frank. Uppity if you ask me, spouting his damned scripture, showing us that he was an educated man, though he ain't.

Cole was right, though. Was a damned fine haul. Bet we made off with better than $15,000. Jesse rolled a wad and shoved the greenbacks in his trouser pocket. He come over to me, slapping me on my back, and laughing.

"We'll be traveling to Minnesota in style, eh, Bill?"

Minnesota was my idea, which Jesse took to like a catfish to stink bait. It was Jesse who brung me into the gang all them years ago, sided with me even though Frank and Cole suspicioned me to my face and called me a Yankee. Jesse, he'd back me all the way, told me so, and, when I said maybe we should head north and rob them Minnesota banks, steal bona-fide Yankee money for a change, he loved the plan. My plan.

"Them banks are just full of cash up there," I said. "Black-earth farmers and wealthy mills, and that rich carpetbagger governor, I hear tell he run back home after mistreating those damned fine people in Mississippi for so long. They almost impeached that bastard."

"They should have hung him," Jesse said.

We was down in Texas when I broached the notion. Jesse didn't say much more about it, maybe 'cause Cole started acting scornful. That had been in late winter, maybe spring, I disremember, but I won't forget when Jesse sent word for me, back in Missouri, to meet him at the cave we hid out in around Monegaw Springs. It was early June. He asked me to tell him more about them Minnesota banks.

"I know Minnesota," I told him, which wasn't no damned brag. "Banks are rich . . . richer than anything we see down here. Fat with cash, and them city folks, there ain't a one of them with any damned sand in their craw. Dumb farmers, town drunks, yellow-bellied businessmen."

For a spell I'd hung my hat in Monticello, had family still living in Minnesota, and I'd been all over southern Minnesota. Sis, she taught school near about Cannon Falls. She didn't want much to do with me, especially after I done that spell in the Stillwater prison, but her no-account husband, he sure liked hearing my stories, and I bet I could have him join the boys if he wasn't so henpecked and Frank and Cole so damned suspicious of anyone from up north.

"Governor Ames, that black-hearted bastard who ruint Mississippi, he and his daddy-in-law, that damyankee General Butler, they got money in them banks. Shit, Jess, it would be justice to steal from them two thieves."

"You know the towns?" Jesse asked.

"Sure. Mankato. Albert Lea. Northfield. Faribault. I know them all. Know every slough, every forest, every tree." I grinned. "Every whorehouse, too."

Jesse didn't say nothing.

"Ain't a man in the state worth a tinker's damn," I repeated.

"We'd have to do some scouting," Jesse said.

My enthusiasm was growing. "Sure, Jess, sure. And Saint Paul, now there's a city for you. Don't have to worry about no law there, long as you don't start trouble. Folks in that town let folks be, and it's got some fine-looking whores and plenty of card tables." I let out a good holler. "Jesus Christ, Jesse, it'll be a vacation for us!"

Well, one of these days I'll learn. Jesse, his eyes went damned cold, and he lowered his voice, telling me that, if I ever used the Lord's name in vain around him, he might just shoot me dead. I offered him my apologies, and he said no more on the matter.

Them James boys, they should have been damned preachers.

Next time we met up was in Kansas City, at a hotel. Jesse had done some more thinking, and he wanted to talk it over with Bob Younger. Bob, he couldn't be much older than twenty, and he thought the world of Jesse. Like I said, I didn't have much use for Cole, and he none for me, but Bob? Now him I liked. Didn't know Jim well, one of the other brothers, him off in California, being a respectable farmer or something.

"Minnesota?" Bob said, damned incredulous. "I don't know, Dingus."

"You sound like your big brother," I said, and I mean to tell you, them hairs on Bob Younger's damned neck stood up. Guess one reason I liked Bob so was that I knew how to play him.

"Cole ain't my keeper, Bill," he shot back

at me, and Jesse grinned one damned cold grin.

"Yankee money, Bob," he told his friend. "Bill, here, he knows the land. He'll guide us through. And the banks there are rich, filthy rich, rich with money stole from good Christian Southerners. It'd be enough for you to buy that farm you got your eyes on, Bob."

Reckon that sold Bob right then and there. Jesse, he never was damned pushy, maybe as he knew Bob would do whatever he said, but we agreed to meet later in the month at Monegaw Springs. "Bring Bud," Jesse told Bob. "See what he thinks."

Hell, I already knew what Cole Bud Younger would say.

"That's a damned fool notion," Cole said when we finally met up. "I come from Texas to hear this? Bob, we ain't going to Minnesota. Not if I have any say in the matter."

Reckon I knew what Bob would say, too.

"Well, you don't have a say in what I do, Brother!"

That started a long spat between them two. The more Cole argued against our plan, the more Bob backed Jesse's play. For a spell there, I thought they'd come to blows, which wouldn't be no good for me and Jess and our plans, 'cause Cole could whup his kid brother as easy as he could blow his own nose.

"You going along with this harebrained scheme, Buck?" Cole turned his rage on his good friend.

"It's a plan," Frank said mildly.

Let's see, Frank and Jesse, Bob and Cole, me and Clell Miller and Charlie Pitts was there. We talked things over, but Cole just shook his head and left, which got Bob's dander up. Bob was all ready to go right then and there, just to spite Cole, but Jesse was always thinking things through, and he said we needed a few more men, and, real soothing like, he put his arm around Bob's shoulder and told him not to worry, that Cole would come around to our way of thinking. I thought so, too, but Cole had one more bean in his wheel that I hadn't figured on.

Seeing he was losing his reins on young Bob, Cole up and fired off a telegraph to his brother Jim.

COME HOME STOP BOB NEEDS YOU
STOP

Them Youngers, they're as clannish as any

23

family I ever met. That wire brung Jim back from California in a hurry, and, at our next meeting, Jim was cussing both his brothers — Bob for his stupidity and Cole for worrying him something bad. Jim had thought Bob had been shot by Pinkertons or something worser.

By then, Jesse had met up with Hobbs Kerry, through Charlie Pitts, I think. Kerry was with us at that meeting, least ways, and Jesse outlined the plan again. We'd ride up to Minnesota, get the lay of the land, see which bank was thickest. Meantime, we'd have ourselves a high old time. Folks wouldn't be so cautious of strangers that far north. And after we robbed a bank or two, I would lead them to safety.

"Him?" Cole snorted, and spat. "I don't know him from Adam's house cat."

"Well, I do," Jesse fired back. "And I'm trusting him."

Tell you something. That made me feel damned proud, 'cause Jesse, he don't trust nobody but himself and his ma. Don't even trust his brother half the time.

"I'm going with Dingus," Bob told his brothers, "and you two can go to hell."

Reckon that did it, 'cause Cole and Jim just shut up after that. Jesse went over his plan one more time, not that he had much of a plan then, and we all fell silent. No more of a plan than I had propositioned him with a month earlier.

"We'll need us some spendin' money," Clell Miller finally said.

Which is how come we robbed the damned train at Rocky Cut, where I got spooked so.

But I mean to tell you, Christ A'mighty, I wasn't nowhere near as spooked then as things got shortly after we made that robbery. Hobbs Kerry, we should have shot that dumb bastard and took his share. He lost all his money shooting dice, or most of it, I hear tell, spent some on women, then got roostered and wasn't long before some St. Louis detectives arrested him for Rocky Cut.

Then he just sang out to the laws, sang out long and too damned clear.

"May God in heaven damn that poltroon's black-hearted cowardly soul to the deepest pits of Hades," Jesse said in Kansas City when we read it in the papers. "May God strike him dead. Or I shall, should ever our paths cross." Jesse started raging after that 'cause Hobbs Kerry had up and confessed, sold us out, the bastard, named every one of us who took part in the robbery.

Jesse wrote a letter to another newspaper, the kind of letter he was mighty good at after ten damned years robbing banks and trains. Wrote that he was nowhere near Rocky Cut on that night, blamed some other fool for the robbery, and called Hobbs Kerry a foul liar. Don't think no one in Missouri believed Jesse none. All that did was sell newspapers.

Things started getting hot in Missouri, hotter than usual for August. Posses was everywhere, looking for us. I took to the timbers, even if nobody really knew me in that part of the country. Jesse said Pinkertons and laws was all over his ma's farm down in Kearney. We heard that Clell Miller got arrested over in Kansas, but that turned out to be mung news. Yet we couldn't help but be edgy.

Frank, he come close to shooting me and Charlie Pitts when we met the boys at Monegaw Springs one last time. "Thought you were a damned Pinkerton," Frank said, "and I had a notion to kill you."

Frank never acted spooked like that, but things changed after Hobbs Kerry got his thirty pieces of silver. Missouri was no place to be, no matter how many friends and family the James boys and the Youngers had. Damned ticklish it had become.

"I think it's time to go to Minnesota," Bob said one night along the Crooked River.

"I reckon you're right," Jesse agreed.

So I was going home, back to Minnesota, and I'd show all them bastards. I'd come visit Sis and her brother-in-law with my pockets filled with silver and gold, more loot that I'd ever damned dreamed of stealing horses or selling whiskey to red niggers. I'd show my sorry excuse of a ma and pa, always praying for my soul when not cussing me or tanning my backside with Pa's razor strop, what a successful man I'd become. Show them sons-of-bitches who up and arrested me and sent me to Stillwater for stealing that damned horse. And I'd even show them skeptics, Frank and Jim and Cole, that I was a man who lived up to his word. I'd get them out of Minnesota. I'd make a name for myself.

Only the damnedest thing was I just couldn't get them hymns being sung on that train at Rocky Cut out of my head. Just kept hearing them over and over again, like a damned nightmare, and I just got this damned feeling, peculiar it was, that somebody indeed had just stepped on my grave.

Chapter Two:

ADELBERT AMES

With pencil in hand, I desire to relate to you a certain piece of heaven on earth, a hallowed community that Father fell in love with years ago. After spending far too long in the Hades that is the South, I have come home to this glorious town, which I, too, hold dear.

Father, who had spent thirty years at sea and circumnavigated the globe twice, arrived in Northfield in the year that saw the bloody rebellion commence. He and Mother came only to visit my brother John, but here the charm of this village, the majesty of the Cannon River, the wondrous principles upon which John Wesley North founded this blossoming village, all conspired to capture my parents' hearts.

That Mr. North began this town just twenty and one years ago is hard to cognize. This city strikes me as one that is as old as truth. By old I do not mean it looks as ragged as the war-torn South, or a town of tenements and vagabonds, but rather as a place that has always been here, always beautiful and bucolic. Mr. North espoused Abolition, women's suffrage, Temperance, and wholesome thinking, and our Lord God shined on this good man, and shined even brighter on a dream destined to become a thriving town. A dam was constructed, followed by sawmills and gristmills, and righteous men and women flocked to his burgeoning metropolis. Today we are blessed with not only the millers and the farmers, but wheelwrights, cobblers, blacksmiths, tinsmiths, a tannery, foundry and plow factory, bankers, bakers, hostlers, tailors, grocers, apothecaries, fishermen, and fishers of men. We have a railroad and a fire department.

West lies the Big Woods, as fine a forest as ever cultivated by God's merciful hand. East stretches an endless prairie. North you shall find Minneapolis (formerly St. Anthony) and St. Paul, and south, Cannon City and Faribault, fine cities all, but Northfield, to me, bests them all. It has become a center for not only business, but one of education. We have St. Olaf's School, founded a year or so ago, and Carleton College, celebrating its tenth anniversary, plus an outstanding public school. We support a lending library, a Y.M.C.A., Masons and Odd Fellows and the Northfield Improvement Association. Temperance has failed, as a few dram shops and other pests of society have sprouted up, but overall I find my new home virtuous and clean.

Northfield easily won over my heart, nigh as easy as beautiful Blanche Butler did. We have been married six years now, six years that should have been joyous except for our long separations due to my duties in the South, and anxieties from those duties. Now, I am home, living in the house that occupies a full block on Division Street. When I saw the plans in *Harper's Monthly,* I knew this would be a perfect home for my parents. This home we share together now that I am no longer the prodigal son, a home admired by everyone in town, filled with wonderful furniture and lovely paintings, some from Maine, a few from Europe, but much from the South, liberated by the mighty hand of the Union, and paid for — not stolen — although I will concede that I received bargains. The only decent items ever to come from South Carolina or Mississippi are the furniture, curtains, oils-on-canvas, china, and silver now gracing our home.

Late summer is a beautiful time of year in southern Minnesota. The hills come alive with goldenrod and gentian, although this year has been surprisingly wet. Fertile valleys are filled with oaks and black walnuts, fine corn crops, wild plums and delightful crab apples, and abundant fish and game. Farmers till the black earth and raise cattle.

No longer am I governor, senator, or general, though neighbors and friends still address me as such. I am a partner with my father and brother in Jesse Ames & Sons. The mill rests on the east side of the river, just across Mill Square near the iron bridge, grinding out better than 175 barrels of flour each day, a number that keeps growing. Why, Father's new process patent flour brought him first prize at this year's Centennial Exposition in Philadelphia, not bad for an old sea merchant.

A mariner I thought I would become, too, and as a lad in my teens I worked my way up to a mate on Father's clipper ship, but the oceans did not call me, and, growing up in Maine during those troublesome years, I saw war coming. Thus, I received an appointment to West Point, and, as fate and glory would have it, I was graduated in May of 1861 — merely days after those fire-eaters in Charleston fired upon our flag in

Fort Sumter, and entered the service of the Union — fighting to preserve our nation and wash away this blight upon the South, indeed, our entire country, that was slavery.

I shall not bore you with my service during the War for the Suppression of the Rebellion. The wounds I received, including the ghastly one at First Bull Run, and the medals I earned, the brevets and the commissions, can be attributed to duty. At first, I served in the artillery, but even the best officer finds advancement hard among the ranks of cannon and mortar, so I returned home to Rockland and went on the stump, befriending men with power and soliciting their help until finally receiving a commission as commander of the 10th Maine Infantry. As the commoners in both blue and gray would say, I "saw the elephant" at Gaines's Mill, Malvern Hill, Antietam, Fredericksburg — oh, the horror of our slaughter and the glory of Union bravery at Mayre's Heights! — Chancellorsville, Gettysburg, Cold Harbor, Petersburg, and Fort Fisher. During those ensanguined times, I had the honor and privilege to command a division in the Army of the James under the watchful eye of Major General Benjamin F. Butler. Because of this act of God's mercy, I had the good fortune to meet General

Butler's beautiful daughter, Blanche, whose hand I would take in matrimony on the 20th of July, 1870. Our paths would not cross till after the rebellion, however, as I would not be humbled by her beauty and grace till General Butler introduced us in Washington City, when he was a representative and I a senator, Republicans the both of us as you can be sure.

The general has been reviled by many in the newspapers, hated by secesh for his actions in Louisiana during the rebellion, but I find him a most honorable man. When the fiend in New Orleans abused the flag under which we served, General Butler ordered him hanged. When that witch of a secessionist dumped a chamber pot on Admiral Farragut, the general issued General Orders Number 28, which declared that any of those harlots who dared disrespect officers and men of the Union would be treated as the unscrupulous ladies of the tenderloin they surely were. I tell you: I would have done nothing differently had I been in the general's place. Benjamin Butler is no Beast; he is a faithful patriot.

I did as much in South Carolina. I punished those men who dared abuse the laws of our nation, who would still fight for their ignoble cause, who would spit on their amnesty oaths and the rights of the Negro, who would desecrate the uniform of the Federal soldier. Southerners do not have to respect me, but they will respect the office, Army, and nation I represent.

War for me, however, began in earnest after the surrender of General Lee and other Rebels. When I was mustered out a year after Appomattox, I longed to visit Northfield, or settle there, but my services remained in need. I vacationed in Europe before returning to duty in Mississippi in the summer of 1867. Almost a year later, I received an appointment as military governor of that wretched state which gave us such fiends as Jefferson Davis and Van Dorn. Later my jurisdiction would reach into Arkansas.

Southerners called me a carpetbagger, one of Grant's scoundrels, a thief, but I stole nothing as senator or governor. My aim was to enforce the rights of the recently freed Negro and punish the scoundrels that dared remain unreconstructed. The Negro earned his freedom, and the 14th Amendment guaranteed his rights, though one would find that hard to believe in Mississippi. In 1874, Mississippi elected me governor, and I vowed to reconstruct this miserable land of swamps and myriad biting insects and reptiles into a vision of New England, yet faced obstacles at every turn. Confederates despised me as much as I loathed the carpetbaggers who plundered the land and gave good Northern men a damning reputation. The Negro proved ignorant, some of those as dishonest as the most perfidious carpetbagger. Even my lieutenant governor, a man of color named Davis, proved to be a dolt.

I desired the see those ill-gotten plantations cut into parcels and sold as farms to men, colored or white, who would work them. This, as well as other plans I laid out to rebuild this dreadful place, led to mobism, acts of violence, murder. During the recent elections, the notorious Ku Klux Klan formed guards at the polls, intent on disrupting due process, and that vile Senator Lamar started a dastardly campaign — nay, a new revolution — in the halls of the legislature. My pleas for help from President Grant went in vain, and thus it came as no surprise that after the elections of November 1875, after Democratic victories by the most foul measures — Negroes were threatened, sometimes attacked, at the polls — Mississippi's hold on me, tenuous as it had always been, was lost forever.

Yet I have never been one to retreat, and,

when the villains began speaking of impeachment, I refused to surrender. I fought, as is my nature. Ludicrous charges — that I had incited riots in Vicksburg . . . that I granted unwarranted pardons . . . of corruption and malfeasance — led to my facing impeachment.

Northern men can find no justice, and certainly no safety, in this cauldron of secession where the mere sight of Old Glory fuels the white-hot blaze of contumacious passion like coal oil. Southerners care nary one fip for humanity, and had I my way, and General Butler his, all those *frondeurs* who wore butternut and gray would be imprisoned, and those holding high office, or rank, perhaps hanged for their transgressions.

On March 28, 1876, Congress cleared my name, yet I knew I must depart the South, leave forever.

I resigned as governor of Mississippi, resigning after winning the fight, refusing to cower to threats, resigning only after my name had been vindicated for the records history might desire. With dismissal of the Articles of Impeachment, I felt, well, liberated.

Those nefarious scoundrels in Jackson and Vicksburg celebrated. I imagine, if I may be so profane, that they cleansed their bowels and kidneys in chamber pots whose bottoms once had been painted with General Butler's likeness but now bore a resemblance to a certain former Union general from Rockland, Maine, forced into politics after the rebellion.

Let the names Adelbert Ames and Benjamin Butler be as reviled in that land of secession as the name William T. Sherman, for I have no doubt that history will praise my attempts at reconstructing the South, at fighting injustice, while Southerners like Frank Blair of Missouri and Lucius Lamar of Mississippi will find their tarnished names reviled, as will many of my unscrupulous Northern counterparts blinded by greed and ambition.

Freed from my years in Purgatory, I came north, to Minnesota, to Blanche and my parents. I tried to shun my experiences in politics, and in the Army, and think as a businessman, as a husband and father and respectful son.

The cool air is refreshing after breathing the sour odor of stagnant water and fighting that oppressive heat. People here are friendly, loyal, and true, many of whom, as did I, proved their mettle on the battlefields in Virginia and elsewhere against the Rebels.

Rice County sent 800 — perhaps more — brave men to fight for the preservation of our union, to fight to free the Negro in the Bloody 2nd and other glorious volunteer infantries. Others remained home to put down the Sioux insurrection. Most earned their baptism in savage battle.

Our business prospers. To my tired eyes, the Cannon River is as powerful as the Mississippi, as beautiful as the Congaree, cleansing whereas those former rivers flowed with scorn, contempt, prejudice, and hostility. I gaze upon the hills and vales of Rice County as Adam must have first admired Eden.

Our new life begins, I wrote Blanche shortly before my departure from that most foul of Southern states.

Only . . . as God is my witness, never in my worst nightmares in Carolina and Mississippi, never could I fathom that the South would follow me to Minnesota, and bring its vile war to my home, to threaten my family and leave the streets of this consecrated city stained with the blood of the innocents.

Chapter Three:

CLELL MILLER

"You-all suggested this," Cole told Frank and Dingus. "I didn't want a damned thing to do with it. I'm just going along with you."

"Ain't no gun to your head, Bud, so you can back out now," Dingus fired back, but Cole just shaken his head — kinda sad, it struck me.

"No," he said. "I. . . ." But he didn't finish, not that it mattered none because I don't think nobody heard him, nobody but me, being closest to him that evening.

We was a-hiding out in the barn on the James farm till full dark. After Dingus and Cole had their little rumpus, Ma James come in. Ma James — though she had married a couple of times since Dingus and Frank's pa got called to Glory by fever in California and now went by the name Samuel, and she wasn't my mama, I still called her Ma James — was a-making a pretense to go milk the cow, in case any laws was in

39

the woods, but really she just wanted to kiss her boys good bye and give us some corn dodgers and cold ham for the road. She was a big woman, right tough. Hell, I'd bet on her in a fight against a man twice her size even if those damned Pinkertons blowed off her arm and kilt her simple-minded boy back in '75. But she loved Dingus and Frank dearly.

From an oaken bucket, she pulled out the hidden wheat sack holding the grub and passed it to Bob Younger, then I set my pipe down and taken the bucket, a-tipping my hat and a-saying how I'd milk that sorry cow for her. That's what I done, too — let her have a little bit of private tenderness with her two sons. When I was just about done with the milking, she come over and put her hand on my shoulder.

"You're a good boy, Clell Miller," she told me. "I'm trustin' you to take care of my sons. I know you'll look after 'em. You and Bud. But I ain't trustin' that damyankee." She jutted her chin over toward the maw-mouth who called hisself Chadwell. Never seen a body with so many teeth crammed into his mouth. Now, personally, I figured Chadwell, or Stiles, or whatever his real name was, he was a good egg, but I ain't one to contradict Ma James, not by a damned sight, so I just nodded and give her the milk to haul back to the house.

I tried to think of something funny to say, but, instead, turned serious. "I love Jesse like he was my own brother," I told her, "maybe more." After she kissed my cheek, I offered her a pinch of snuff, which she taken.

Wasn't no fib, neither. I thought highly of Dingus. He liked a good joke, same as me. Way I see things, Dingus and me, and Frank, Cole, and the boys, I felt closer to them than my blood kin. Hell, Dingus and me was blood kin. Baptized by the blood of the Confederacy. We'd been together since we robbed the Corydon bank about four years ago, but I had known them during the war.

Folks say the war ended more than a decade ago, but don't hold no truck with that balderdash. No, sir. I was there when Bloody Bill got kilt over in Ray County, and I heard what they done to his body, them damyankee bastards. Cut off his head, they did, put it on a telegraph pole, drug the rest of his body through the streets of Richmond, didn't even give him no fitting Christian burial after they was done with their pleasures. Them same Yanks locked me up in a prison, left me there to rot. Reckon they

41

would have, too, if I hadn't told them I was a loyal Union boy — reckon that was one of my best jokes — and my pa, Moses, he swore on a stack of Bibles that Bloody Bill had kidnapped me, that I had been true to the blue during the entire rebellion. They believed him, because Pa had taken the damned oath hisself, and he sobbed like a gal when he found me in that jail, Yankees just a-hankering to hang me. Reckon they would have kilt me but for my tender age, and 'twas by God's grace that they spared me after they kilt poor Bill. I was only fourteen that October. Still, they didn't let me out of that privy of a jail till April once word came that Bobby Lee had given up the fight, and only then after Pa had gotten some high-ranking Yanks to speak on my behalf.

Yet I ain't one to quit no fight once I've started the ball. Folks call me fun-loving, but not when there comes a ruction. Hell, I had rode with Bloody Bill, Arch Clements, and the boys. Enjoyed it, and later I got pleasure a-keeping the fight alive, a-robbing banks and trains with Dingus. Sure beat a-sweating on that Gentry County farm with my younger brothers.

I come of age riding with Bloody Bill. That's where I met up with Dingus. Hell, I was there when we give him that name.

He wasn't much older than me when we met, near Plattsburg, him a-cleaning this old Colt's Dragoon when it went off, as them old horse pistols be prone to do, and taken off the tip of his middle finger on his left hand. "That's the dodd-dingus pistol I ever saw!" he snapped, dodd-dingus being something he could say whereas Ma James would have nailed his hide to the barn for a sacrilegious god-dangedest. We got a good chuckle at that, and, afterward, all the boys called him Dingus.

Yet after such an auspicious beginning, Dingus sure proved hisself a soldier to the cause, and I grew to respect and admire him, so when he propositioned me with this plan to ride up to Minnesota, well, it didn't take much propositioning. I'd done all right with him since Corydon, was plumb proud to be in the company of a man like Jesse James. And, since I'm a-being all truthful here, I was right ready to get out of Missouri by the summer of '76. Reckoned things would be a mite quieter for us amongst the Philistines than at home with the Midianites amongst us.

"It's time," Frank announced an hour or so after Ma James had gone back to her house, and we crawled into the back of a buckboard with our dusters and saddles and gear and such. Dingus, Frank, and Chadwell covered us up with a canvas tarp, then Frank called out to their nigger boy: "Perry, you may open the door!"

The James boys mounted their horses, Chadwell climbed up onto the buckboard driver's bench, released the brake, and once Perry Samuel, who had been a-keeping a eye on things outside, had the doors flung wide, we left the farm afore the moon rose.

That's how our little adventure to Minnesota begun.

We had met at the farm one last time, to see if anybody wanted to turn yeller and quit the job, but nobody did. Cole had his little say, that he wasn't for this plan, no, sirree, Bob, and that it was mighty poor judgment to be at the James farm when half the laws in Missouri was after us, and we bickered a mite, but we was all in this together. Frank and Dingus wanted to ride their own horses all the way north, but Cole called that pure folly even though Frank said he had just bought a mighty fine dun horse over in Kansas City and he wasn't about to trust no plug mule they'd get in Minnesota, and Cole allowed the dun had a lot of heart and bottom but he hisself was too damned old to ride 400 miles to Minneapolis. And Frank, he just grinned and said: "Bud, it's closer nigh to five hundred miles to Texas, and you never complained about your ass all the times we rode down there."

"Well, the rails suit me now," Cole said.

"You might regret that come September," Dingus said, "when you're trusting a Northern horse to get out of a fix."

"I thought you said there wouldn't be no fix, Dingus." Cole's temper started a-festering again, but before they could commence a-fighting, Chadwell, he said horses wouldn't be no problem at all up yonder. Jesse then said he'd ride his own damned mount anyhow, and Bob Younger didn't know what to say or do, just kept a-whipping his head toward Dingus and then Cole and back again. So the argument went 'round and 'round till Ma James come in to say her fare-thee-wells.

Anyway, how things turned out was we rode out of the farm that night in a wagon and, with Frank and Dingus on their horses, rode on till dawn and then some, off the big roads, all the way to Council Bluffs. Frank, he wanted to go see his honey, as pretty a thing as they come, over in Omaha, so he left. Dingus and Chadwell rode out, too, said they'd rendezvous with Frank that night. Rest of us would catch a train, us decked out in our finest business suits we bought from our Rocky Cut takings, and we'd meet up at Albert Lea.

"Who's Albert Lea?" I asked before we split up at Council Bluffs.

"Not a who," Chadwell barked back, not a-knowing that I was just a-making a joke. "It's a town. They got a good livery there."

I taken out my pipe and whistled. "Now, that's something a body should aspire to. I'd like to have a town named after me . . . a big town with a fine livery. McClelland Miller, Missouri. Kinda catchy, don't you think?"

Only Jim Younger thought I was funny, but that was all right. We shaken hands, Dingus rode off with Chadwell, a-leaving us near the depot. So as not to draw much attention to ourselves, the rest of us separated. Bob Younger and Charlie Pitts found a hotel, Cole wandered over to the wagon yard by hisself, and Jim and I headed to the man and bought ourselves tickets to Albert Lea. Train would be along in an hour, the fellow told us, so we just waited on the bench, sharing an airtight of peaches. Rest of us train riders would probably follow the next day or thereabouts.

"You know what?" I asked Jim while

a-rolling up my ticket stub and a-pushing it through one of the bullet holes in my hat.

"What's that, Clell?"

"I'm a-thinking this'll be the first train I ever rode that we wasn't gonna rob."

Jim chuckled a mite over that one, then flicked a finger out at my plug hat.

"You might want to consider buying yourself a new hat, Clell."

"I like this one."

"Those three holes might draw unwarranted attention."

"Damn' right," I said. "It'll show them Yanks what a good pistol fighter can do." I held out that hat for Jim's inspection because you could cover them holes with a dollar coin.

"That speaks highly of the man doing the shooting."

"Damn' right," I said again. "I done it. Didn't I tell you about it? Naw, I reckon that was Dingus I told."

So I up and retold the story. I'd been at Uncle Bill's after Rocky Cut, went upstairs, hung my hat on the bedpost, and turned in. Long about three o'clock, I waken up, but still half asleep, and I see this figure, mostly shadow, and, hell, got spooked that it's some law dog. Now I admit that earlier Uncle Bill and me had shared some "nockum stiff" he

47

had brewed. Anyhow, I rolled over, a-pretending I'm still asleep, ripped my Remington from underneath the pillow, and put three bullets into that law's head. Quick as you please, I'm a-hitching up my trousers and a-trying to find my boots when Uncle Bill come a-barging in, just a-blasting me for being a damned fool a-waking up the family and all. That's when I realized I had just kilt my hat.

Done with my tale, Jim drained the peach juice and tossed the empty tin in a trash box. "I left California to put my life in the hands of Dingus, who blew off the tip of his finger, and you, who shot your own hat." He taken off his hat and run his fingers through his hair. "It's a wonder I ain't been killed yet."

I laughed at that one, stretched out my boots, and waited for the train.

Minnesota was a mite cooler than I had expected, but I warrant hell's cooler than Missouri in August. Albert Lea seemed to be a pretty fancy city, too, and we lugged our saddles and tack over to this big old brick building called City Livery, Feed & Sale Stable over on Broadway and Clark.

Chadwell, he hadn't told no stretchers when he spoke highly of Minnesota horse-

48

flesh. We hadn't been there five minutes before Jim taken a fancy to a blood bay thoroughbred.

"You gentlemen want reliable horses, you've come to the right place. Name's Hall." We turned from the stallion and shaken hands with a balding feller in a green and black checkered suit, giving him a couple of aliases.

"Fancy rigs." Mr. Hall nodded at our saddles.

"I like to be comfortable," Jim said, "when purchasing grain all over Freeborn County."

"You two gents dealers?"

Nosy fellow, I thought, but allowed Jim to palaver with him.

"Out of Chicago. Just got into town. My partner and I, newly employed with Abbott Flour, will be visiting farms throughout the county. You might be able to guide us in the right direction."

"Might," Mr. Hall said.

"And you might also be able to give us your rock-bottom price on that sore-legged piece of glue bait." He tilted his head at the thoroughbred.

Mr. Hall, he let out a belly laugh. "You sure you're not a horse trader?"

Jim give him an easy smile. "I'm a speculator, Friend Hall, in many things."

"Well, why don't you speculate on this . . . you won't find a better horse between Duluth and Omaha. If you want something sore-legged or bound for the glue factory, I'll direct you to Balch's Wagon Shop. A.J. doesn't do much horse trading, but, on occasion, someone swindles him with a lame horse. But this prime example of horseflesh, well, he's only four years old and I wouldn't lead him down the ramp for anything short of two hundred dollars."

"That's funny," Jim said, "I was thinking more along the lines of fourteen years and twenty dollars."

Well, that's how things went. Jim Younger, he knew horses, but so did that Mr. Hall, and they wound up agreeing on $110. Over the next three days, we bought eight horses, three good ones plus the fine blood bay, along with four others we figured we'd do some trading for. Me and Jim also bought a spring wagon from a Dutchy named Drommerhausen at a carriage shop over on Clark Street, a-putting two of Mr. Hall's least reliable horses in harness.

By and by, the boys come along and joined up with us — Cole first, then Charlie Pitts and Bob Younger, finally Chadwell, Frank, and Dingus. We scouted about around Freeborn County, over around

Mansfield Township. Albert Lea was right close to the Iowa border, but the bank didn't look fat with cash, and, besides, wasn't many of us so jo-fired to rob a bank right at the get-go, Jim and Cole a-being the exceptions. Dingus, he wanted to do some consorting in Minneapolis and St. Paul, but Frank deemed it wise to get these "reliable" Albert Lea horses accustomed to our ways before a-getting too comfortable in Minnesota.

It always amuses me when I read them newspaper articles about us bushwhackers or hear paper-collar men speculate on us outlaws at some tonsorial parlor. Lots of folk figured it was Frank James who called all the shots, others said Cole Younger could lead a handful of men through the gates of Hades, but most believed Dingus to be leader of the gang.

Truth be told — weren't no leader. Oh, we had our certain jobs during a robbery. Cole, he liked being an outside man, Dingus didn't have no druthers, but Frank was more of the inside person. Like as not, he'd be one of the boys inside the bank because he was ready. He carried a Remington revolver like me, but he had carved out a notch in his holster — and it was a pretty rig, black, with a narrow shell belt and a mighty fancy brass buckle — so he could thumb back the hammer before that .44 cleared the leather.

But the point I'm a-making, nobody really led us anywhere. We come as we pleased, did what we wanted, and fought like me and my brothers done oftentimes. I can't tell you how many times I thought Dingus and Cole would come to blows, and since Rocky Cut, well, Bob had been a-treating his brothers like Yankees. Chadwell didn't have much of a temper, but he and Frank, normally the peacekeeper amongst us, taken to each other like a match to gunpowder, while Charlie Pitts just sided with Cole and kept his mouth shut.

Me? I found it kinda amusing. Hell, I was here for the adventure, and it didn't mean much to me whether we was at a whorehouse in Minneapolis, poker table in St. Paul, or the bank in Mankato.

So there we was one afternoon, on some sorry country road near nothing, a-waiting on Charlie Pitts to finish his business in the woods, and arguing, for the umpteenth time, on which way to travel. Dingus said we should spend a while in St. Paul, and Chadwell agreed, allowing that we'd be safe there, Cole and Jim a-spouting off their complaints, Bob a-cussing his brothers.

Frank said it didn't mean a damn to him if they done St. Paul or Mankato but we'd sure as hell better get our horses trained or find better mounts. I hooked a leg over the saddle horn, lighted my pipe, a-trying to figure out who I'd bet on once the fists started a-swinging.

Yes, sir, we was in the middle of the damned pike, a-bickering like we done most of the time — wouldn't them damned Pinkertons loved to have come along on that scene — when that farmer came a-trotting down the road and scared the blazes out of all us.

Chapter Four:

JOE BROWN

Just wasn't paying attention is all. Coming from town like I always do after selling produce and buying coffee, flour, and sugar, plus ordering those plowshares at the mercantile, following my wife's orders, I didn't see the men in the road till I topped the hill and rounded the curve. No, actually, I didn't even see them then. Mind was wandering, and I was looking down, trying to cut off some tobaccy with my jackknife, because you could ride betwixt my farm and town and not see a soul nine times out of ten, so the men saw me before I heard them.

"No, Dingus!"

That's when I looked up to see those strangers. The name struck me as funny — Din-gus — but I thought maybe I misheard. Could be that man's name is Darius, which was my grandfather's name.

Well, there they sat on their horses like they owned the road, seven of them, all

54

looking at me. One fellow, the one called Dingus or Darius or maybe it was Augustus or could have been just Gus, he had been reaching inside and behind his duster, and only slowly pulled his hand back after the taller man with the beard kept talking to him, whispering now.

"Hold up there, mister!" one of the other men shouted, spitting out his pipe and trying to control his skittish mare, and only then did I realize that I was still riding right toward them, and if I didn't rein in Ol' Jezebel, well, I'd either ram those horses or they'd scatter, and the men, except for the one riding the nervous brown mare, didn't look like they had any notion to scatter.

"Sorry," I said, tugging on the reins. When I stopped, I set the brake and reached down to pick up my knife and the tobaccy I had bought and was in a hurry to have my afternoon chaw before I got home to Matilda. She didn't care for my habit.

"Dropped my tobaccy," I said, without looking up, and, when I sat up straight and tried to give the strangers a smile, well, practically every one of them was looking hard right back at me. Three of them had dismounted so that I couldn't see nothing but their hats and legs, and most of the rest had reached inside their dusters.

Struck me as odd. So did the fact that I counted eight horses, but only seven men, every mount saddled, too. Maybe they were highwaymen, I thought, but if they held me up, it would be downright comical what they got. Still, I was nervous. Like I said, the men were strangers, fancy rigs on their horses, and dressed in linen dusters and good clothes. And, like I said, as lonesome as this country was, if they killed or maimed me, nobody would find me for a 'coon's age.

But the taller man, he had trotted his big dun horse over toward me and bowed. He wore a gray hat and black broadcloth suit, with a silk tie. Shamed me, what dressed in muslin and duck trousers, boots covered with mud and muck from all the rain we'd been having. Surely admired his saddle. Never seen something so fancy, not in Minnesota, maybe not even in Kentucky. What's more, there he sat, leaning over a mite, offering me Navy plug.

"Thanks," I said, "but I found mine."

"But mine hasn't been lying in manure." He grinned, and I glanced at my boots and all the filth lying down in the wagon. So I tossed my tobaccy aside and took his, carved off a small bite, and started my chaw. When I give him back the plug, he bit off a mouthful, and held out his hand.

"Name's Wood," he said. "Ben Wood."

"Joe Brown."

I couldn't think of anything else to say, so we just sat there, working our chaws, till I finally asked: "You-all lost?"

"Wouldn't say that," Ben Wood said. "Debating on which way to go. On our way to find some timberlands."

"That would be north of here," I shot back. "Long way north."

Ben Wood had an easy smile as he looked over the rolling plains. "Yes, sir, I'd dare say this is country for farming, not logging. Grew up on a Tennessee farm myself, yet my calling led elsewhere."

"Tennessee, huh?"

"Land of Crockett and Houston and Jackson. Some say Eden."

"I grew up in Kentucky, come out here, though, before the rebellion."

Said this because I was still suspicious of these guys. They spoke like Southerners, and I wanted to see how they'd react to me calling the war a rebellion, secesh being touchy on that subject.

"Lot of good Union men in eastern Tennessee, Mister Brown," Ben Wood said, like he was reading my mind. And with that, the rest of the men come up over to the wagon, walking their horses now, and shook my hand, telling me their names. Seven of them. With eight horses. Really friendly gents, though I couldn't recollect most of their names. There was a Horton and a Howard and a Chadwell, but I couldn't tell you which was which five minutes after introductions.

Well, we started talking about the timber-lands, and my suspicions faded. War was over, had been for ten, eleven years, and they were most interested in hearing all about northern Minnesota, so I talked and talked till I had worn out my first chaw of tobacco and Ben Wood offered me another. I like to talk. Takes me a while, but once I get started . . . just ask Matilda.

"Timber seems to be a sound investment," Ben Wood said.

"Better'n farming, I warrant," I said.

"Oh, farming's a noble endeavor," Ben Wood said. "Practically all of us grew up on farms, except Mister Chadwell there. He's a city boy, but has lived some up north of here. Why his tales of all that forest, that's what led us out of eastern Tennessee."

"There's some fine woods in that part of the country, too."

"Indeed. Well, sir, we've kept you from your home too long. Let us bid farewell and we'll be on our way."

"No rush," I said, enjoying the chance to converse with someone other than Matilda or Jezebel or that miser of a mercantile owner back in town. "My place is just a mile up the road."

"Still, it's getting late."

"You're more than welcome to spend the night at our place," I said. "My Matilda, she sets a nice table, 'specially this time of year."

Thunder rolled in the distance. "We won't impose," Ben Wood said. "Mister King, he's a fine cook . . . his food not as dour as his face would lead one to believe."

"No imposition," I said.

"Well." The thunder cracked again, and Ben Wood turned to look at his colleagues.

"Ain't nobody ever accused me of a-being a duck," said one of the guys whose name I had already forgotten, the one on the brown mare dusting off his pipe, and he started poking a finger through holes in his hat.

"Then, Mister Brown," Ben Wood said, "lead us to Camelot."

I released the brake, and rode on down the road, when there come a commotion — man alive! — and suddenly a wagon bolted out of the woods, driven by some fellow in a duster, too, and I almost stopped to see just what the blazes was going on here, but Ben Wood rode up alongside of me. There was that eighth man, he'd been hiding all along.

"That's Sam Wells," Ben Wood told me, pulling the extra horse behind him. "Don't mind him none. He's shy is all." He lowered his voice, tapped his temple. "Little touched in the head."

"What's in the wagon?"

"Our supplies. Long way from Tennessee, sir. Sam's harmless, Mister Brown. I give you my word."

My suspicions had returned, but that Ben Wood could talk so smoothly, politely, it eased my apprehensions about them. I just didn't know what Matilda would think.

Well, that's not entirely true.

"First things first, Joe," Matilda said, wiping her hands on the apron and blocking the front door. "There's tobacco flakes stuck in your teeth, which is brown as molasses. Didn't I ask you not to buy none of that devil's chaw? Rot your mouth out, it will. Didn't I tell you we don't have money to squander? You don't see me buying sassy-frass tea."

"Mister Wood over yonder, he offered me his own plug, Mama," I told my wife. Which was the truth, I figured, pushing my own dirty store-bought plug deeper inside my mule-ear trousers pocket.

"And that's another thing. How many times before you get it through that thick skull of yours that we don't have enough food to spare? You meet any fool on the road, you invite him over for supper, then work your jaw till midnight. Gracious, Joe, how many are there over yonder? Nine? We can't spare no food for nine, ten men."

"It's only eight, Mama, and they're strangers, on their way north. From Tennessee. Said they wouldn't take no food from us. Got their own."

Rain started to sprinkle, but she still blocked the door, staring over my shoulder at the camp Ben Wood and his friends had made in the field by the barn.

"I don't like it when you bring strangers home, Joe. Don't like strangers." She was looking at me again. "Did you order the plowshares?"

"Yes, Mama."

"Get the coffee?"

"Yes'm. And sugar, and flour."

"How much did Ziegler give you?"

"Same as last time."

She snorted. "Well, best bring in them sacks before they get ruint by the rain." When she looked up again, her face hardened and she let out an angry bark. Knew she wasn't snapping at me no more, so I turned around to see Mister Wood standing by the well with a bucket, him just smiling at us.

"What do you want?" my wife hollered at him.

"Fetching water, ma'am, to boil potatoes."

"Well, if it's water you're after, fetch it. Don't just stand there paralyzed." She looked back at me. "What is it them men are doing here?"

"Heading north to the logging country," I started to say, but only got about halfway when Matilda was barking at Ben Wood again.

"Missus Brown. . . ." Ben Wood swept off his gray hat. "The Good Book says in Saint Matthew, Chapter Twenty-Five, Verse Forty-One . . . 'Then shall he say also to them on the left hand, depart from me, ye cursed, into everlasting fire, prepared for the devil and his angels. For I was hungered, and ye gave no meat; I was thirsty, and ye gave me no drink. I was a stranger, and ye took me not in naked, and ye clothed me not, sick, and in prison, and ye visited me not.' "

Setting the bucket by the well, he reached inside his coat pocket and pulled out one of them little Bibles, the kinds soldiers often-times carried with them off to war, and he started thumbing through the pages as he walked toward us till he was protected somewhat from the little drizzle of rain under what passed for a porch at our place, and he was telling my wife, who on most Sundays didn't cotton to having her toes preached on, to turn with him to Chapter Seven of the same Gospel.

" 'Judge not, that ye be not judged,' " he read. " 'For with what judgment ye judge, ye shall be judged; and with what measure ye mete, it shall be measured to you again.' " With that, he closed the Bible, put it back in his pocket, and walked back to the well, where he drew his water.

My wife, she wasn't never at a loss for words, and she wasn't struck dumb too long by Ben Wood's preaching.

"That man is a preacher!" she told me, watching him sling a strap over his shoulder and haul the water bucket back to their camp, before reminding me to bring in the sugar, coffee, and flour.

Thought they'd be gone come first light, but Ben Wood met me at the door with a handful of greenbacks.

"I know we said we would not intrude, Mister Brown," he told me, "but some of our horses are a little green, and my colleagues do not wish to travel all the way to the northern timbers on skittish mounts. We'd like to leave our wagon here, ride off to do some training, and return by evening."

Preacher or not, I figured Matilda would raise Cain about that, but before I could say one word, Ben Wood pulled a gold coin from his vest pocket and wrapped it inside the greenbacks, which he pressed into my hand.

"Ain't no need . . . ," I started, but Ben Wood had already turned around and was heading back to their camp.

Which is how things went over the next three or so days. Matilda, she sure had no complaints because Ben Wood — directly, we started calling him Preacher Wood — paid us each and every morning they was there, and he'd read Scripture with her of evenings. Like having a camp meeting at our place of evenings. And a horse ranch every afternoon, because, after the first day, they done some training at our place after they had come from wherever they rode off to each morn. Appeared to me they were teaching the horses neck-reining, jumping fences. Some of the horses seemed hopeless, but others learned fast, and those boys worked them animals, I mean to tell you. 'Course, if I had saddles and bridles like they had, I'd want my horses well trained, too.

They all seemed nice fellows, even that Sam Wells who had startled me so when he come riding out of the woods with the wagon. Preacher Wood would come over of evenings and read Scripture with Matilda and me, and Matilda even baked an apple pie to share with his friends. 'Course, Preacher Wood, he insisted on paying for the pie, and Matilda didn't protest too much.

I'd come out to their camp each night, after Preacher Wood did his preaching, make sure they didn't need anything, and we'd talk some more. Talked about lots of things, not just the country around here, but religion and science and farming and the War of the Rebellion.

"Where are the biggest banks?" the serious fellow, the one who did the cooking, asked one evening.

"Oh, I don't know. You mean in the forest country?"

"No, closer to here."

"Never really trusted banks," I said, which got all of them to laughing, and I grinned and chuckled myself.

"If there were more people like you, Joe," the one with the Gus-sounding name said, "then men like us would. . . ." He just grinned like I knew what he meant, though I didn't, and the men busted out laughing again.

"The banks?" Mr. King, the serious one, asked from the cook fire where he was getting coffee ready.

"Oh, hear there's a big one in Mankato. Reckon there must be a nice size bank in Northfield what with that big Ames mill on the river there."

"Ames?" The big fellow, the one with the pale blue eyes and thinning hair, straightened up. "As in Governor Ames from Mississippi?"

"I told you that already, Cole!" said the clean-shaven one, the gent from somewhere here in Minnesota.

"Hold your tongue, Stiles," Preacher Wood said, and nobody was laughing any more.

"Well, I think it's his daddy," I said, breaking the silence. "But, like I said, I know farming, not banking."

Preacher Wood's grin returned. "I don't know, Joe," he told me, tossing me a new plug of Navy tobaccy. "Were we to stay much longer, paying our way as the Lord sees fit, you might have to start your own savings and loan."

"Wouldn't that be something!" I slapped my knee.

"Then we might bring our business to yours," Gus — Howard he was — said, and the laughing fit erupted one more time.

Nice fellows, like I said. Plumb sorry I was when they announced the next morning that they had to be on their way, had to make their way north to see if that timberland was as glorious as they had been led to believe. They left behind a stack of silver coin and a couple of pouches of tobaccy, which I wouldn't find till they had ridden off.

Even Matilda was sad to see them saddling their horses and hitching the team to the spring wagon, complaining that, had she known they was gonna leave, she would have made up some victuals for them to eat along the trail.

" 'He that soweth the good seed is the Son of Man,' Christ said," Preacher Wood told us as he mounted his dun horse. "You have a fine farm, Mister Brown, ma'am, and we have been blessed by your generosity. You loveth the stranger, you gave him food and raiment. And we feel we are strangers no more. May the Lord bless you."

They rode north. Never saw a one of them again.

CHAPTER FIVE:
MOLLIE ELLSWORTH

If you whore long enough, nothing surprises you, and I have worked the tenderloin a long, long time.

Jesse, he surprised me. Christ, he scared the shit out of me. He always did.

With evening's approach, I had retired to my upstairs room to get dressed, and, while pulling up black stockings, a loose floor-board squeaked. Looking up, I made out the form in the shadows, the form of a man, spying on me, in my room, in my bagnio.

"Listen, mister," I said, tying my kimono over what my mother would modestly have called "unmentionables" — but my modest days remained a far distant memory, much like Mother. "I entertain gentlemen, and gentleman do not spy on a woman in her bedroom. So get the hell out of here before I whistle for Fish and have him stove in your skull. Or fork over fifty cents for the peek show."

The shadowy figure barely moved, as if enjoying this, but I am not one to make empty threats, and not until I stuck finger and thumb to whistle for my bouncer, did the man speak. The accent was soft, Missouri, and his words chilled me.

"Didn't you run a house in Saint Louis, where you were called Kitty Traverse?"

That took my breath away, and, as he stepped into the light, grinning, I uncontrollably stepped back against my dresser.

"Jesse!"

Jesse Woodson James was handsome — no woman could ever deny that — and I have never seen blue eyes so mesmerizing. Tall, usually smiling, quick with a joke and laugh, I might have looked forward to pleasing a man like him, per chance having him please me, but I had known Jesse for thirteen years. Silently, like a cat, he approached me, smiling his sweet smile, shaking his head at the irony of meeting me up here, after, by my tally, five years.

At first he had been just some green kid riding with men, a bushwhacker perhaps, but still nothing more than a boy — shy, silly, devoutly religious, but equally insecure. After the war, or maybe during it, he had changed, and, when I looked into those penetrating eyes, I no longer saw beauty, only death.

"Guess I should call you Mollie, and you should call me W.G. Huddleson."

"All right, W.G." Now, this is my house, and I had worked hard to secure a reputation and a foothold, and no bushwhacker, not even Jesse James, would ever see fear in Mollie Ellsworth's eyes. Let a man see that, he shall trample you, sure as spit. So I turned, found the decanter and glasses, poured him a brandy, and myself a larger one, over shaking hands.

"You frightened of me, Mollie?"

His breath warmed my neck, and his long, smooth fingers topped my trembling hand, and he helped me set the decanter on the dresser, guiding me around to face him, rubbing my hand, tracing my fingers until our hands — his hands were so small and pasty with long, probing fingers — interlocked and he pulled me close to him.

"Why would I be afraid of you, Mister Huddleson?" I said at last. "Hattie Floyd wasn't."

He let go, taking his brandy, and laughed. "I haven't heard that name in years." He drank, trying hard to suppress that boyish cough because Jesse had never been much of a drinker.

■ ■ ■ ■

Years ago, perhaps shortly after the war, Hattie had worked for me in St. Louis, and Jesse had been sweet on her. At least, Hattie was sweet on him. Oh, sure, Jesse was a devout Baptist, son of a preacher, practically betrothed to his cousin and his cause, and his mother would have whipped the bitter hell out of him had she known he consorted with lewd women. But, hell, he was a man, a man often away from his home and lover. No different than any other gent I have known. Hattie did not have much experience, as a demimonde or anything else for that matter. Her man had been killed in the war, leaving her with two kids to feed, and, since her man had been a bushwhacker with Quantrill, and St. Louis was far more Union than Rebel, well, she did what she had to do. But she loved Jesse James, and, at the time, I thought maybe this young, good-looking Missouri boy and she would escape the bowels together, but I did not really know Jesse well, not then.

He came in one night, gave her this shawl, and not just something his mother had made. This was fancy, as fancy as they come, and, when she wore it on the street a couple days later, proud, pretending, dreaming, to be some refined lady, the constable arrested her. It had been stolen, worth a veritable fortune, and they demanded she tell who had given it to her. Poor love-struck Hattie would never consider selling Jesse up the river, and they put her in prison. For five years! For wearing a stolen shawl.

"Whatever happened to Hattie?" I asked.

He turned the empty glass over with a flourish. "She died years ago, Mollie. You open for business?"

Without waiting for my answer, he removed his coat and unbuckled a belt that holstered three large revolvers. That I had not expected. This was Minneapolis, not Missouri.

"Jesse," I said. "You are not on some case here, are you?"

"I'm about to be on your case, Mollie."

I gulped down my brandy and hurriedly closed the door, found my courage, and came back to him, putting my hand firmly on the butt of his Schofield. Eyes blazing, he pressed his hand on top of mine, pressed hard until I thought my fingers would break against the walnut butt, but I refused to cry out.

"I run a good place. And if you think you

can pull something like you did in Saint Louis. . . ."

He let go. "If you ever touch my revolver again, Mollie. . . ."

We let our threats go unsaid, and he unbuttoned his pants while I remembered another one of his cases, five years back in St. Louis.

One of my girls and I had been drinking with a big banker before leading him upstairs. I think that man had more interest in forty-rod than fornication, and he had loved showing off his money more than his manhood. He kept flashing his big stocking around. Try and figure that one out. This banker, chief teller at one of the largest institutions in St. Louis, carried his money around in a silk stocking. Likely skimmed it off the books, I figured. Contemptuous bastard, but we doves can never be choosy.

Jesse had been there, and I recognized that look in Jesse's eyes. He had left the bar, put his arm around me, and whispered: "Stand aside, while I drop into that."

Next thing I knew, he and the banker were fighting, and Jesse had clubbed the buffoon, grabbed the stocking, and made a beeline for the door. I had started to stop him, but again those blue eyes unnerved me, so I had

73

let Jesse flee into the darkness.

That's really why I left St. Louis. When that teller, thief though I am certain, complained that Kitty Traverse's house was not safe for rich gentlemen, those fool men listened to him. When word, even a lie, like that gets out, you might as well be running a hog ranch than a parlor house. So I sold out, moved north. Whoring is a gamble. I am certain of that, as sure as I am that had I remained in Jesse's way, tried to stop his case, block his retreat, and protect my own investment, he would have killed me.

He lay quiet when he had finished, rolled over, and curled up in a ball. A few minutes later, I heard him whispering a prayer, and I knew I had better leave, figured he was thinking about that new wife of his, how he had betrayed her, how he had failed sweet Jesus. Quickly I dressed and went downstairs, glad to be free of Jesse James for a while.

His brother sat on a corner sofa, debating Shakespeare with a Minneapolis butcher and an Eagan apothecary. Always the gentleman, Frank rose when he saw me, swept off his hat, and bowed.

"The man at the Nicollet House said the women at Madam Mollie's have no equal. I am John Wood, of Virginia, have seen much of the world, yet the man at the Nicollet House did not prepare me for your beauty." He kissed my hand, while the butcher and apothecary applauded his bravado.

"Nicollet House," I said. "The best in the city."

"We would have it no other way."

"May I buy you a glass of champagne, Mister Wood? At the bar?"

"To be seen in your company is an offer I cannot refuse." He excused himself and escorted me to the farthest, quietest corner of the parlor, where Fish brought our flutes of champagne.

"How long have you been in town?" I asked when Fish had left.

"But a short while. Trying to buy good horses."

"Saint Paul's safer than Minneapolis," I told him.

"Are you desiring we take our leave, Mollie?" He smirked, something his kid brother never could do. "We paid a hack to transport us from the Nicollet in style, and young Bob Younger's upstairs now partaking of some horizontal refreshments with that plump redhead."

Bob Younger. God, this might be worse than I ever figured. If Bob had tagged along with the James brothers, that meant Cole had to be with them, and who knew how many others.

"All I am saying is Saint Paul is safe for men of . . . of your . . . particular breed, Mister Wood."

I could easily picture Frank, Jesse, and Cole in St. Paul. That was Jack Chinn's town. Chinn had ridden with Quantrill and Morgan during the war, now ran a gambling den, pretty much controlled all of St. Paul's gambling parlors, and St. Paul did not have much law, as long as you never raised much hell. On the other hand, my bordello was about as ill-reputed as Minneapolis allowed. The city had a new Farmers' Market, which had opened up only that year. We had the Nicollet House just a few blocks from my place, we had the Pence Opera House, and an exploding population. All I could think of was Lawrence, and Centralia, Liberty, Gallatin, and Lexington — all those towns stained with blood. I dreaded the sight of Minneapolis turned into some battleground.

"Yes, well, Bob has lauded Saint Paul since his arrival. Stiles took him to a baseball game at Red Cap Park, and he seems fascinated with that damyankee game. I fear Stiles may have corrupted the poor lad."

Stiles. Bill Stiles. I knew, detested that

name, recalling Bill Stiles, a petty criminal and horse thief who had frequented my parlor years ago. That would explain why they came north to explore Minneapolis and St. Paul.

"I would rather be corrupted by baseball than. . . ." I shook my head. "The Red Caps have a good team." I winked and finished my champagne. "And some of my best customers." I let him drain his flute before turning serious. "I told, uh, Mister Huddleson, that I hope he has no designs on dropping in on any cases here."

Frank slid the empty flute down the bar, shaking his head. "Miss Ellsworth, we are simply taking in the sights, enjoying ourselves. Poker. Horse trading. Not exactly the kinds of cases you seem to be laying on our doorstep. Lord knows, we haven't had much time to enjoy ourselves of late, and we have been rather quiet, don't you think?"

I doubted that. You hear a lot in my line of work, and I had heard much over the past few days, rumors and bits of stories that did not concern me until seeing Jesse, and now Frank.

A First National Bank gentleman I entertained had mentioned how he happened upon two men sleeping at Sibley and Fifth, well-dressed men, not saddle tramps, but wearing so much iron it frightened him. Another story, out of one of Chinn's gambling dens, went that two men, before sitting down to play five-card stud, had removed their coats and gun belts, placing revolvers on the table while one of them announced — "Just want to make sure you sharpers don't play us for fools." — and I could hear Cole Younger's voice. Some stranger had bought a black horse off a farmer right in front of a mercantile for $110, then raced his new purchase up and down Wabasha Street. I heard of flashy men in dusters tipping far too much at the Nicollet House and Merchant's Hotel. I heard of men dropping fifty-cent and dollar coins from their balcony at the Nicollet on passers-by, simply to amuse themselves.

Quiet? Not Jesse and Frank. Not hardly.

"Did I tell you I have married?" Frank suddenly blurted out.

"No." Of course, many of my customers had wed, but Frank seemed overly proud of his accomplishment, and I have to give him credit, for he remained downstairs, enjoying showing off with his wit, not his wick.

"Yes, a lovely lass from Jackson County . . . used to teach school . . . though her father despises me. We eloped."

"My best wishes for happiness to the both

of you. Sometimes marriage tames the wildest, though it never turned out that way for me."

"Nor for my brother," Frank said, and I detected a trace of sadness in his voice, though he tried to hide it with his grin.

And here is something you might find peculiar, especially if you read below of what happened later that evening, but, as I headed back upstairs, I realized Frank unnerved me more than Jesse. Jesse I could never predict. He would be laughing one minute, then exploding, but Frank, he always seemed so calm, and that scared me. Jesse could not hide his emotions for long, but Frank, he bottled everything up, and I feared I would be in his path when the cauldron finally boiled over.

As soon as I closed the door, Jesse's small hands felt like iron as he struck me in the back, and the air rushed from my lungs as I fell.

"Whore!" he shouted. "Whore of Babylon!"

He picked me up and threw me on the bed, straddling me, slapping me left and right. I tasted blood.

"You tell anyone we're here, whore, and you'll be deader than Hattie Floyd, you miserable whoring bitch."

"I would never. . . ."

He hit me again. Blood rushed from both nostrils.

Someone pounded on the door, and I heard Fish's concerned voice. "Mollie! Mollie! You all right?"

I also heard the click of one of Jesse's revolvers.

"I am fine, Fish!" I called back.

"Open the door!" he yelled, unconvinced.

"He is a paying gentleman, Fish. Go away. Everything is all right."

Then I started laughing. Hard to explain. Maybe I went a tad crazy, but, with a man-killer beating hell out of you on your own bed, I imagine most women would lose control of their faculties. Jesse stared at me, bewildered, but I just laughed till my ribs hurt, looking at the little sampler on the wall, the one I had packed with me from brothel to brothel from Missouri to Minnesota:

IF AT FIRST YOU DON'T SUCCEED, TRY, TRY AGAIN

"How you feel?" Jesse asked later, as close to an apology as he would ever come. I pressed his handkerchief against my nose till the bleeding stopped. A little rouge would hide the bruises, and I could lie away the split lip.

"I have been hurt worse. This is nothing."

A light tapping sounded on the door again, and Jesse leaped for his arsenal, but Frank's voice called out: "Mister Huddleson?"

"Yeah?"

"That little row from this room earlier has cast a pall on the evening's entertainment. Mister King and I are taking our leave, and you might find it prudent to leave via the back stairwell. The gentlemen in the parlor are anxious to see Miss Ellsworth, and their numbers grow at an alarming rate. If she does not show her face soon . . . well, one of your cases might just drop in on you, sir."

"Directly," Jesse said caustically. He filled a glass and gently placed it in my hand.

The brandy burned like blazes. While I drank, he slowly withdrew an envelope from his coat pocket and placed it on my bed. It was addressed to a Mrs. David Howard, in care of General Joseph Orville Shelby of Page City, Missouri. His wife, I suspected, living a lie, living under an assumed name, with mail delivered through a second party, an old Confederate war hero like Jo Shelby, someone Jesse could trust. Sometimes I think whores have it rough, but, really, ours is an easy life. I felt for Mrs. Jesse James then, and Mrs. Frank James, though I try hard not to feel for anyone, even myself.

"If you hear of my death, would you mail that for me, Mollie? Only though if I'm dead, certain sure."

"Sure, Jesse, but you'll never die."

"Oh, I shall die like a dog, or eat the hatchet." He placed five gold pieces on the letter, kissed my whore's forehead, and left.

The next afternoon, after learning for sure that Mr. W.C. Huddleson of Baltimore, Maryland had checked out of the Nicollet House, and left no forwarding address, I located a policeman on Hennepin Avenue. Knowing the boys the way I do, I figured they would continue to split up into groups of two or three, scouting for the perfect target, then joining forces, and when those forces joined — well, I did not care to think of that.

I told the policeman that some strangers had been playing cards in a public house, armed like bandits, and arousing suspicion.

"I wouldn't concern yourself," the copper told me.

"Do you know who I am?"

"I am familiar with the goings on along

North Second."

"Well, I do not want to be implicated for not speaking up if these banditti try something here or in Saint Paul."

"Like I said, don't worry yourself."

So much for a whore's duty, I thought. No one would believe me. Maybe I should have expected that attitude, probably did, deep down, but I figured this would clear my conscience, or at least my name, because I knew Jesse James well enough to know he did not go anywhere without, as he would put it, dropping into some case. The man was a thief, and always would be one. A thief and a killer, temperamental, cold, unpredictable, frightening. As I walked away, the copper called out my name.

"Did these suspicious men give their names?"

Well, I just saw Jesse again, the time he charged out with that stocking of money in St. Louis, and him straddling me, beating me to learn me my place, though I think it had more to do with his own guilt, and him laughing about Hattie Floyd's death.

"I never asked their names," I said.

CHAPTER SIX:

COLONEL THOMAS VOUGHT

I had just stepped onto the shadiest part of the porch to enjoy an after-dinner pipe when I spied two riders riding slowly down Buck Street. Watching them, wondering if they would stop or ride on, I admired their horseflesh, hoping they would ask for accommodations, for not only did their horses interest me, but so did these strangers. Their hats were broad, black, their faces full of character, and they had an easy way of sitting in the saddle, slouched but alert. I dare say they rode with the cocksure attitude of a cavalier, and though I had detested horse soldiers during the War for the Suppression of the Rebellion, I enjoyed stimulating conversation.

Which is why I am a hosteler.

The biggest of the two — or so he seemed to me, though perhaps the way he carried himself influenced this perception — gave the other one a nudge, and both reined up but made no move to guide their horses toward my porch. They merely studied the building.

"I like a shady porch," the big man said to no one in particular.

"As do I," I added with proprietary pride. I gestured to the trees along the front of the building. A line of young ash trees grew right next to the boardwalk and porch. Others sprouted as if from the porch itself. "My wife told me, when I bought this establishment, that I should chop down these trees, that they were too close to the hotel, but I said I would not kill a tree."

When the big man sniggered, I realized the absurdity of my statement, which the stranger latched onto like a snapping turtle. "That's a mite interesting," he said, and I could only shake my head at my folly, waiting for his verbal, though humorous, challenge. "Wooden porch. Wooden columns. Wooden sign. Wooden doors. Wooden windowsills. Wooden rafters. Two whole stories of wooden sides." He glanced upward and, although he could not see the roof from his position, chanced a guess. "Wooden shingles, too. Yet no trees got killed."

"It's a house made of cards," I said. "Simply painted to resemble wood."

The big man's bluish gray eyes twinkled,

accented by a well-groomed mustache and goatee and that fine black hat. Broad-shouldered, with a ruddy complexion, he had to pack, by my guess, more than 200 pounds on a solid, six-foot frame.

"I've been pining for a real hotel," the second man said, which surprised me. I could find wisdom and humor in the first man's features, but never would have expected wit from his companion. His hair was blacker than a raven at midnight, his face so bronze, I would have thought him a savage Indian were it not for the thick mustache and Van Dyke. An intimidating man, his face a scowl even while enjoying this play on words, almost six feet in height, but seemingly thinner, less solid than the rider with the goatee. In fact, I did not notice their similarity in height until they had dismounted a few minutes later.

"Since the Big Woods." The first one nodded. "The lumberjack we met told us that . . ." — he pointed at the wooden sign, red and blue lettering on the curved plank hanging from the wooden columns like an archway — "the Flanders Hotel had the hardest beds this side of the timberline."

"Not so," replied I, keeping my face a mask, enjoying this repartée.

"Not so." His head bobbed and he asked

the second one. "What do you think?"

"I don't know. He said that rather woodenly."

My rejoinder: "Would you rather I bark out my answer?"

"No," said the first man, "but perhaps we should branch out in a different direction. How is the food in this hotel?"

"I suggest you try our cherries. Or maybe walnuts."

"Are you leaving anything out?" the second one came back.

"Merely the maple syrup."

"Well," the first one said, turning to his companion, "my head is burning like pitch pine. You. . . ."

"You never could see the forest for the trees, Capt'n," the second one fired back, excited to have come up with something to keep this silly exchange going.

"That's my cross to bear. Want to stay?"

"Oh, wouldn't I!"

They swung from their horses, and the first one, now grinning widely, shook my hand and announced: "We're running the white flag up the pole and quitting this game."

With a curt nod, I told him: "It was becoming a bore."

He shook his head, and bellowed, then

asked seriously: "Are you Mister Flanders?"

"Thomas Vought," I said. "I bought Joe Flanders out three years ago."

I whistled for the stable boy to take their mounts away, and led the two men to the register, wondering how they would sign their names, for if they tried some tree or wood allusion, I would be suspicious of them, branding them highwaymen or, worse, men who didn't know when to end a joke. I can read a signature upside down.

The big man was J.C. King. The dark-faced one, Jack Ladd, which seemed to amuse him, but, at the time, I thought he was merely reliving one of his plays on words.

In seriousness, the man I would know as J.C. King said they had come to Madelia in search of farms to purchase.

"You don't look like farmers," I said, and they didn't, not with those big black hats, black coats, linen dusters, and the heavy golden watches, big chains, large fobs. Farmers are frugal, with rough, calloused hands.

Mr. King removed his hat, revealing thinning hair — auburn, a few shades brighter than his facial hair. "Ten years ago, I didn't look like I'd be bald, but take a gander at me now."

At ease again, I informed Mr. King and Mr. Ladd that I would find much delight in showing them around Madelia, telling them of the farms that I knew might be for sale. After handshakes, I offered both a long nine cigar, which they took with relish.

Thus, we exited the hotel, turned down Buck Street, and walked along, enjoying the sunny day.

"First things first," Mr. King said. "I ain't willing to pay more'n one dollar an acre."

"No need to haggle with me, sir," I answered, "for I am not selling."

Presently I introduced them to Doc Cooley, and the good physician joined our troupe, selling Madelia and the surrounding farms as if he were a land agent.

"Lot of sloughs, lot of water, lot of woods," Mr. King said, addressing Doc Cooley. "What concerns me most is getting my crops to market. Tell me about the land around here . . . to the north, and to the west."

They had asked me the same question moments earlier, and I could not help but notice how their interest seemed much more intense when hearing descriptions of Watowan County. Naturally Mr. King's reasoning made sense, and were I buying a farm in a strange area, I would not take one man's word on paradise. I would seek opinions from everyone.

We told them about the Army Road, which ran southwest across the ford of the Watowan River. They asked about the river, the ford, and Doc told them we might have a bridge put up sometime; at least, that notion kept resurrecting itself in town meetings. We told them about the two other fords, the ferry, the hard-working nature of every resident for miles. We told them about Lake Hanska, and they asked more about bridges, so I told them about the bridge over in Linden Township, up in Brown County. We told them about Linden Lake, and again Mr. King expressed his concern about getting crops and cattle to market, about not wanting to get bogged down or flooded out. We told them a lot about Madelia, although naturally we never once mentioned St. James, the town southwest of Madelia, hell-bent on stealing our county seat.

They asked about a bank, and Doc told them that the Yates brothers gave credit at their store. They asked about a hardware store or gunsmith, and again Doc referred them to the Yates' mercantile, although saying he rarely carried anything other than a shotgun and, as far as we knew, had never been asked to repair a firearm. "Shotgun's fine," Mr. Ladd said, winding his big gold watch. "Just saw some prairie hens riding into town."

"That's about all we ever hunt," I informed them.

They asked about the law, and we said that James Glispin was a good Irishman, though we never had much trouble. They asked about the woods, again, and the sloughs, and the roads and terrain, and which farmers might be most interested in selling.

Then Mr. King asked: "Is that croquet?"

Which stopped me. I stood there blinking, confused, then Mr. King pointed to the vacant lot, and sure enough, the ladies — including Hester, my lovely wife — did have a game of croquet going, girlishly laughing as they'd try to send those balls through the wickets. Their efforts were as lamentable as mine on a baseball field.

We introduced our visitors to Hester, Mrs. Corley, Miss Ivers, Inez Murphy, and Horace Thompson's niece. Hester asked Mr. King if he would care to join them in the game. Mrs. Corley asked Mr. Ladd to join in as well, but the Indian-looking man shook his head and said he'd watch, but Mr. King said he would be delighted to join the contest. Now that, I tell you, was a sight, watching this towering man handle the curved stick, enjoying himself or maybe enjoying the admiration or adulation of those ladies. By jacks, he asked the ladies a bit about the country around Madelia, too.

"Landlord," Mr. King told me, "this has been a most enjoyable day."

We were sitting on the porch after supper, enjoying cigars and my pipe once more, listening to the ash trees rustling in the evening wind.

Mr. Ladd spoke. "Got a nice town here."

"That's why I settled here."

Withdrawing his cigar, Mr. King exhaled and pointed the burning end of his long nine in my direction. "We've practically talked ourselves out about Watowan County and the farms for sale. Never learned a thing about you." With a wink, he added: "And I reckon a tenant should know something about his landlord."

What could I tell him? I was forty-three years old, a New Yorker by birth. I had left the East before I had seen twenty years, tried farming and raising stock in Wisconsin, at Bryce Prairie, which is where I had met, courted, and married Hester. She was a Bryce Prairie Green. Then came the rebellion, and I had marched off with the 14th Wisconsin. After the war, restlessness gained control of my heart, so in '66 Hester and I moved to Madelia. I tried farming, tried raising cattle, even tried a stagecoach business, but nothing took root until the railroad reached Madelia, and I bought the hotel from Joe Flanders.

"You said end of the hostilities . . . you really think the war has ended?" Mr. King asked.

I had paid scant attention to my words. So, with a shrug, I said: "Lee and the other secessionists surrendered. Ten years have passed. I'd say the war is over."

"Secessionists." Mr. Ladd spat. "War was about a lot more than that."

"I take it you both fought on the side of the Confederacy," I said with no malice to my voice, mere curiosity.

"We're from Kentucky." Mr. King said this too quickly, though I did not really detect anything suspicious about our conversation, indeed the entire day, until a few weeks later. "Border state. Saw men in blue and gray, and, as you said, Lee surrendered. A man's past and his past allegiances are his own private matters."

Which could have ended the discussion, but Mr. Ladd asked: "See the elephant?"

My head bobbed ever slightly, and I wished I were describing Lake Hanska or that German farm down the Army Road or the country west of town. We had mustered in at Fond du Lac on a bitterly cold day in '62, reporting to Savannah, Tennessee, with Grant's army. See the elephant? Our first blood came at Pittsburg Landing. But twenty-nine, never had I imagined such slaughter, heard such savagery, taken part in such barbarity. Mayhap, I've often thought, I would have forgotten the carnage of battle, except after the Rebels retreated, the 14th had remained behind as provost guard. Other regiments moved on, in pursuit of the enemy or to lick its own wounds, leaving the unspeakable horrors behind, but we, or at least I, saw reminders of the terrible battle every damned day.

See the elephant? Corinth followed, in many ways as ghastly as Pittsburg Landing. Afterward, the misery, monotony, brutality of Vicksburg and the capture of Natchez. The bungling disaster of the Red River Expedition in '64. Tupelo, then Nashville. Down to Mobile and Spanish Fort. Finally Atlanta, now with Leggett's Division, Savannah and into the Carolinas. I rode in the Grand Review as a colonel, but found little glory in our triumph.

See the elephant? I had seen too much. I thought of my experiences in the war that I have described above, but, in my answer to the strangers, I merely said I had seen several battles with the 14th Wisconsin.

"I figured you as some peace lover," Mr. Ladd said. "I mean, man who won't kill a tree ain't likely got the gumption to send another fellow to hell."

"If I believed in hell, I would answer that I sent many men there. Men I killed wearing butternut and gray. Men wearing blue whom I ordered to their deaths."

"You were an officer?" Mr. King inquired.

"A colonel."

He whistled. "They stuck the rank of captain on me, though it didn't mean much to me, or the boys." He still did not name his allegiance, but I knew he had fought for the South.

"War is terrible," Mr. King added. "I wonder why God tolerates us foolish men."

When I said nothing, Mr. King leaned forward, using the cigar as a pointer once again. "You say you don't believe in hell. You're not a religious man, sir?"

"I find fallacies throughout the Bible."

"How so?" Eyes full of interest, he leaned back to study my answer.

"Jesus preaches peace, but the Old Testament is filled with more slaughter than I even saw at Pittsburg Landing or Corinth, or even the misery marching with Sherman. There is no consistency to this book."

"Sure there is," Mr. King said. "When Jesus preaches, he is using the teachings from the Old Testament."

" 'He teacheth my hands to war,' it says in Samuel," I retorted. "The Old Testament is full of war. . . ."

"That's why folks love reading it!" Mr. Ladd interjected.

Ignoring his colleague, Mr. King continued. "Full of war, but also full of God's message, Colonel Vought. Remember Psalms, Chapter Forty-Six. 'He maketh wars to cease unto the end of the earth; he breaketh the bow, and cutteth the spear in sunder; he burneth the chariot in the fire.' And in Samuel, the same chapter from which you quote, there is a message of love. 'God is my strength and power; and he maketh my way perfect.' "

I was not about to surrender. " 'And I have pursued mine enemies, and destroyed them; and turned not again until I had consumed them.' That's not exactly Jesus Christ's message. Is it?"

He nodded, somewhat sadly, eyes vacant, as if my Scripture had reminded him of something. For the longest while he did not speak, finally bringing the cigar to his mouth and sucking hard, then spitting, and fishing out a match from his coat pocket to re-fire it.

"Many men pursue their enemies with the wrath of the Old Testament. It's a damned shame, isn't it, landlord? Society remains intolerant. That's why Christ was put to death on the cross. That's why Lee may have surrendered, but the war is not over. Intolerance. Power. Religion. Wait a few years, and we shall be fighting again, probably for the same reasons, but maybe using some other words, Abolition or states' rights, the Indian question or the Texas border. You're a free-thinker?"

"I merely have doubts to the veracity of the Bible." I tapped my rosewood pipe against the arm of my rocker.

"Fascinating." He leaned back and stretched out his boots. "I have a friend of mine, my best friend, name of . . . well, we call him Buck . . . and he and I get into these debates all the time. Now, his mama and his brother are about as hard shell as they come, and his daddy was a Baptist preacher, though he died years ago. But Buck? He's neither agnostic nor atheist nor Bible-back. What about you? Come from a religious family? You must, the way you can recite Scripture."

"My parents were Catholic. Mass every week, and I served as an altar boy. My doubts began at Pittsburg Landing. They have not been erased."

"No offense, sir. My curiosity can get me in trouble, and if I have dredged up horrible memories or intruded on your privacy, my apologies, landlord. Religion is a favorite subject of mine, but I shall drop it."

Actually I enjoyed the debate. Not many men had the courage to argue religion, at least, not in Madelia. Even I lacked the courage to tell Hester of my doubts. I found myself glad these two men had decided to stay in town, at the Flanders Hotel. My reading of their strong faces had not been in error.

"What about the war?" Mr. Ladd asked, his voice a hard drawl. "You got any notion how the South lost? They had the best generals, best soldiers."

"Overconfidence," I said perhaps too quickly. "Lee came to Gettysburg thinking he could not lose. I think history may tell us this is also what happened to General Custer in that battle this past summer against the Sioux. It happened to Napoléon. And to many of your kings in your Bible,

Mister King."

"You weren't at Gettysburg," Mr. Ladd snapped, "and you damn' sure wasn't with Custer."

"And you were?" My own voice had turned angry.

Mr. Ladd's face flushed, but Mr. King slapped his thigh and pushed himself back in his rocker. "Overconfidence, eh? That's an interesting theory."

"Custer," I said, "won his laurels at this place in the Indian Territory . . . I disremember the name . . . but from reports I have read, he never faced real Indian warriors, not until June of this year. Remember, Minnesota had its run-in against hostile Sioux during the late war. Many were hanged just over in Mankato. I have neighbors who fought against the Indians. Many more of my friends and neighbors served in the late war. We have all seen the elephant. Certainly Lee had been tested against valiant soldiers, but he never should have ordered that charge. The war was lost then and there, if not before. Overconfidence. Seeking glory. That has killed more good men than anything."

The next morning, to my sadness, the newcomers checked out, paying their bill and shaking my hand. I handed Mr. King a list of farmers who might entertain purchase offers and wished them luck. The stable boy brought their horses, and they mounted up.

"I wish you success," I told them.

Mr. King nodded. "May the God of peace be with you," he said, and trotted his fine horse out of town.

Peace. Well, that I would not find, not for a while, my mind suddenly stoked with images from Tennessee, Mississippi, and Alabama, with nightmares brought about from childhood memories of Bible stories, of vengeful nuns and stern priests. Later, I would smell the brimstone, taste the sulphur, feel the heat of battle, my last campaign. I would come to think that a merciful God saved me in that battle, a matter I would eventually discuss with Mr. J.C. King.

Only then, approximately three weeks after our first meeting, I would address him as Cole Younger.

CHAPTER SEVEN:

JIM YOUNGER

Never turn your back on family. That's the most important thing. At least, it's the way we Youngers have always been raised. Only, Bob, my kid brother, he forgot, just wouldn't listen. Not to Cole. Not to me. Not to anyone. Nobody but Jesse, and Jesse wasn't family. Land's sake, Charlie Pitts was closer to blood than Dingus. Only the way Bob, who ordinarily didn't act so damned mule-headed, talked, Jesse James had the most brilliant mind since Mephistopheles, and we'd make a big haul in Minnesota, where nobody would be expecting the Jameses and Youngers to raid, and we'd avenge our father's murder. We'd make the Yankees pay for all the torment they caused our family. We'd come away wealthy men.

I didn't buy a word of it, but I came to Minnesota. Had to, since Bob wouldn't turn back, wouldn't listen to reason.

Family.

After a little respite in St. Paul and Minneapolis, we parted company. Cole and Charlie Pitts rode one way, Bob and Bill Stiles went another, and I stuck with Frank and Jesse and Clell Miller. Stiles had suggested we rob the bank in Mankato, so Cole and Charlie agreed to scout the land out west of there, but Frank had the notion that maybe Red Wing would be easier, so we eased our way in that direction.

From the beginning, I knew Red Wing wouldn't work. Oh, the banks were mighty enticing. The city supported three of them, including the First National at Plumb and Main with, word went, $100,000 in the till. Plus, upstairs sat the Goodhue Savings Bank, and Jesse — Mephistopheles that he is — said we could rob both banks at the same time. Wouldn't work, though. I'll give the James brothers credit. They had a peculiar talent, and, most times, Jesse or Frank planned everything real careful. That's why we had been in business for the ten years since the war's end.

You have to take a lot of things into consideration robbing a bank, especially since we found ourselves in a foreign country.

The way things worked, we always plotted our escape route, and that didn't look good in Red Wing. With only two roads in and out of town, robbing a bank or banks in Red Wing would get us all shot to pieces or hanged.

My job in these forays typically involved the hardware stores, to see what kind of guns they might supply. Red Wing had more than a few hardware stores selling double-wheel hoes, Acme cultivators, and Granger seeders. The city had Whitney's Gunshop, where I bought a few boxes of .44 cartridges. Weasel of a clerk made the comment that he didn't sell many shells that large, but he stocked them, along with a few Winchesters, too, even a Remington Rolling Block and one traded-in percussion Sharps, not to mention the little popgun pocket pistols and shotguns. Jesse didn't like that, either. Too much firepower. If the alarm spread that the bank was being stuck up, we might find ourselves leaking like sieves, shot to pieces.

So Frank and Jesse rode to Northfield, and Clell and I headed to St. Peter.

Sometimes I thought we'd never rob anything in Minnesota, that this grand adventure would turn out to be nothing more than a sabbatical, that we'd have our fun tossing coins to wide-eyed children, playing poker, and poking whores, race some horses, buy some sound stock, run out of money, and light a shuck back to Missouri. Then, I'd bid good bye to Cole and Bob and ride the rails back to La Panza, where no one knew me as an outlaw. Start over. Start a family.

Family.

I'm the worrier of the Youngers. Cole, he's the kind-hearted one, though most people, those who don't know him, would likely figure him as the hardest of the hard rocks. Bob? I don't know. If you'd asked me before the summer of '76, I'd call him the kid, the follower, but he sure made a stand, against Cole and me, against all reason. Against the family, damn it all to hell. Impetuous. Guess that's how I'd label him now. And me? Like I said, I'm the worrier.

Which is why I started drinking.

Cole, he'd seldom pull a cork, certainly never when we were hitting a bank or a train. Liquor robbed a man of reason, and Cole demanded we be alert and ready when on a case. That's another reason we had been in business so long, despite turncoats and Pinkertons and other laws. My older brother could preach temperance like some circuit-riding Methodist. Nor would Cole ever take a hand of poker if Bob and I were sitting at the table. Figured it would lead to repercussions.

Neither St. Peter nor Northfield held much interest to us, not at first, not after hearing all that flapdoodle Bill Stiles, or Chadwell as he sometimes was called, spouted off about money for the taking in Mankato. Those stories reminded me of all that talk about buckets full of gold just waiting to be picked in California and Colorado.

I knew better. I started drinking after we rode up to St. Peter. Some of the boys were supposed to join us there, but, when they didn't show, my nerves began tormenting me. I'd buy every newspaper I could find, and spend breakfast or supper reading every item, slurping coffee, trying to learn of any arrests.

Nothing.

So I'd sweeten my coffee with John Barleycorn. After a day, I quit with the coffee. Finally Bob and Stiles showed up, but we still hadn't heard anything from Cole and Charlie Pitts, scouting, we believed, somewhere around Watowan County.

"The hell with this," Jesse said. "Let's do Mankato and be done with this damyankee state."

So we rode to Mankato, meeting up at last with Cole and Charlie.

It was September 2nd.

City was a-bustle when we came riding in from the South Bend Road. After breakfast, I inspected the hardware stores, then watched as Frank entered the First National Bank to change a $20 bill and get the lay of the bank, the vault. I snuck a few swallows from my flask, hating the prospects. Like I said, folks had packed into the city, and the bank looked no better than the three in Red Wing. It was a frame building, and about a half dozen carpenters were already at work.

"Banking business is good," said Stiles, who had walked up to me. "They're adding on. Need more room for all that money we're about to withdraw."

And he was sober, the damned fool.

Ask me, the First National Bank of Mankato was a deathtrap. But nobody asked me.

"I think the teller suspicioned me," Frank said later that day when we met in a patch of woods by the Minnesota River to talk things over. "He kept staring at me while counting out the change he made me. I think he saw me looking at the vault and the windows."

"Most of those windows are boarded up," Clell Miller said. "That could be a problem."

"You two have become cautious old

106

women," Jesse said. "Boarded up windows." He snorted. "Nobody could see in."

"We couldn't see out, either," Frank fired back.

I had another drink.

"Town was crowded," Cole said.

"Shouldn't be so bad tomorrow," said Stiles.

Our debate carried an edge, more so than usual. Even Frank sounded a tad raw, and I'd never ridden with a man as cool in the heat of battle as Frank James. Frank and Cole, only Cole just frowned.

Tense, things were. Yet maybe, I thought, Jesse was right. Get the damned thing over with. Get out of this damyankee state.

Jesse and Bob checked into the Clifton House on Front Street, while Clell and Stiles got a room at the Gates House. Cole and Charlie bunked at this place on Washington Street, and Frank and me rode over to Kasota and paid some farmer for a night's lodging. Didn't want everyone in town, you see. That was another way we operated.

"Might I ask your name?" the farmer asked.

"No questions asked," Frank said, his words somewhat slurred. "No lies told."

■ ■ ■ ■

Next morning, we decided to make our play.

Things went to hell in a hurry.

"By god, Jesse James!"

Jesse and Bob were mounting their horses, when this gent shouted at them, or rather, Jesse, from across the street.

"You've sprouted some chin whiskers since I last saw you, old hoss. How the hell are . . . ?"

Jesse made no reply, didn't even look at the man, just rode toward the river, followed quickly by Bob to the river bottoms, where they stopped to fix coffee, awaiting the rest of us.

I emptied my flask as Jesse told us the story. Wasn't much rye left in it, anyway.

"Fellow in town recognized me," Jesse announced after we had finished our coffee.

Frank chuckled, and I suspicion that he had been drinking more than was his custom, too. His tone didn't have the sharpness of last night, and his eyes shone like a drunkard's, like mine.

"You are ubiquitous, Dingus," he said.

I don't think Frank believed Jesse. I know damned well Cole didn't, could tell by the scowl on his face, but I'm not sure. Bob wouldn't lie to me, and Jesse had no reason to tell some stretcher, though his vanity often got the better of him. 'Course, Bob used to listen to his brothers.

"Price of fame," Jesse said, far too casual for my liking, but he turned serious. "I didn't reply, just rode out with Jim. But this puts us at a crossroads, boys. If we ride into Mankato, it could be a trap."

"I'm betting we'll be safe," Stiles said. "Man in southern Minnesota cries out . . . 'I've seen Jesse James!' . . . nobody believes him. Nobody at all. Hell, who would?"

"You recognize this fellow, Dingus?" Clell Miller asked.

"Didn't study his face. Just rode out, pretending I hadn't heard him."

"Let's just get this damned thing over with," Bob shot out, and, for once, I agreed with my kid brother.

"Damn' right." I walked to my horse.

The plan we had laid out worked this way. Three of us would ride into town, straight to the bank, followed by two more to watch things in front of the bank. If they liked the look of things, they'd start the ball. The rest of us would follow, keep a watch on the streets, and, if shooting commenced, we'd keep the townsfolk scared, keep their heads

109

down by firing shots and cutting loose with Rebel yells.

We rode in at noon, finding way too many folks outside to our liking, so we circled back to the river, passing the time, then, an hour later, returned to the bank.

Land's sake, the crowd seemed even bigger.

"The game's afoot," Jesse said. "Let's get out of here."

We left Mankato at a healthy lope.

"This ain't worth a tinker's damn, Stiles!" Jesse shot out. "I'm half broke, spent most of the money we got from Rocky Cut trying to plan this damned robbery."

'Course, Jesse had spent his money tossing coins to kids, flaunting his wealth on whores and whiskey and the finest hotels and finest duds. He liked spending money. Well, so did Bob, even Cole.

"You said it would be easy pickings," Jesse went on, his face flushed with irritation. "But we don't have a thing to show for it. Might as well go back to Missouri."

I was all for that.

It fell silent for a moment, broken when Stiles suggested: "Northfield."

"Jim?" Frank asked. I thought he was inquiring about my thoughts of Northfield.

There were two hardware stores — least, that's what Frank and Jesse had reported to me, for I'd never even set foot in Northfield. But I didn't find cause for concern, in my cups like I was. The nearest hardware shop to the bank — Manning's was the name, I remembered — didn't have the stock of the Red Wing gun shop, and the other store was even smaller. Plus, Yankee mill workers and college professors didn't impress me as warriors.

"Piece of pie," I said and, hearing the sniggers, looked up to see Frank shaking his head, holding out his hand, waiting for me to pass the jug of wine we had bought in New Ulm. Frank didn't care a whit what I thought about Northfield, just needed a snort. I passed him the Bordeaux.

"Northfield." Jesse's head bobbed.

"Rich town," Stiles said. "Like I said before, it's where that bastard Ames lives. We could put a hurt on him, and make ourselves rich."

"You boys better sober up," Cole snapped, "before we try anything."

"We will," I said, smiling a drunken smile. I had no intention of listening to my big brother. Reckon I had forgotten all about family, too.

■ ■ ■ ■

We're not soothsayers, not Merlin, not God, can't see the future. Well, we talked things over, and were all agreed. We'd try Northfield, but we took our time getting there, scouting the roads, the farms, the forests. I still had a map I had bought at some bookstore in Minneapolis, and Stiles had a compass.

The next night we rode into this little burg called Cordova, and the following night found us in Millersburg, even a smaller dot in the road than Cordova. I spent most of that night sick with worry, alone in my room at the old Cushman House. Worrying. Well, maybe the whiskey and wine had me off my feet, not just the worries.

It was September 7th, a Thursday, when we rode to Northfield, making a little camp in the woods outside of town.

"Bank's busy," Stiles said after a little scout of things. "Like I said, this one should be easy."

"Two hardware stores," Cole said. "Not what I'd call an arsenal."

To get a feel for the town, a few of us crossed the railroad track on Third Street, turned on Water, and trotted our mounts over the iron bridge into Mill Square. They were changing shifts at the Ames mill, and we turned right onto Division Street. The First National Bank stood on the river side of the street, between a general store and an undertaker's.

Undertaker. Bad sign. More forewarning when we picked up a copy of the newspaper, and the first thing I noticed was a front-page advertisement.

THEODORE MILLER
UNDERTAKER
Have the Largest and Finest Stock of
COFFINS
On Hand to be Had in This Town

More bad sign. I was too in my cups to take note.

Rob the bank, ride out, cut the telegraph wires, get back to Missouri. It would be as easy as the train at Rocky Cut.

Shortly after noon, Bob, Jesse, Charlie, Frank, and me had dinner at this place called Jefts' Rail Road Restaurant.

"Eat hearty, boys," Jesse said, and he did. So did the rest of us. Most of us, least ways. Not me. I didn't have much of an appetite until Jefts himself brought us a bottle of whiskey. Frank had ordered it. I hadn't heard him.

"This used to be a Temperance town," Jefts said. "But we've reformed."

"That's good," I said, helping myself to three fingers of the worst forty-rod to blister a man's throat.

For some reason, Jesse, contrary as he liked to be, tried to bet Jefts $1,000 that Minnesota would vote Democratic that fall. Damned fool. Talk like that would arouse suspicion. I knew that, even drunk and worried as I was.

Jefts didn't take the bet, said it was a damned stupid wager. It was, too. This is Yankee country.

After lunch, we rode back to the woods, waiting on Cole, Stiles, and Clell to join us. Hell, neither of those had been drinking, and I bet if Cole had known that we were all pretty drunk and intent on getting drunker, he would have called the damned thing off.

"Town's getting crowded," Cole said.

"The hell," Jesse shot back. "Let's get her done."

"Yeah," Clell agreed. "I'm down to my last dime."

"Only if it looks good," Cole said.

"Right." That came from Stiles. He pulled out a piece of paper he had torn out of some newspaper. The bank had some new Yale chronometer vault and safe. "You boys might want to read this, those of you who'll be inside the bank."

He passed it to Frank, who didn't even bother reading it.

"Bob," Jesse said, "you'll be inside. You and Charlie and my brother." He turned to Cole. "Bud, you and Clell, you follow them into town." Back to face his brother. "If it looks good, you go inside the bank, do the business. If not, ride out." Back to Cole. "If things get ticklish, fire a shot in the air. That'll bring Jim, me, and Stiles into town. Otherwise, we'll wait here, make sure nobody blocks our retreat. Then, when we're done, Bill will lead us out of here. We'll cut the telegraph wires. Sound good?"

Nods all around.

"Nothing to worry about," Stiles said. "I told you boys this would be easy, and you'll soon find out just how easy it is."

Clell Miller let out a little laugh, but I think he was all bluster. "I'm a-gonna smoke my pipe through the whole shebang," he said. "That's how easy this'll be."

"All right," I said, gathering the reins to my horse, watching Frank, Charlie, and Bob mount up and ride down the street.

Cole called out to them, and to us, maybe

to himself, and to his conscience. I guess Brother Cole worried, too. "Nobody gets hurt. Whatever happens, we don't shoot anybody if we can help it. I won't have any innocent blood on my hands."

CHAPTER EIGHT:
ALONZO E. BUNKER

What kind of joke is this?

Those first thoughts flashing through my brain seem childish at best, idiotic at worst, looking back on that horrible day, but you must take into consideration that Northfield, Minnesota is not St. Alban's, site of that dramatic secessionist robbery in Vermont during the war to free the slaves and preserve the union. When three men announced their intentions of robbing the bank that Thursday afternoon, I thought it had to be in jest, an almighty poor joke.

I am not a man who will allow whiskey to pilfer me of my faculties, but although I abstain from intoxicating liquors, not all of my friends have proselytized the heritage and teachings of John North, our town founder. For the most part, the men who honor me with their friendship prefer beautifying their gardens, working on their homes, understanding the gospels, bettering their minds and souls, but Northfield is not without its "bum" element. One needs to merely happen by that wretched Jeft's bucket of blood by the depot or wander down the boardwalk in front of the Exchange Saloon on pay day. And, yes, some of my acquaintances have been known to decorate their noses with the suds of a beer. Inventing a diversion like this would not be beneath them.

Pen in hand, I left my ciphers and turned at the sound of the door opening shortly after two o'clock that afternoon, not even looking up until I reached my position at the teller's counter facing the front lobby. Then I saw them. Blinking, trying to comprehend the sight of three men brandishing horse pistols of an immense caliber I had never imagined, I registered my first thought: What a foolish joke! But which fool is playing it on me?

Suspicions immediately targeted J.S. Allen, who, minutes earlier, had left the bank after bringing in a deposit slip but having forgotten the money. Only I would only rarely associate jocundity with Mr. Allen, especially raw, foul humor.

The three men wore no masks, but long linen dusters covered their clothes as if part of some uniform. One man was dark, a brooding, vicious specimen. All were tall. All sprouted facial whiskers in one form or another. I did not recognize them. They had left the front door open, but, through a glimpse, I spied another man, also clad in a duster, slam it shut. When the three gunmen jumped over the counter, I still thought this to be some ill-thought attempt at comedy. Even when one of the inside men cried out — "We're robbing the bank! We've got forty men outside!" — even moments later when I heard J.S. Allen's shouts from the front door, even then, I could not accept the reality of the situation.

Robbery? In Northfield? No. Never. I am twenty-seven years old, in my first year of marriage to a wonderful schoolteacher, employed at the First National Bank for the past three years. I am a graduate of the St. Paul Business College, a former student at Carleton College here in Northfield, the second son of fine New England parents. This could not be happening.

This wasn't even the permanent home of the bank. We were operating in the Scriver Building. Our cashier, Mr. George M. Phillips, was not even in Minnesota on this day. Maybe it was Phillips who was behind this joke. Joseph Lee Heywood, my friend and fellow worker, the First National Bank's bookkeeper, had revealed to me a conversation he had had with Mr. Phillips about what actions he might take if our bank were to be assaulted.

Certainly, Joe and I never dreamed a robbery would ever happen. Could this be Mr. Phillips's hand? No, he would do nothing so preposterous. Yet it couldn't be a real robbery.

A long-barreled revolver pressed hard against my face.

"Which one of you sons-of-bitches is the cashier? Is it you?"

I found myself that afternoon working as the teller. The lobby was empty, had been since J.S. Allen left to find his deposit. Working with me that day were Joe Heywood, acting cashier during Mr. Phillips's absence, and assistant bookkeeper, Frank Wilcox, all fine colleagues, industrious men of high principles and solemn living.

"Hands up, damn you. Now open that safe, or I'll blow your damned brains out." Only then, their curses finally registering as the cold barrel pressed harder against my cheek bone, did it strike me then that Joe Heywood, Frank Wilcox, and I faced desperate men. In addition to the dusters, all three donned hats (two black, one gray) and spurred boots, with more pistols shoved into shell belts that I would think possible. They stank of whiskey, but their pupils did not hold the dull ignorance of a drunkard's. The eyes looked cold, deadly, merciless.

Fear numbed me. This was no dream, no joke.

"I asked you a question, you son-of-a-bitch. Which one of you two is the damned cashier?"

Two? They had not noticed Joe Heywood, couldn't see him from his position in the corner, partially hidden by the cashier's desk, and, when the smallest of the trio bounded for the vault and stepped inside, Joe, bless his brave heart, bolted out of his chair and tried to slam the heavy door shut, trapping one of the three inside.

He failed, for the outlaws screamed, and one leaped forward, slapped Joe with brutality and curses, and flung him against the partition.

"You bastard! Try that again, and we'll kill you!"

Outside came more cries. "Robbery! Robbery! Get your guns, boys, they're robbing the bank!"

Too real. Too real. Too real.

"Are you the damned cashier?" the third

121

man asked me.

I tried to answer, but couldn't. My head shook. They asked Frank Wilcox. They asked Joe Heywood. Both heads shook, but they singled out Joe as the most likely cashier, as, indeed, he had been stationed at the cashier's desk.

"You're the damned cashier! Open the safe . . . quick, or I'll blow your head off!"

"Murder!" Joe cried. "Murder! Murder!"

Outside, shots rang out.

"Shit!" one of the bandits inside yelled. "I'll show you murder, you lousy bastard."

The other two dragged Heywood toward the vault.

All during this time, I had not moved since raising my hands at their vile instruction upon understanding the seriousness, the essence of the situation. Now realizing that I still held a pen in my hand, I tried to place it on the counter, but the youngest of these fiends swung his revolver in my direction. "I said keep your damned hands up! Get down on your knees."

The pen slipped from my fingers, dropping at my feet, while my right hand shot up again.

These brutal men continued to torment Joe, and, when the young man guarding Frank and myself turned his attention on that torture, my eyes spied the .32 Smith & Wesson near my ledger.

Could I reach it in time?

I never got the chance, because one of the wicked souls torturing Joe had looked up to see me, perhaps read my mind. He was the most savage-looking of the three, with a face darker, eyes cruel, thick mustache, and small under-lip beard.

"Hey, you bastard!" He shoved Joe's face onto the floor and, leaping from a crouch, raced toward me, brandishing his big Colt revolver. Spotting the .32, he shoved it into his waistband, laughing drunkenly as he told me, and his companions: "You couldn't hit anything with that little Derringer anyway."

The savage man, who resembled a half-breed, returned to the tall, gentlemanly figure, and drew a big Bowie knife against Joe's throat. "Open the safe now, damn you, or you haven't but a moment to live. I'll cut your throat. Cut your damned head off!"

Never have I seen a man as brave as Joe Heywood, as cool as he was that afternoon. Since his cries of murder moments earlier, he had regained his composure, had resolved to do his duty. The blade cut him slightly, and blood trickled onto his paper collar, but he replied in an even voice: "There is a time lock on, and the safe cannot be opened at this time."

"That's a damned lie!" the tall man, proving he was no gentleman, shouted.

Well, yes and no. The safe did have a time lock, but all those fools had to do was pull the door open. The door was shut, but we had not turned the combination dial to secure the locking mechanism. Nothing should have kept those three rogues from some $15,000.

Nothing but their ignorance, their drunkenness, and Joseph Lee Heywood's bravery.

"Hell," the tall man said, nodding at the dark one. "Go inside and try the safe."

"All right, but don't let that son-of-a-bitch lock me inside, Buck!"

"He won't do a thing," said his tall colleague.

More shots outside. And more. Screams of men, women, horses.

Suddenly, with a wicked oath and no warning, the tallest man slammed the butt of his Remington revolver against Joe's head, a sickening, heart-breaking sound, and the poor man, my good friend, crumpled in a heap. The two brutes dragged him into the vault, ordering him once more to open the safe, but I didn't think Joe could answer. I truly thought that such a blow would not only render him senseless, but kill him.

A shout from outside: "For God's sake, boys, hurry up! They're shooting us all to pieces!"

The Indian-looking one fired a pistol shot at Heywood's head, and, when I flinched, fearing they had killed my friend, the youngest one decided to brutalize me.

"Where's the money outside the safe?" he asked. "Where's the cashier's till?"

I summoned my courage, inspired by Joe Heywood, and pointed to the box of loose change atop the counter.

"There," I said.

"Horseshit!"

Yet he withdrew a grain sack, and dumped the nickels, pennies, and silver inside, never noticing the drawer underneath the box, the cashier's drawer that, by my guess, contained perhaps $3,000.

"You get anything, Bob?" the tall man asked.

"My claim ain't panning out much, Buck!" he said with a mirthless laugh, but, when he turned toward me again, anger flashed in his blue eyes, and I thought I would die.

"There's more money than that here, and you damn' well better tell me where it is, you son-of-a-bitch! Where the hell's that cashier's till? And what in hell are you standing up for? I told you to keep down."

He shoved me to the floor, and jammed the cold, hard barrel of his revolver at my temple.

"Better show me where that money is you son-of-a-bitch, or I'll kill you."

It's a cliché, I know, but I closed my eyes and thought about my life. I saw my mother. I saw dear Nettie, and wondered how long my wonderful bride would wear black, to grieve for me after these vile, wicked men killed me. I thought of God, and the Streets of Gold. I thought I was dead, and as I mouthed the Lord's Prayer, I realized the young brigand had returned to the counter, rummaging for paper money and coin.

I looked up. If I could make it through the director's room, I could hurl myself out the back door — pretty much nothing more than blinds — dart down the alley, maybe warn Mr. Manning in the hardware store. If I wasn't killed inside the bank, or shot down from all those gunshots I kept hearing outside.

Something else flashed through my mind. The savage Indian-looking man kept growling, and the tall man, scattering papers from Joe's desk, whirled at him and yelled, screaming at him to try the damned safe. If

126

he pulled on the handle, the door would open, and Joe's bravery would be for nothing. I had to act. Now.

Frank Wilcox remained on his knees, staring in my direction although I doubt if his brain registered anything — his face ashen. Still, I motioned for him to move a little closer to the counter, to give me room to make my break. They had killed Joe Heywood; at least, that is what I feared, and, had I known Joe still breathed life's air, had I known what would happen once I fled, I would gladly have traded my life for his, would resolutely have stayed inside the bank, but, as God is my witness, I thought Joe was already dead and feared that, if I did not make my play now, both Frank Wilcox and I would join him as victims, unless I acted immediately.

I shot to my feet, and ran, pushing past poor Frank Wilcox, ran hard through the back door.

"Shit!" The dark man's voice rang out, followed with sacrilegious curses from the youngest of the trio, and the tall man's orders: "Stop that bastard, Charlie!"

Then . . . a gunshot!

My ears rang as I hurried, seeing the bullet splinter the blinds right before I pushed through them, crashing outside, hearing the cannonade of the attack from all around Mill Square and Division Street.

From inside the bank: "Kill that son-of-a-bitch!"

Outside — shrieks, hoofs, gunfire that surrounded, it seemed, the entire town.

Feet churning, flailing stupidly, I ran as hard as I could, heard the dark man's vile cursing, heard the click of his revolver, or at least imagined I did.

An instant later, a bullet slammed into my back.

CHAPTER NINE:

ANSELM R. MANNING

Try as I might, my hands would not quit trembling.

I am not a soldier, not a young man. I am a forty-three-year-old Canadian-turned-Minnesotan, an Episcopalian and Freemason, a Northfield businessman with a lovely wife and three-month-old daughter. For all of those things I have mentioned above, albeit not in that order, I found myself fighting when bandits attempted to sack our town. My town. My home for the past twenty years. I would not be deterred, no matter how frightened I was, no matter the danger of the situation. My life meant nothing, not in the grand scheme of things.

But . . . gee willikins! I acted as naïve as most citizens on that Thursday afternoon. Even the first shot did not alarm me.

"What was that?" R.C. Phillips asked.

Phillips started walking toward the entrance of the hardware store, where I sat working on the books, but I waved him off. Earlier, I had read in the Rice County Journal that some Thespian group was performing at the Opera House that evening, and I warranted the actors in this combination had gotten permission through the local constabulary to ride up and down Division Street and raise a ruction, to draw up interest for the sordid melodrama that appealed to teen-age boys and ne'er-do-wells with too much time on their hands and an imagination whetted by the half-dime novels published by Beadle & Adams.

Yet when I heard the panicked shouts, and J.S. Allen's warning — "Get your guns, boys, they're robbing the bank!" — followed by muffled curses and an explosion of musketry, I understood the gravity of the afternoon.

At that moment, J.S. Allen, who owned the hardware store next to my own, ran inside my store, it being closest, out of breath, terrified but unfaltering. "Robbery!" he cried out. "Robbery! Robbery! We've got . . . to get the . . . guns."

He tried to explain what was happening to R.C. Phillips, but I caught only bits and pieces. Allen had walked to the First National, temporarily being housed in the Scriver Building. One or two men had stopped him, struck him, cursed him. He had fled. They had fired at him, maybe in warning, perhaps with the intention to maim or kill.

I didn't hear the rest. John Tosney and John Archer rushed inside as R.C. made his way to the door, pushing him away from the door and windows. "They're robbing the bank!" one of them shouted. "Better stay off the streets!"

Yet I had no intention of doing such. Gunshots popped outside as I grabbed a handful of ammunition, picked up the Remington breechloader with which I had been practicing for the fall hunts, and stepped out of the store over stunned protests and made my way to the corner of Mill Square and Division Street.

"Get off the streets! Get back, you sons-of-bitches!"

At first glance, I knew more than two men were taking part in this affair. I spotted two men in front of the bank, three others galloping on horses, firing six-shot revolvers, yipping a bloodcurdling yelp, cursing. Desperate men.

"Better jump back now!" came a friendly if petrified voice near me. "Or they shall kill you."

With trembling hands, I took careful aim.

I squeezed the trigger, and shot a horse tethered in front of the Scriver Building.

This action aroused the wrath of one of the men in front of the bank. He wore a broad black hat and linen duster, as did all of these plunderers, and I could tell he sported long side whiskers, an auburn mustache and goatee. He snapped a shot over my head, screaming to one or all of his companions: "Kill that white-livered son-of-a-bitch!"

I tried to extract the shell from the rifle, but it remained stuck, so I hurried back inside the store, drew a ramrod, and, with R.C. Phillips's help, rammed it down the barrel, pushing the hot brass cartridge out. In my haste, I had grabbed the wrong ammunition, but now I rectified this situation, and, armed with the appropriate caliber, I returned to my position, sweating, shaking, pale, but determined.

"Get in, you sons-of-bitches!" repeated the vile cry of one of the brigands.

More gunfire, and I realized my defense of Northfield was not a lone act. A shotgun roared, and across the street I saw men and boys of our town hurling stones at the men on horseback as they thundered past, firing pistols, ducking behind the necks of their mounts like red Indians. Impressive warriors . . . I will say that much for them, and brave, I suspect, but not as courageous as the people of Northfield, who rose to meet the threat. Boys and men, young and old, throwing stones at highwaymen firing huge pistols. Comrades, that is what I define as grit.

Another shotgun blast. And another. Rifle fire from across the street. Another shot from a nearby window upstairs. The popping of small pistols. Shattering glass and pounding hoofs.

Grit!

We were not prepared for a murderous invasion. We are peaceable city folk, but we would account well for ourselves on this day.

The man with the goatee jumped up from behind the dead horse serving as breastworks, pounded on the bank door, and shouted: "For God's sake, boys, hurry up! They're shooting us all to pieces."

At that moment, his companion in front of the bank tried to mount his horse, but a lad — Elias Stacy, I would later learn, a fine boy of strong Canadian stock with two brave brothers — ran forward and shot him in the face with a fowling piece.

"Cole!" the man cried, falling back into the dust. "Cole! I'm hit, Cole! I'm hit!"

Elias Stacy whirled and ran back to find

cover behind the crates stacked in front of Lee & Hitchcock's store.

Grit, indeed. What bravery he had shown, and he was not finished. "Help me load this piece or give me another gun!"

"Keep your head down," I told him, and took aim.

In front of the Scriver Building, the man with the goatee squatted beside his friend, who was halfway sitting up, shaking his head, not seriously wounded for Stacy's weapon had been loaded with only chicken shot. I took aim again. A bullet whistled over my head. "Get back inside," bellowed a man on horseback, "you damned bastard!" I rushed my shot, did not have a proper target, anyway, and saw the wooden post splinter, then the man with the goatee crumpled, whirled, snapped a shot. My .45-70 bullet had gone through the post and struck him in the hip, a scratch shot, but one I'd gladly take.

I leaped back as a bullet ripped past my ear.

The shakes worsened.

"Be careful," another voice told me, calm but firm. "They have been shooting merely to warn us, frighten us. Now they are intent to kill."

I blinked. Governor Adelbert Ames, newly

134

returned to Northfield from his stay down South, stood beside me. "Take a deep breath," he said to me. "Don't stay in plain view too long." He smiled. "You are doing fine, Anselm."

"Would you . . . ?" I offered him the breechloader.

His head shook. "You are the better shot, Anselm. Continue the fight, my good man. Can you shoot the other horses in front of the bank?"

I reloaded, drew back the hammer, and prepared to chance yet another shot as Elias Stacy darted across the street and dived through an open door, pleading again for someone to give him a weapon to use against these bushwhackers. I aimed at one of the other horses, but the rifle shook violently, and I ducked back, the breech-loader unfired. "I can't," I told Governor Ames. "Not the horses. I . . . just. . . ."

"It is all right, Anselm," the governor said soothingly. "I fear I could not kill a horse, either. So kill the men who ride them."

That I felt I could do.

"Take careful aim," the governor coached.

I stepped into the street again.

Up the road about a block, perhaps 130 or 140 rods away, I spied one of the outlaws, popping shots at our townsmen, hiding behind the neck of his horse. He was one of the few clean-shaven ruffians raiding our town, and I drew a bead on where I thought he might lift his body and give me a clear shot. When he did appear, just for a second, I squeezed the trigger, thought I saw him flinch, and leaped back behind the wall to reload.

Governor Ames smiled. "Great shooting, Anselm," he said. "We could have used a man with your eye and pluck during the rebellion."

My mouth felt too dry to even attempt a response. My hands trembled with such force it's a wonder I hit anything that day.

"Chadwell! Stiles!" one of the outlaws yelled. "Stiles! Bill! Bill! Christ A'mighty!"

I worked another shell into the Rolling Block's chamber, returned to my position, and saw the clean-shaven man lying dead in the dust. His horse trotted along casually, turned down Fifth Street as if heading for the Northfield Livery. Only then did I know for certain that my bullet had flown true.

I felt no compunction, no need for penitence (except, much later, for the horse I had slain), not even fear, not any more. I fired again, ducked back, heard the man with the goatee pounding on the door with the butt of his revolver, screaming: "For

God's sake, boys, come out! It's getting too hot for us!"

The man with the goatee limped to his horse, swung into the saddle, firing, shouting at his rowdy friends inside the bank to finish their business. The man Elias Stacy had shot in the face with the shotgun had also remounted.

Horses thundered past us again. Smoke burned my eyes. My ears pounded from the roar of the battle.

Then a cry came from a voice I did not recognize, but it had to be from one of my neighbors.

"They've shot Alonzo Bunker!"

Chapter Ten:

CHARLIE PITTS

I'd ride through hell for Capt'n Younger.

Best friend I ever had, but then, when I think about it, I never met many men I'd label a pard, and damned fewer who'd call me his pal. Capt'n Cole, though, I reckon he'd ride through hell for me, too.

So when that pip-squeak of a bank teller scrambled to his feet and dived through the flimsy back door, I let out with an oath and took after him, mad more at myself than that paper-collar man, mad for letting the capt'n down.

'Course, it was young Bob who was supposed to have been watching him at the time. I had just stepped out of the vault to holler something at Frank when I heard the teller's shoes pounding the wood floor and caught him out of the corner of my eye. "Shit!" I yelled, and Bob whirled, yelling something stupid. I ran after the fool Yank, snapped a shot, jerking the trigger at the last moment because I recollected that Capt'n Cole didn't want us to shoot anyone iffen we could help it. 'Course, with all those shots coming from out in the streets, I wasn't so certain nobody was following the capt'n's orders no more.

"Stop that bastard, Charlie!" Frank James hollered at me, but I was already chasing the teller. He had pushed through the blinds, gone down the steps, and was raising dust through the back alley. Only twenty feet ahead of me.

"Kill that son-of-a-bitch!" Bob's voice boomed inside the bank.

Which is what I figured, now, I had to do.

I raised my Smith & Wesson, pulled the trigger, figuring the capt'n's rules didn't apply no more that things had gone to hell. Nailed that running son-of-a-bitch in the back, through the shoulder blade, heard him gasp, saw him stagger, blood spurting, but damned iffen that rascal didn't somehow manage to keep his feet. He was running south, had a funny way of running, like his legs wasn't bending or something, maybe from fright. I thumbed back the hammer on my .44, but the banker was gone.

"Damnation!" I said, heard Bob Younger's shouting from inside, and I rushed up the steps and back to the vault.

The older banker, he remained where I had left him, on his knees behind the counter, eyes wide, hands raised but shaking like some drunk's. The younger guy, the one with the dark beard who had tried to lock me in the vault, he lay inside the vault, bleeding from where Frank had practically stoved in his head with his big Remington pistol.

"You get him?" Bob asked.

"Chicken fled the coop," I answered.

"Well, hell, Charlie, that's all right!" He grinned slightly at the noise from the battle being waged outside. "Seems the alarm's already been given."

Bob is Capt'n Cole's kid brother, not a bad fellow at all, and I'd call him a man to ride the river with. All of them Youngers was.

I growed up near Commerce down in the Indian Nations, one of a dozen kids, though I had been pretty much on my own since the summer of '60 when I got adopted out — bartered, reckon you'd have to call it — to work on a farm, our family being dirt poor like most folks down in the Nations. Mama was a Cherokee. Pa was a squawman, farmer when he wasn't running whiskey for some white fellers over in Fort

Smith. That left me nothing more'n white trash. Or a red nigger. Half-breed. Injun. Puke. Ruffian. You name it, but iffen you do it to my face, or if even I just gets word of it, I'll kill you. A year or so later found me in Missouri, and that's where I come across Cole Younger's daddy.

He had been shot dead, thrown in some bar ditch. Me and the wife of this farmer I was working for — Washington Wells was his name, and I'd later come to use Sam Wells as one of my handles when on the dodge. Anyway, me and Mrs. Wells seen the body, and I'd covered him up with my saddle blankets and waited while Mrs. Wells rode to Westport to fetch help. It was one of them sultry days in June, threatening to rain. I just stayed with the body, by lonesome, to keep animals from the poor soul. Nothing anybody half decent wouldn't do, but these wasn't decent times in Missouri. Mr. Younger had been a wealthy man, a powerful one, with sons favoring Southern sympathies, same as me, and I reckon that's why them Kansas Redlegs or Union vermin or Abolitionists or whoever killed him. That unfortunate circumstance is how I come to meet Thomas Coleman Younger. Later, Mr. and Mrs. Wells brung me over to Lee's Summit to meet the Youngers. Capt'n Cole

141

wanted to see me, to thank me personal for staying with his daddy. Capt'n Cole, he shook my hand, said he'd never forget what I done.

Shook my hand.

Me, Charlie Pitts, piece of squaw trash from the Nations, shaking hands with a rich feller like Cole Younger. Man had a strong grip.

Damned right I'd ride through hell for the capt'n. And his brothers.

"For God's sake boys, come out!" It was Capt'n Cole's voice. He pounded on the door with one of his pistols. "It's getting too hot for us!"

"Frank?" Bob and I called out at the same time.

Frank James, about the coolest man in a fight I'd ever laid eyes on, let out with a curse, and kicked at the man he had buffaloed.

"The hell with this," Bob said, grabbing the wheat sack of coin he had collected, and marched toward the door, not waiting for Frank's orders. Mind you, Bob wasn't scared. None of them Youngers never understood the meaning of fear, but I suspect Bob felt concern from his brothers, wondering how they fared out on the streets where the shooting was hotter than the gates of Hades.

Frank started to say something, but Bob barked out first: "My brothers are outside, Buck! Yours, too!"

Frank just stood there, gripping that big .44 till his hands shook and his knuckles turned white.

Wasn't nothing like we had expected.

When we first left Missouri, we'd had a hell of a time, buying and racing horses, playing poker, whoring. One reason I always rode with the boys wasn't just because of the capt'n and the way he had treated me, but because we had a fandango wherever we hung our hats. Some right interesting jollifications. We laughed a lot, too, even during the most desperate of situations. Sure, we'd fight amongst ourselves, but that was just natural. Mostly, we took things in stride, figured we wouldn't live forever, but we'd have some laughs, spend some money, make a name for ourselves, and die game when the time come. I remember the capt'n and me, pretending to be on the scout for farms, having that exchange with the hotel landlord in Madelia about woods and such, and me, signing the guest register as Jack Ladd. Figured that'd get a chuckle out of the capt'n when we was in our room, and it sure had — Jack Ladd being one of the Pinkerton men who had raided the James farm a year or so back. I had meant to tell Frank and Jesse about that, make them two laugh, but had never gotten around to it.

Wasn't sure now I'd ever get the chance to tell them.

Wasn't nothing funny no more.

"It's all gone to hell!" Frank said. "Let's get out of here."

He didn't have to holler them orders at me more'n once.

"Yankee bastards!" Bob bellowed from the doorway. "They killed my horse."

They had, too. Just shot it at the hitching rail where we had left it in front of the bank. Takes one low son-of-a-bitch to kill a horse. We never cared much for that down in the Nations or Missouri.

Capt'n Cole was hollering at his brother, telling him something, but I couldn't make heads or tails out of nothing from all the shooting.

All right, I'll confess that we was drunker than Hooter's goat when we walked inside that bank, but I guaran-damn-tee you that I felt sober as a Mormon when I ran out, stopping at the door, taking in the scene. Savagerous, it was. The capt'n was bleeding from his left hip. Clell Miller's face had been peppered by bird shot. Jesse sat on his high-stepping white horse riding up and down the streets, cutting loose with Rebel yells, firing pistols in both hands, reins in his teeth. Jim Younger galloped by, his trousers torn by pellets from a scatter-gun, and somebody from an upstairs window damned near blowed his head off. I didn't see Stiles, the guy who had told us how easy this affair was gonna be, not at first, then saw him lying dead.

Well, I let out a little cry of surprise right then and there. Bill Stiles — Chadwell he sometimes called hisself — was dead, him the fellow who was gonna guide us out of this place, get us home safe and rich.

"Shit and hell's fire!" I said.

Which is what we had stepped in.

A bullet clipped the post nearby and sent splinters into my face. I snapped a shot at some kid throwing a rock as Jim Younger galloped past again, screaming at us to get on our horses and light a shuck out of this battleground.

The capt'n was there in my face, madder than a hornet. "What the hell kept you?" he hollered.

I give him a feeble answer, some excuse, ashamed of myself, and looked back inside the bank, yelling at Frank to get the rocks out of his drawers. "The game's up, Buck!"

I told him. "We got to get out of here. Bill's dead!"

What I saw next haunts me, and I ain't never been a man scared of apparitions and consciences and such. That cashier, the one whose throat we had nicked with a knife, whose skull we had cracked, who we had tortured and threatened to no avail — man was game as a bantam rooster though quiet and soft like most city gents — he had somehow climbed to his feet after Frank left him in the vault.

Frank busied hisself stuffing some paperbacks and silver in his trouser pockets, flung himself over the counter, made a beeline for the door where I waited.

"Frank!" I called out, and pointed my revolver's long barrel at the cashier. He moved like he was asleep, the cashier did, his dark beard matted with blood, staggering for his little desk in the corner in front of the vault. I thought he might be trying to fetch a pistol, like the man I had shot had been eyeing just a few minutes before he made his break. I still had that little .32 in my waistband. Of course, as soon as I called out Frank's name, it occurred to me that I didn't need to holler no warning. That gent wasn't doing nothing. Like I said, he was almost walking in his sleep, staggering, and he pitched toward his desk, trying to stop himself from falling hard to the floor.

He might have been all but dead already.

Frank, though, he whirled and fired. Missed, but Frank wasn't done. God as my witness, I never knew Frank to act so, not when his family wasn't threatened. It was like he was riding with Quantrill again, under the black flag, giving no quarter, expecting none in return. Maybe it was all that whiskey and wine we had been drinking before we went inside this damned bank. Maybe it was something else, the pressure from all we'd been through. But Frank, he went back to that cashier, like a man with a purpose, cocked his Remington, leveled the barrel.

The shot caused me to flinch. I've killed my share of men, but I always given them a fair chance. They was armed. They was intent on killing me iffen they could find the chance. This guy wasn't doing nothing, nary an intention of anything but trying to keep from falling.

Frank shot him in the head, scattering blood and bits of brain and bone all over the poor bastard's ledger and desk.

Murder. Ain't no other word for it, and I wondered iffen Frank would slay the other banker, the one still on his knees on the

147

floor, but Frank didn't give him no second notice. Almost made me sick, it did, seeing that brave city feller get his head practically blowed off, but Frank was moving toward me — nothing I could do, not now — and I bolted outside, gathering the reins to my horse.

I sat in the saddle, crouching, covering Frank, making sure he didn't get left stranded, didn't see Bob Younger no more. Didn't hardly see nothing but dust and gun-smoke and Frank James. Heard the capt'n shouting my name, saw him kneeling beside Clell Miller, who had just gotten shot off his horse, bleeding like a stuck pig. I started to ride over that way, but then Frank, he flinched, grabbed the saddle horn, somehow managing to keep a grip on his new model .44 Remington Frontier, and I knew he'd been hit.

"You hit?" I asked anyway.

"In the leg," he said through clenched teeth, but, game and brave, he pulled himself into the saddle, cursing, wheeling his mount, and firing one way and t'uther.

"Let's go, Charlie!" he screamed, and spurred his big dun, riding into the hell that awaited all of us on the streets of North-field.

CHAPTER ELEVEN:

COLE YOUNGER

"For God's sake, boys, hurry up! They're shooting us all to pieces!"

I pounded the butt of my Russian on the door, whirled, snapped another shot over the head of one of them damned fool locals. They had killed Bob's horse, peppered Jim's leg with bird shot, turning things hotter than a summer with Quantrill. A second later, a shotgun roared close by, and I turned to see Clell Miller, that faithful servant, falling from his saddle.

"Cole!" he yelled. "Cole! I'm hit, Cole! I'm hit!"

Some town puke, wielding a huge shot-gun, took off running and dived behind the crates stacked in front of this mercantile just as Dingus thundered past and popped a shot in the general area of his hindquar-ters.

I run over to Clell, figuring to find his head blowed off, but he was sitting up, stunned more than anything, bleeding from the forehead, nose, and cheeks.

"Bird shot," he said, shaking out the cobwebs, and let out a little laugh.

"You're lucky," I told him.

I wasn't. The bullet tore through the post and slammed into my hip, knocking me backward. Well, maybe I was lucky. If that big shell from some old buffalo gun hadn't gone through that post first, I expect it would have blowed my leg clean off.

"Get back inside," Bill Chadwell — Stiles — yelled as he rode past, raking his horse with them fancy spurs of his, "you damned bastard!"

I don't know who he was yelling at. Could have been anybody. Seemed like half of Minnesota had poured onto the streets.

"I seem to have lost my pipe, Cole," Clell said, trying to find some humor in our desperate fight, pulling himself to his feet, grabbing hold of the stirrup. I helped him back into the saddle, then run to my own horse.

Right about then, that white-livered son-of-a-bitch who had killed Bob's horse for no good reason shot Chadwell out of the saddle.

"Stiles!" Jim hollered, reining up, but only briefly. "Stiles! Bill! Bill! Christ A'mighty!"

Bill Chadwell, Bill Stiles, whatever his true name was, he couldn't hear nothing no more.

I stopped at the door again, pounding the frame so hard it shook, screaming at those boys to hurry up. Our plan had gone to hell. "For God's sake, boys, come out! It's getting too hot for us!"

Not long afterward, I hear one of the Yankees yell: "They've shot Alonzo Bunker!"

Well, I always knowed this had been a bum idea. Didn't like it when Dingus laid things out down in Missouri, and sure didn't like the looks of things when we rode in to Northfield that afternoon.

The deal was supposed to go like this: Brother Bob, Frank James (Buck, me and others called him), and Charlie Pitts would ride into town first. If things pleased them, they'd enter the bank about the time Clell and me rode in. If not, they'd just keep riding out of town.

"I'm a-gonna smoke my pipe through the whole shebang," Clell had said back in the woods when we had talked things over one last time. "That's how easy this'll be."

True to his word, Clell was pulling hard drags on his corncob pipe when we eased our horses down Division Street, and I seen

Frank, my best friend, Charlie Pitts, and my kid brother lounging on them crates in front of the mercantile near the bank. I also seen a passel of people all over the square, all over the town. Two o'clock on a Thursday afternoon — streets shouldn't be so crowded. What's more, a couple of folks just sitting out front by the big hotel was eyeing Frank, Bob, and Charlie with some suspicion.

"Surely the boys won't go into the bank with so many people about," I told Clell. "Wonder why they didn't just ride on through town."

As one of the church bells rang out with the time, I muttered an oath when Bob shot up from his perch on a peach crate, muttered something, and Frank, with a shrug, followed suit, Charlie Pitts right behind them.

"Hell," Clell said, still puffing his pipe, "they're a-goin' in."

"If they do, the alarm'll be given sure as there's a hell," I told Clell. "So you'd better take that pipe out of your mouth."

It went to hell in a hurry. Damn, Charlie Pitts forgot to shut the damned door, so we swung out of the saddle, me pretending to tighten the cinch while Clell, still smoking, hurried to the door and shut it, then stood at the door, arms folded across his chest, pipe stem being chewed on something fierce.

Wasn't more than a moment later that this fellow crossed the street from over by the Dampier Hotel, headed straight for the bank door.

Clell grabbed his collar, shoved him aside, and told him that he couldn't go inside.

"Listen," the man said, "I have business there, mister."

That's when Clell pulled out his revolver and jammed the barrel under the gent's nose. I give up pretending to tighten my saddle cinch, and drew the .44.

"Don't you holler, you son-of-a-bitch!" Clell was telling the fool. "Or I'll blow your damned head off!"

The man pivoted, leaped off the board-walk, and run, yelling at the top of his lungs: "Get your guns, boys, they're robbing the bank!"

"Hell," Clell said, snapped a shot at the fellow's feet, and I started firing, too, shooting in the air, yelling for everyone to stay off the streets. Pigeons flew off from the roofs of the buildings on Division Street. For some reason, they caught my fancy, and I couldn't forget just how pretty that sight was, them pretty birds lighting a shuck across a clear blue sky.

I whirled, squeezed the trigger.

Somebody from across the street let out a scream. "Robbery! Robbery!" Just then, Dingus, Jim and Chadwell come riding across the bridge, cutting loose with curses, shots, and Rebel yells.

The fellow over by the hotel, who had just shouted out, turned, and, in the corner of my eye, I saw Clell aiming his pistol at him. "Let him go!" I hollered. Man running wasn't no threat, though, if I'd knowed what that feller would wind up doing, I might have let Clell shoot the son-of-a-bitch in the back. He disappeared inside the Dampier House Hotel.

"Bank robbery! Bank robbery!"

Now gunfire from all directions echoed the shouts and screams, the yelping dogs, our own curses. That's when I give my first warning at the bank door.

I'd wind up yelling at those inside the bank three times. Bob come out after the second time, when that horse-killing son-of-a-bitch fired again from the corner of the square and Division Street.

"Get that bastard, Bob!" I shouted. "Charge him."

Previously I had said there wasn't to be

no killing, but by now I figured we'd have to kill or we'd be shot to pieces.

Bob took off running, firing his .45 Colt, and Charlie Pitts finally stuck his head out of the door. Still no sign of Frank James.

Jim rode past, and a bullet come too close to his liking, and mine. He let out a little gasp, trying to spy who had damned near killed him, and looked at me, crying: "Let's light out!"

"What the hell kept you?" I yelled at Charlie, and I seldom, if ever, rose my voice to a loyal comrade like Charlie Pitts.

"We botched things up, Capt'n," he said, and looked back inside, yelling at Frank.

Botched things up. He smelled like a walking whiskey vat. I started to curse him for being a fool, for drinking when I told him and all the boys there shouldn't be no John Barleycorn, not when we was on a case, but a gunshot roared inside the bank. Another.

Then I saw Clell Miller, leaning over, adjusting his stirrup, and straightening in the saddle, yelling out in surprise as a bullet slammed through his shoulder.

He tumbled on the ground again, his horse — damned traitor — skedaddling over to Fourth Street where some citizens was shooting at us, and I run to that gallant Missouri boy who had rode with us for so long.

"Clell!"

He pulled himself on his knees, his shoulder already drenched with blood, and tried to tell me something. "Charlie!" I shouted. "Charlie." Charlie Pitts, who had stepped into his saddle, started toward me, and I yelled one last holler at the bank: "For God's sake, Buck, come out! They're killing our men out here!"

Buck come out, cool as you please, and Charlie held up, to make sure my friend made it into the saddle. I saw him get hit — Frank James, I mean — in the leg, above the knee, but he didn't fall, just pulled himself into the saddle about the time Clell collapsed in my arms, and I laid him gently on the boardwalk.

"Clell!" Dingus yelled as he galloped past.

"He's dead," I said.

Clell Miller, sporting a few days' growth of beard stubble, no pipe around anywhere, looked at me with those pretty blue eyes of his, only he couldn't see nothing no more. Poor Clell. I unbuckled his shell belt, strapped it loosely across my duster. Grabbed his other revolvers, too, shoving one in my waistband, holstering my own, using his little .32 Moore rimfire to shoot.

"Bob!" I shouted, looking up.

Bob and that bearded fellow who had

most recently laid Bill Chadwell low was playing a game of chicken, using the stairs as a sort of barricade between them. Neither could get a real good shot at one another, but that fellow who had shot at Jim moments earlier, who was perched somewhere upstairs at the hotel, he drew a clean bead on my kid brother. Same fellow, it would turn out, that had run off the streets, shouting — "Robbery! Robbery!" — same fellow that Clell was about to back-shoot, same fellow whose life I had ordered be spared.

He put a .52-caliber ball into Brother Bob's elbow.

Now, Bob, he might be the youngest, but he ain't lacking game, not one whit. No, sirree, Bob. Soon as the bullet crippled his right arm, he tossed his Colt into the air, caught it in his left hand, spun, snapped a shot at the upstairs window.

Then Brother Jim wheeled in the saddle, dropping his long-barreled Colt, grabbing his shoulder, finally the saddle horn to keep himself from being pitched into the dust.

"Ride out!" I yelled. "Save yourselves!"

"I won't leave you!"

"Ride out, damn you. You ain't leaving nobody!"

I started for my horse.

Dingus come by, jerked the reins from

Jim's hands, screaming at Jim to hang on, and they thundered down Division Street. That wasn't the way we planned on lighting out, but we felt certain sure nobody would come out of here alive if we tried to cross the big bridge by the mill.

I had to take my time, keep from getting my head blowed off. Charlie and Buck were down the street, offering some covering fire. I kept one eye on my horse, the other on Brother Bob, still in the corner, by the stairs.

"For God's sake!" It's Bob who was pleading now. "Don't leave me! Don't leave me here!"

"I ain't leaving you," I told my brother.

Only now I spotted this other person, just standing in the street, looking at me. Drunk or a fool. I couldn't tell. He said something, but my ears were ringing pretty bad, and it ain't no language I could savvy no how.

Someone downstairs yelled at him. "Come down here, Nicolaus!"

But Nicolaus wasn't listening. A bullet clipped my hat, and that's when my patience was shot. Nicolaus jerked his finger at me; over the barking dogs, screaming horses, gunshots, and everything else, I heard him laughing at me. The son-of-a-bitch was laughing at me.

So I shot the bastard in the head with the .32.

He fell down the stairs, rolled down toward the basement.

Another fair-skinned face popped up from the stairs, eyes wide, and I pointed the Moore at him. "Get back down, you son-of-a-bitch, or I'll kill you, too!"

Me? Thomas Coleman Younger, the fellow who had told everyone we wouldn't shed no innocent blood. Me? I'd just shot an unarmed citizen in the head. 'Course, Clell Miller had practically died in my arms, and I'd just seen my two brothers get bad shot, seen my pard Frank Buck James take a hit in his leg. I was smarting some, too, from a big slug in my left hip. No excuse, though. I can't put the blame on anyone but me, 'cause it was me that shot that fellow. Shot him for no reason, other than he — like the rest of them Minnesotans in Northfield — just wouldn't listen to me.

Like Bob wouldn't listen back in Missouri when I told him this was a damned fool plan.

Bob was screaming again. "Cole! Cole! Don't you leave me, Cole, for God's sake, don't you leave me here alone!"

"Bud!" Frank's shouting from down the street. "Get the hell out of there, Bud!"

159

Rest of it, I see like a dream that just keeps on coming to you, slowly, clearly, too damned real. Just too damned real.

I shoot the Moore dry as I run, pull myself into the saddle, and ride by, shoving the empty .32 in a pocket and drawing my Russian. A bullet takes my hat off. Another clips my left rein. Quickly I draw my knife, slice the other rein close to the bit, will have to guide this gelding with my knees, but he's a good horse. Yet another shot slams into the saddle horn, shredding it loose. This is hell! Using only my legs and spurs to guide my horse, I ride hard, wheel up at the corner, fire a shot at the second-story window in the hotel and another past the bearded horse-killer's head, reach down, and grab Bob's gun belt, pull him up behind me. Hurts like hell, for both my brother and me, but I get her done. Ain't got no choice.

Then I'm spurring my horse, emptying my .44, riding down the street toward Charlie Pitts and Frank James. Dogs bark. Bullets fly overhead. I see some kid, not even in his teens, step out of an alley, wooden pistol in his left hand, a chunk of brick in his right. He lets the brick fly. Damned near tears my nose off, missing it by inches. Then, he's aiming his toy pistol, mouthing: Bang. Bang.

Bang. . . .

A few rods up ahead, Charlie doubles over, hit in the shoulder, and finally I've reached them, and we're riding — riding toward Dundas, leaving Clell Miller and Bill Stiles, alias Bill Chadwell, leaving them two boys and I don't know how many dead citizens in the streets of Northfield.

Riding to . . . where?

Chadwell, he's the one who knowed this land. Sure, we've studied it a mite, but this is a foreign country. Soon we'll be hunted.

We catch up to Dingus and Jim. Keep riding hard, five horses abreast down the street. Five horses. Six men.

Bob almost slips.

"Hang on!" I yell to him. Suddenly I remember something else. "The telegraph wires!" I shout.

"No time!" Dingus yells back, and he's right.

We were supposed to cut the lines, but now the whole damned state will be alerted.

"Hold on, Bob!" I cry.

"For God's . . . sake . . . don't . . . leave me!" He's choking out them words like feeble sobs, crying, whimpering.

"I ain't leaving you, Bob!"

My horse stumbles, and Bob's whining more. "For God's . . . sake . . . don't . . .

leave me." I figure he's in shock now, thinks he's still on that damned boardwalk, trading shots with the bastard who killed his horse.

"Which way?" screams Charlie Pitts.

"Just ride, damn it!" Dingus answers. "Ride or get buried!"

Chapter Twelve:
JOHN OLESON

Nic and I had been share wee taste of *sprit-dryck — mycket liten,* not much, two, three swallows, no more — when shots began. We down in Bierman's basement, Bierman being man who owned furniture company who had ask me to hang door. Odd. You think furniture company fellow could hang own door, but he hired me, and I am carpenter.

Nicolaus Gustavson, he new to this country, live in Millersburg. Swede, like me, he comes to better place, to start life new, see something better than in old country.

But he like strong drink. Like me. Maybe Nic like it better. I mean . . . *liked* . . . Nic, he dead now. Man killed him. Well, Nic not quite dead, but I told there is nothing to do but wait. So I wait. Wait for Nic to die.

He got shot this way. We hear gunshots when we sit on stairs to basement. Nic say something, start up stairs, but I tell him, no. This not right. Something wrong.

Maybe Nic had more drink than before I share *spritdryck*. He pull away from me. I crawl up steps after him. Beg him to stay down.

Nic tell me it some theater show. He has hear of it. I tell him, no. I speak all of this in old language. Nic, he not understand English much. His nephew and others in Millersburg tell me this because too much *spritdryck* Nic drink. Maybe so.

"Nic," I plead to him. "This real."

Mr. Manning, I see, fire big rifle. It boom. Mr. Manning, he no in theater company. Own hardware store. Mr. Ames, big government man, he run up beside Mr. Manning. I see that Mr. Manning has killed *häst* in front of bank. Other men, strangers in town, keep shooting.

"Nic . . . Nic! They rob bank."

"Nej," Nic tell me. He wave me off. Call me *dumbom.*

"Brottslings!" I point at mounted men who thunder past.

"Get off the street," shout one, "you sons-of-bitches!"

I almost soil myself.

"Feg stackare," Nic tell me, and he laugh.

I climb down stairs, cringing at whine of bullets. Men curse. *Feg stackare?* I no coward, but nor I *dumbom.* I screw open flask, have long drink.

How much time pass? I know not. Seem hours, but only minutes, *ja*. Nic yell again at me, still calling me *feg stackare, dumbom*, and I climb slowly steps, like cat. Nic, he *berusad*. Stinking drunk, like they say here. Not from my flask, though. He point again, laughing loudly. Now I see two men in long coats worn by cattlemen. I see them in streets, one near us, other toward corner of square. Another man, he cry out, hiding under stairs, throw his pistol into air, catch it with other arm. He shoot at window in hotel.

More curses. Dogs bark. Men gallop past us. Bullets whine. Feel hot.

"Nic!" I yell.

Then I see man, he crouch, he fire, he yell at Nic: "Get down, you son-of-a-bitch!"

Nic, he cannot understand, but I know it not his no good English. Two men dead. *Häst* dead. Guns. Shouts. Cursing. That language clear enough. No act this is. Get down! But, Nic, he drunk.

I see Nic laugh at highwayman. I see man's cold eyes flame with anger. He cusses. He shoot Nic in head, and Nic, he fall down stairs, roll past me. For some reason, I look up, maybe to see if man, if he come to shoot me, too.

He see me. He yells: "Get back down, you son-of-a-bitch, or I'll kill you, too!"

I come down. All way down. I bang on door to Bierman's, but it locked. I bang and bang. And then I hear no more shots, and when I look up, Nic, he gone.

Slowly I climb stairs into streets. Men and boys, they point down Division Street, but that way I see nothing. I look around. Two men on street, dead. *Häst* dead. Some men run into bank. Mr. Manning and Mr. Ames, they walk slowly. Others run. To bank. To livery. To dead men.

"We need a posse!" someone yells.

"Get a telegraph off to Dundas. That's where they're headed!"

"They shot Alonzo Bunker!"

"I heard. How is he?"

"With the doctor now."

"Somebody go fetch his wife!"

Wheeler boy, one studying to become *doktor,* he step out of hotel, holding big long rifle in arms. He yell at some boys standing over body of one of dead *brottsling.*

"By God," come cry from bank. "Joe Heywood . . . he's been murdered!"

I remember Nic. Maybe I am drunk, too, no? No, I think it is just fear.

"Nic! Nicolaus Gustavson! Where are you?" I cry out for him in English, in Swedish. No answer.

Someone point toward Cannon River, by mill pond. "The Swede run off that way!" he yells.

"Tack," say I, and I hurry to river.

There, I find Nic. His head all bloody, and he try washing blood off his face. I cannot believe he dead not.

"Nic," I tell him. I grab him by his arm, pull him from water's edge. He look at me. He vomit.

I wrap his arm around my shoulder. Nic, he sob. I tell him he will be fine, that we must find *doktor,* and lead him to Norske Hotel. It where newcomers from old country stay often. Nic, he stayed there. I stayed there. By then, Nic, he asleep. Other men help me, they carry him to bed. *Doktor* look at me, look at Nic.

I wait.

Doktor, he say Nic will die. "The bullet fractured his skull, pierced his brain. There is nothing I can do, nothing anyone can do."

So now I sit by my friend, Nicolaus Gustavson.

I wait him to die.

CHAPTER THIRTEEN:

HENRY MASON WHEELER

"Hey, boy, you stop that. Put that pistol down!"

Still in my stocking feet, I raced across Division Street, from the hotel to the body of the man I had killed. This pockmarked kid — I didn't recognize him — held a big Colt's revolver in his hand — a pistol dropped by one of the outlaws, I expect — aiming it at the dead man's face, and I wasn't about to have his body ruined so. As a medical student, I envisioned a much higher calling for this young desperado. And his friend lying up the street, also.

"I said . . . put it down!" The boy obeyed, started to keep the gun, but J.S. Allen wrenched it from his hand, and told the kid to show some respect.

"Man's dead. He can't hurt you now. And we might need this pistol in the inquest and trial of those murdering b'hoys."

The kid took off running. I made sure he

didn't detour toward the other corpse.

"My word," someone said, staring at my handiwork, "look at all that blood."

Another: "Like a hawg killin'."

The man stared at us with unseeing blue eyes, his curly, reddish hair matted in sweat and drying blood, one side of his linen duster soaked in blood. No gun belt, but I remembered one of his companions relieving him of his weaponry. A drummer, visiting from Faribault, bent over the dead man and began going through the pockets of his striped britches, under the pretense of learning the deceased man's name, but I think he just wanted to touch a slain outlaw. The search revealed only a map, a battered Waltham no longer ticking, and 10¢. Not much to show for his life, I thought. A young man doomed to die an early death because of his outlaw ways. Fate had let me kill him.

"Still can't believe a shoulder shot would kill that poor bastard," someone else said.

"My bullet severed the subclavian artery," I explained. "No way he could survive. He bled out in seconds."

"Your shot?" The Faribault man looked up, sounding skeptical.

All you did was touch him, I thought to myself with some vehemence and irritation.

You certainly didn't kill him. I patted the Smith carbine's stock, pointed its barrel at the second-story window at the Dampier House.

Dr. Dampier crossed the street now, and he overheard this conversation, came forward, and patted my back, saying: "Brave lad, brave lad. That was some shooting, too."

"Yes," I said, trying to sound immodest.

Nor do I wish this to sound as brag, but I suspected these strangers were up to no good when they rode into town.

Northfield is home. Well, technically, I was born in New Hampshire but have lived twenty of my twenty-two years here. Father runs an apothecary shop on Division Street, and, last year, I was graduated from Carleton College here in town, then went off to Ann Arbor to study medicine at the University of Michigan. Having returned home between semesters, I found myself relaxing in front of Father's store, boots off, whetting my appetite on soda crackers while reading the Rice County Journal with only passing interest.

Three strangers rode into town, tethering their mounts to the hitching post in front of the bank, then moved down the street and sat on some boxes in front of the mercantile.

One produced a bottle, flask, something, and passed it amongst themselves. The first things I noticed were the quality of the horses, the fine saddles, out of place in a farming and milling town like this. The men did not look at home, either. They wore long dusters, buttoned for the moment, boots, spurs, broad hats. One sported an auburn mustache, a dark-skinned man had a thick mustache and Van Dyke, and the third man, tall, cocksure, wore a full beard, evenly cropped. He glanced often at the bank. The dusters, I thought, would be fine to hide sidearms, and I thought to myself — *These men bear watching.*

From that moment, my eyes did not leave them for more than a few seconds.

A while later, I noticed two other men, also well mounted, coming down the street. They, too, donned long dusters, and, when the first men saw them, the bearded man said something, but the youngest of the trio — the one with the auburn mustache — jumped to his feet and headed for the bank door. The dark man shoved the flask into his pocket, and all three entered the bank, leaving the door open.

Yet not until later did I know with all certainty of their evil intent. The two riders swung off their mounts. One pretended to be adjusting the girth, while the other, puffing a homemade pipe, hurriedly slammed the door shut and stood blocking the entrance. Seconds later, J.S. Allen stepped into the scene.

When the pipe-smoking man rough-handled Mr. Allen, I leaned forward in my chair.

"Father," I called inside, "something is happening!"

Then I saw the pipe-smoking man unbutton his duster and draw a huge revolver, cursing at Mr. Allen, who turned and fled, shouting: "Get your guns, boys, the bank's being robbed!"

The men fired, although their shots at this time were aimed at the heavens, and I leaped from my seat. "Robbery!" I yelled. "Robbery!"

"Get inside, you sons-of-bitches!"

As if on command, three other riders galloped across the iron bridge, yelling like savage Indians, firing their guns this way and that. I leaped from my chair, into the street, still amazed at what I seemed to be witnessing. "They're robbing the bank!" I yelled.

The men in front of the bank turned to me. "Get in," one said, "or we'll kill you!"

Now, since I turned fourteen I have been

hunting, and am more than a passing shot. I knew I needed to get my hands on a rifle, but my own Enfield hung above the door inside my house. Blocks away. A bullet smashed into the column beside me, and I realized I'd never make it to my house. Where? Where?

Mr. Allen's hardware store? Perhaps Mr. Manning's? No chance. I'd have to cross the street, now filled with chaos, with galloping outlaws firing pistols, and over to Mill Square. I'd be dead before I got halfway there. Suddenly I remembered the old Army carbine Dr. Dampier had shown me at his hotel. He kept it, he said, and a sack of cartridges behind the counter in the lobby. So I raced to the hotel, hearing gunshots, hoofs, screams, and a booming voice: "Let him go!"

Well, if that man-killer was referring to me, I am grateful they let me go.

Inside, a stunned Dr. Dampier did not comprehend the situation.

"They're robbing the bank!" I told him. "I need that rifle of yours. And the shells!"

"Son," the kindly man said, "they're just play-acting. Part of some troupe coming through, performing at the Opera House. . . ."

"I tell you they are robbing the bank, sir.

Please!"

I imagine the bullet that shattered one of his windowpanes changed his mind, and he quickly retrieved the carbine.

"Cartridges!" I demanded. "And caps."

He moved slowly, put two on the counter, then another. "I can't find the danged sack," he said, but handed me a tube of percussion caps.

"I'll take these." I raced to the front door, stepping outside, met instantly with a shot that sang past my left ear.

"Get back inside, you Yankee bastard! Stay inside, or I'll blow your damned head off!"

Good advice, I thought, and retreated deeper into the Dampier House. What had I been thinking, stepping onto the streets like that? Upstairs! I bounded the steps three at a time, knowing that a perch on the second floor would provide good cover and a clear aim.

The weapon was an old Smith breech-loader, .52 caliber, firing foil and paper cartridges with a percussion cap. Dr. Dampier had carried it with him during the War of the Rebellion. When I reached the second story, I charged into a room, opened a window, and took in the scene. Five men on the streets, all in dusters, shooting, cursing, screaming. A man raced across the street with his son and took cover inside El-dred's Confectionary. Another man climbed out from the stairs leading to the basement offices of Bierman's furniture store. Just stood there like a dolt, either drunk or in shock.

For a moment, I simply stared at the battlefield below, seeking out a target, but these men moved rapidly. Elias Stacy, I believe, drew first blood when he charged like a lancer, lifted a shotgun, and blew the pipe-smoking man from his saddle.

The outlaw landed on the boardwalk, yelling something, and Elias pivoted and beat a hasty retreat, diving behind the crates in front of the mercantile while a scraggly bearded fellow on a high-stepping horse galloped past and fired, splintering one of the boxes but missing young Stacy.

I fired twice, rushing my first shot, missing my second by inches at some passing rider. The third cartridge I dropped, and it broke on the floor, spilling powder on the hardwood. Needing more ammunition, I darted out of the room and met Dr. Dampier on the staircase. He handed me a flour sack, and I grabbed it and returned to my fortification, withdrawing another foil and paper cartridge, working it into the breech, capping the nipple, looking out the window, taking it all in again, still hard to fathom.

A man in a duster lays sprawled down Division Street. Men have left the bank. The streets are chaos. Gunsmoke. I hear dogs barking, the musketry of savage fight. It's like no hunting trip I've ever been on.

A rider galloped past, cursing, snapping me from my state of shock, and I fired, missing, but scaring the hell out of him. And then I saw my chance. The pipe-smoking man, who had miraculously survived Elias Stacy's shotgun charge, was back in his saddle. I took aim, but he bent over, and I cursed, holding my rifle steady. He adjusted his stirrup, and, when he straightened himself, shifting his revolver in his hand, I squeezed the trigger.

A good hunter knows when he has scored a hit, and I did not hesitate, swinging down to reload and recap the Smith. When I looked out again, the pipe-smoking man, who had long ago spit out his pipe, was down, being attended by another outlaw, but I had no clear shot at him. Another outlaw I spied, by the corner stairs, aiming his pistol, trying to get a clear shot at Mr. Manning. I chose him for my next target, drew a bead, let out my breath, fired again.

This time, foolishly, I tried to watch,

rather than take cover and reload. This mistake almost got me killed, for, amazingly, my bullet slammed into the outlaw's right arm, but he tossed his revolver in the air, caught it with his left hand, whirled — somehow must have spotted me in the window — and let loose with a shot. It shattered a pane, inches from my head.

I ducked, reloading, cursing my stupidity.

When I chanced another look outside, I found the man I had wounded in the right arm, screaming something, still by the stairs. Another man, the one who had been adjusting the saddle girth, mounted his horse. I'd kill him next.

Some people, I believe, are blessed with the armor of the Lord. I fired. Mr. Manning fired. Others shot at this scoundrel. The man's hat flew off, and I am certain my shot tore his saddle horn asunder, while yet another clipped one of his reins. Previously the man had been wounded in the leg, but he did not act like a suffering soul. No, he drew a lethal Bowie knife with one hand, sliced the other rein with the blade, then kneed and spurred his brave horse to his wounded comrade.

I am a man who admires courage, and this man showed more grit than anyone I have ever seen. He got his horse to stop and wheel at the precise moment it reached the stairs. I fired again, but still God's armor protected this brigand, and, with amazement, I watched him grab the wounded man's gun belt and lift him into the saddle behind him. Then, without benefit of reins or a saddle horn, riders and steed exploded down Division Street, toward Dundas.

Like that, it was over.

I grabbed the sack of ammunition in one hand, the Smith in the other, and hurried downstairs, outside.

"Grosser Gott!" a gray-haired German lady cried out. She stood in front of Gress's shoe store, where she broke out sobbing, pointing, not at the dead men, but at the horse Mr. Manning had killed.

I remained standing guard over the body of the young outlaw I had felled when I heard news that Alonzo Bunker, the teller, had been shot and was being treated by a doctor. Then someone yelled inside the bank that Joe Heywood, acting cashier, had been murdered.

The street became a frenzy of activity once again. Men and boys stepped forward with their weapons, from pocket pistols and fowling pieces to rocks and wooden toys. I noticed one man, a coward to be sure, climb sheepishly out of the ice house, his hair and clothes covered with sawdust and mud, and attempt to sneak away toward the river. A mother rushed her child away from the carnage. Dogs came from all directions, sniffing at the corpses.

Conversations broke out about an inquest, about the dead men, who they might be, about the robbers who had escaped. Others still stood around as if dazed, confused, unable to understand what had happened — how long ago had it started? I checked my watch. Not even ten minutes ago.

Others cried.

"We'll put the bodies of these vermin in the granary for now," one man said.

Ira Summer, who had opened his photography studio in town shortly after the war, said: "Perhaps it might be best to photograph these two specimens before too long."

Naturally there were rumors, flying as wild as some of those gunshots only minutes earlier.

The Swede that had been shot had recognized one of the robbers. . . .

The outlaws were riding down Division Street to kill Governor Ames's family in revenge. (This got Mr. Ames racing down the street to the huge mansion he shared with his family and parents.)

The James-Younger Gang was behind this. (That struck me as pure poppycock . . . for the time being.)

"We need a damned posse!" Mr. Allen shouted. "Get a wire to Dundas. Maybe we can stop them!"

"How much money did they get?" another voice asked.

"Damned little," banker Frank Wilcox answered in a cracking voice as he was helped outside. "Joe wouldn't open the safe."

Jack Hayes quickly mounted the horse of the bushwhacker I had killed, which a kid had fetched after catching it in front of Mr. Cook's place on Fourth, and Dwight Davis rode toward us, mounted, ironically, on the other dead bandit's horse, which he had recovered at Northfield Livery. "We'll follow them," Mr. Hayes said. "Try not to let them out of our sight."

"Don't get too close, boys," George Taylor cautioned. "They are desperate men. They have laid Joe Heywood low and shot that Swede from Millersburg."

"What about Joe Heywood?" Mr. Manning asked. "Someone should inform his wife. And we should get his poor body home."

"Best clean it up first," said a pale gentleman, rolling a cigarette in front of the bank door. "Sons-of-bitches blew his brains out."

"Take my buggy," Mr. Davis said, pointing toward the livery. "You boys catch up, soon as you can get a posse together."

With that, Mr. Davis and Mr. Hayes took off in pursuit of the outlaws.

"We need to send a telegraph to Sheriff Barton down in Faribault," Mr. Allen suggested. "And Minneapolis. And Saint Paul. We must trap those desperadoes!"

"Let's get a damned posse up, now, boys!" Mr. Taylor shouted. "Time's a-wasting. You with us, Henry?"

I will admit that I did not have a strong desire to ride with the posse, but there is a matter of duty. I had two. "All right," I said, but detecting my friend Clarence Persons, standing near Skinner and Drew's Drug Store, I shouted at him: "See if you can get the bodies!"

Excellent cadavers are hard to come by in medical school.

They say up to 1,000 men took part in the search for the Northfield robbers over the following weeks, and I pride myself that I served as one of those, albeit not for long. The Northfield posse was ill prepared, and I cannot be called an exception. One gentleman turned back after losing his dentures. Another lost his gun in the Cannon River. At least neither Principal Mohn, nor posse leader Mr. Taylor, would allow the young boys at St. Olaf to join us.

Twenty-one rode out of Northfield, Mr. Taylor and four others leading the way in a double rig, the rest of us on horseback. We caught up with Mr. Hayes and Mr. Davis at Millersburg, and followed the trail to Shieldsville.

As for me? I felt mighty foolish riding an old plug mule in my stocking feet, gripping the Smith carbine in my hand with the sack of cartridges tied around my horn.

The clouds opened shortly thereafter, a downpour that would continue most of September, and I soon found myself soaked through to the bone. I had no slicker, not even a hat. Luckily my mule gave out (so did I), and with no great reluctance I returned to Northfield the following day, changed into dry clothes, ate a filling supper, and sought out my friend Clarence Persons.

After a coroner's inquest and exquisite photography by Mr. Sumner, and a while the following afternoon to let the trainloads of tourists come and gawk at the dead men, the two outlaws had been buried in our town cemetery's Potter's Field shortly before my return, but the constable and undertaker had promised to bury them shallow. Grave robbery is not a noble endeavor, but I am a medical student and I killed one of those fiends. I figure I deserved him more than anybody else, and nobody was claiming the man Mr. Manning had slain. As I have previously mentioned, those men had a higher calling than outlawry.

On the evening of September 8th, my friends Clarence Persons and Charles Dampier hired out a buckboard and a Negro, and we began our nocturnal business at Northfield Cemetery. The Negro did not care for it, but did his duty, although he would not leave the wagon. Charles and Clarence lacked much enthusiasm for the idea, as well, but the ground was soft from all that rain — it still drizzled as we set to work around midnight — the graves fresh, and, as the undertaker and constable had promised, shallow.

A dirty, detestable job, but we worked quickly, and few people inspect graveyards on rainy nights after midnight. Our conspiracy went undetected. We dug up the bodies, stuffed them into barrels marked *Paint,* and had the Negro drive them to Minneapolis depot, where the "paint" was shipped to the University of Michigan Medical School in Ann Arbor.

On September 10th, I attended the funeral of Joseph Lee Heywood, with most of Northfield, but my mind, I admit, found itself weeks ahead, wondering what would happen back in Ann Arbor.

To answer that question, dear reader, I will skip ahead. Well, I became something of a hero when I returned to school in October. Even the Ann Arbor *Courier* proudly advertised my coup.

The Students of the Medical Department
Will This Winter Have the Pleasure
of Carving Up
TWO GENUINE ROBBERS!!!,
being members of the
Northfield, Minnesota gang.

The two cadavers were first-rate, impressing not only my fellow students, but also my professors, who singled me out for providing the *pièce de résistance.*

"A prime, young specimen," one classmate said after we had worked on the pipe-smoking man. "Practically flawless. How, pray tell, did you obtain such a corpse in this remarkable condition?"

With pridefulness, I answered — "I shot

184

him!" — savoring the startled expression on the young gent's face.

CHAPTER FOURTEEN:

LIZZIE MAY HEYWOOD

Pretend they're shooting fireworks. I like to watch the pretty sparkles in the sky when it's nighttime. Don't you? I like to pretend. Usually. Pretending's fun. Most times, I pretend I'm a mommie and my dolly is my baby. Sometimes we're baby animals. I'm the mommie horse and dolly's the baby pony. Or a mommie cat and baby kitty. Or a mommie rooster, which causes Papa to laugh, and a baby rooster. Or, without my dolly, I pretend by myself. I pretend I'm singing in church choir. I pretend I'm pouring tea for the ladies at the church. I pretend I'm talking to Mommie Martha. I pretend lots of things. I have to pretend today, too.

I heard the fireworks today, but it wasn't nighttime like it was yester-night because I looked out the window in my room where I was playing with my dolly. Her name's Martha, which Papa says was my real mommie's name. Now my mommie is Mommie Lizzie

— she has the same name as me; how can that be? I never knew Mommie Martha, but sometimes I pretend I did.

So, today, I played by myself in my room while Mommie Lizzie sat in the parlor where she worked on a quilt. She couldn't let me help because she says I might stick myself and I'm just a baby, though I told her I wasn't a baby, that I was a baby last year, but now I am five years old. I'm a kid. A little girl, like Papa calls me, though he sometimes tells me I'll always be his baby girl, but I'm not a baby any more. Not a baby! Babies are four or stuff.

So, when I heard all the popping, I got excited, and I grabbed my dolly and ran to find Mommie Lizzie, and I yelled at her: "Fireworks! Fireworks! Let's go see! Let's go see!"

Mommie Lizzie, she put her stickpins down and rose, smiling, saying: "Lizzie, it's not fireworks. Not in the middle of the day. See? And Independence Day has long passed."

"Maybe it's special fireworks," I said.

Now we heard lots of fireworks, and Mommie Lizzie listened harder and walked toward the front door. "It sounds," she says, "like corn popping."

"What could it be?" I asked her. Then:

"Let's go see!"

She opened the door, which made the popping sound louder, and I tried to go down the steps to the edge of Third Street, our street, but Mommie Lizzie grabbed my arm and jerked me back. She was right, though. It couldn't be fireworks because it was still not dark like it is when we go see the pretty sparkles and it couldn't be special fireworks because I looked up in the sky and didn't see any sparkles or things like that.

We heard some other noises, too, but they were too far away for us to understand. More popping. And then Mommie Lizzie got this terrible look on her face, and she brought her hand to her mouth and she gasped for breath, and I asked her if she was all right, but she turned around, and her eyes were so wide, and she shoved me inside, yelling at me: "Get inside, Lizzie! Oh, my God! Get inside, now! Now!"

And we were back in the parlor and Mommie Lizzie was slamming the door shut and sliding the bolt, and I started crying because Mommie Lizzie never pushed me and she never yelled at me and I wanted my Papa, and I cried that I wanted Papa, and Mommie Lizzie knelt beside me and pulled me close and she whispered in my ear: "I want Papa, too." Then she told me she was sorry for scaring me, but I was still crying, and I told her I had left Dolly Martha on the porch because I had dropped her when she had pushed me.

"She'll be all right," Mommie Lizzie said.

"But I want her. I want. . . ."

"Hush."

"But. . . ."

"Hush!"

I wanted to run to my room, but what about my dolly? She's the bestest dolly in the whole wide world and is special to me.

I listened. There was still popping, but I don't think it was corn popping.

"I hope . . . ," Mommie Lizzie started, then bit her lip, and she was crying, and I kept crying, and then she hugged me, and scooped me up and took me to the rocker and just rocked me like I was a baby, like I was her baby, but I've told you already that I am not a baby any more, and she's not my real mommie but my new mommie but I love her and she's a special mommie, but I'm not her baby.

Well, Papa says, like I've told you, that I'll always be his baby.

But that's all right because I love Papa.

Papa's name is Joseph Lee Heywood. He works at the bank. Do you know him? I bet you do because he knows everybody in town. He's been working at the bank as long as I can remember. He was a hero, too. During the old war he almost died fighting the mean Rebs. I don't remember the war because I wasn't born yet, and I never met a mean Reb. Papa told me not to worry, that mean old Rebs don't come to Minnesota much and aren't as scary as witches and warlocks, and the war is over, right prevailed, and we'll never see something that horrible again.

I think Papa is the most handsomest man that ever was, and Mommie Lizzie, she says so, too. He has fur on his face, and it's dark and sometimes it pricks me, but mostly it's soft. Other men in town have fur on their faces, too, but only Papa lets me touch it when he comes home after working at the bank. Mommie Lizzie came here a little while ago back when I was just a baby, maybe three years old, to be my mommie because Mommie Martha is in heaven. Papa says we'll all see Mommie Martha sometime in heaven. He says heaven isn't the place where we go on Saturdays to place the flowers where Mommie Martha's sleeping, the special place with all the crosses and stone things in the ground at the edge of town. He says heaven is in the sky, like the clouds and the stars and all the pretty sparkles when they shoot off fireworks. Mommie Martha went to heaven after I was born and was just a baby, and then I didn't have a mommie except for the times when I'd let my dolly be my mommie and I'd be her baby until Mommie Lizzie came to see us and live with us and be my new mommie.

"Listen," Mommie Lizzie said.

We were still sitting in the rocker, and I listened, but the popping sound wasn't making noise any more.

"I don't hear anything," I told Mommie Lizzie, and she said — "I know." — and we both got off the rocker and moved toward the door again.

I hoped Dolly Martha hadn't gotten scared from all the daylight fireworks and run off and hided. And I hoped that bad dog, June, that lived next door hadn't taken my dolly and run off with her like she run off with the wooden spinning top that Papa had bought for me and warned me not to leave it outside, but I did, and it was an accident.

Dolly Martha was right where I dropped her and I ran and picked her up and told Mommie Lizzie: "Look!" Only Mommie Lizzie didn't look, not at me, but kept looking down the street, and I looked down the street to see who was coming — maybe,

Papa! — but no one was coming.

We didn't hear any popping. Some dogs barked, maybe puppy June was one of them, and heard some other noises, but nothing much else. I wondered what had happened to the daytime fireworks. They hadn't lasted very long.

I asked Dolly Martha if she had seen anything, and we started talking, and then Dolly told me she wanted me to comb her hair, so I pretended that I had a comb and started combing her hair, which is what I was doing when Mommie Lizzie stepped down the steps.

"Where are you going?" I asked, but she must not have heard me. She just walked a few paces and then she looked down the street again, and, when I looked up, I saw some people coming, and I got excited because I hoped one of them was Papa, but no, these men didn't have any fur on their faces, and Mommie Lizzie, she came back and put her hand on the rail on our porch and was stepping up toward me.

Then one of the men running down the street began yelling: "The bank's been robbed! The bank's been robbed! We're getting a posse!"

Mommie Lizzie swayed a little, then ran up the steps and started to go inside, then just turned, and I saw she was crying again, and she just flattened herself against the wall, and I didn't know what I was supposed to do, but I stopped combing Dolly Martha's hair, and, when my dolly asked me why I had stopped, I told her to just hush, and kept on looking at Mommie Lizzie.

She was acting crazy. She never acted crazy. Mommie Lizzie acted kind of scary, like witches and warlocks and mean Rebs.

"Was that man talking about Papa's bank?" I asked Mommie Lizzie. She didn't answer, so I asked her again, and even again, and had to shout it before she looked at me, but still didn't answer, just blinked her eyes, and then she took this long deep breath and held it for the longest time, and I thought she was going to hold her breath forever like I did sometimes when I was a baby and was mad at Papa or somebody for something.

She breathed out, and shook her head, and then she knelt beside me and asked: "I'm sorry, Lizzie, what is it that you asked?" She was still crying, not loud or anything like that, just tears flowing down all her cheeks.

"Is that man talking about Papa's bank?"

"Pray that it is not so, sweetheart," she said. "Let's go inside and pray."

"But it's not nighttime or breakfast or dinner or supper."

"Let's pray anyway."

"But it's not church."

"Come," she said.

"What's a posse?" I asked.

"I'll explain later. Let's pray. Let me find our Bible."

She was opening the door when another man in a checked suit came running down the street, and started pounding on the door of the house near ours, the house where Mr. Karl — he comes from some place called, oh, I can't remember — but Mr. Karl lives in that house and the other man was yelling — "Robbery, robbery!" — and Mr. Karl, he opened the door and said: *"Guten Tag. Was gibt es Neues?"* He talks funny, I think.

"Robbery!" the man in the checked suit said. "Robbery and murder!"

"Wie bitte?" said Mr. Karl.

"Robbery, I said!" The man in the checked suit was waving his arms and he was sweaty and icky stuff, and I kept waiting for Mommie Lizzie to go inside with me, but she just stood frozen. And then I heard the man in the checked suit say this: "Robbery and murder! They robbed First National and murdered Joe Heywood, shot Alonzo Bunker."

194

"Grosser Gott!" Mr. Karl said. *"Der Meuch-elmord?"*

"Yes, sir," the man in the checked suit said. "Foul murder. We're forming a posse. Come with me to the square!"

"Ich komme sofort!" Those are funny-sounding words Mr. Karl says, but Papa tells me that's all right and that Mr. Karl is a fine Christian gentleman and good neighbor, but he didn't even remember then that he was our neighbor, I guess, he was so excited because Mr. Karl took off running after the man in the checked suit. They were running toward the railroad tracks, which Mommie Lizzie and Papa say I mustn't play on, and toward the river and the square, which is where Papa works.

Mommie Lizzie jerked me inside and slammed the door. She was holding her stomach with one hand, covering her mouth with the other, like she was going to be sick, and I hoped she wasn't going to be sick.

"Mommie Lizzie," I said. "They were talking about Papa. What were they saying about Papa?" When she didn't answer, just stood there, I started crying, and Dolly Martha was crying, and Mommie Lizzie finally knelt beside me and she pulled me tight and almost crushed me, and then she scooped me up again and we ran into the parlor, and she stumbled on the quilt she was making, but didn't drop me, and then she sat me down in the rocker and she was sitting, kneeling, just right there in front of me, and she took another one of those deep breaths, and she wiped her tears and suddenly she wasn't crying no more.

"Lizzie May," she said.

I nodded.

"I need you to be very strong. I need you to be a big, big girl now. You can't be a baby any more."

"All right, Mommie Lizzie. I'm not a baby. I'm five. But where's Papa? I want Papa!"

"I know." She paused again. It seemed like the longest time, and I felt I would start crying again, but then she squeezed my arm, squeezed it hard, but not too hard so that it hurt.

"Lizzie May, do you remember when Papa's friends from work came over a little while ago and were talking about the secessionists during the late unpleasantness?"

Well, I remembered Papa had a party, but I don't remember anything about it.

"You remember one of Papa's bosses asked what Joe, your father, would do if bad men wanted him to open the safe like the bad Rebels had done at that bank in Vermont during the war?"

I didn't say anything.

"Joe said he'd never open the safe for such scoundrels. Do you remember that?"

"I think so." But I didn't.

"Your father is a hero."

"He was a hero in the war. When he fought the mean Rebs."

"I fear he was a hero today, sweetheart."

"Is Papa coming home soon?"

"I pray so, but. . . ."

Somebody started knocking on the door, and Mommie Lizzie shivered and it wasn't even cold. She stood up, but not before she kissed both of my cheeks and wiped my face with the hem of her skirt.

"I miss, Papa," I said. "I love Papa. I want Papa to come home . . . now."

"I love him, too."

Preacher Leonard is with Mommie Lizzie now. She is wearing a black dress, and Mrs. Ames says I'll have to wear a black dress, too. She says Papa was a hero. I tell her Mommie Lizzie and I knew that. I heard the man tell Mommie Lizzie, when she opened the door, that Papa had been a hero, that he would not open the safe for the bandits, and I heard Mommie Lizzie, being strong, say: "I would not have had him do otherwise."

"You are a courageous lady," the man said.

Mommie Lizzie pretends good, too.

They would not let me see Papa. They brought him home in a buggy, and covered with a white sheet, but there were some icky spots on the sheet, red and brown and nasty, and I knew it was blood, but I didn't touch it. Maybe, I thought, Papa was pretending to be a ghost, but they told me that Papa was in heaven, that that was just his body, nothing in the scheme of things — what is a scheme? — and that God has a reason for everything, even this.

Papa's in heaven with Mommie Martha.

Does that mean I can go to heaven, too?

"You shall, dear child," Preacher Leonard told me, "but not for a long, long time, God willing."

"But I want to go see Papa now."

But I can't. They won't let me.

They tell me that after Mr. Miller had Papa all fixed up, maybe tomorrow, that maybe I can go see him and kiss him good bye, but I don't want Papa to leave. I want him to read me stories and let me feel his fur and I want him to bring me my dolly and my spinning top and let me play on the piano and sometimes the clarinet because I like music, too, and Papa says I have a gift.

I want Papa to take me to see where Mommie Martha's sleeping when she's in heaven at the place at the edge of town. I want to hug Papa again.

"Your father had so many friends," Mrs. Ames tells me. "And how heroic. You must be brave, too. Brave and strong."

"Mommie Lizzie tells me I must."

"Your stepmother is such a strong young lady."

I pretend to rock my dolly to sleep. She's crying, too, because she misses Papa.

"Your father will have two services, child," Mrs. Ames is telling me. "One in the high school hall. That will be for all of Northfield, all of Minnesota, I warrant. And another here. It will be a trying day for all of us, you dear, sweet child. I hope you will continue to show this God-given strength of yours. You and your stepmother. It says in the Good Book . . . listen, Lizzie May, did you hear that?"

I look up. It is dark again. Maybe fireworks. No?

"Thunder. Hear it roll. Blessed rain. I think angels of the Lord are shedding tears, or will soon shed tears, tears of joy for bringing a brave, brave man like Joseph Lee Heywood into the fold. Do you hear?"

Thunder. I don't hear it, but maybe if I

tell her that I do, maybe then they will let me see Papa.

"Yes, ma'am. Can I see Papa now?"

She gives me a sad look. "In time, Lizzie May. In time. You do not wish to see him now, not in that ghastly state. Remember your father alive."

I am good at that. I can pretend. I like to pretend. I think I will pretend that Papa is not in heaven, and that he'll let me play with his fur, and he can tell me stories and make me laugh. Yes, I will pretend. I will pretend that.

I will pretend that I am not sad.

Chapter Fifteen:

FRANK JAMES

Men at some time are masters of their
    fates:
The fault, dear Brutus, is not in our stars,
But in ourselves, that we are the under-
    lings.

Fate had dealt us a cruel hand, or, as Shakespeare wrote in *Julius Caesar,* we dealt it
ourselves, choosing the bank in Northfield,
leaving behind Bill Stiles — no sorrowful
loss — and Clell Miller; Jesse and I felt
mighty pained to lose a top hand like Clell.
What's done is done, however, and there
ain't no turning back. As Bob Younger, if he
weren't so bad shot up, might say: "We
played a good hand but we lost. Spilt milk.
There are more pressing matters."

Staying alive.

So we rode, rode like hell, running some
white-haired sodbuster off the road in his

spring wagon. "Take the ditch, damn you!" Charlie Pitts screamed at him, and we didn't give the old farmer any choice.

We rode.

"Let's take a damned horse!" Cole cried out, him smarting some, bleeding bad, saddle, reins, and brother all shot to hell, but Jesse wouldn't listen, and I can't blame my brother at all.

"Too soon! Too soon!" he yelled. "We need to get past that little town first. Might have wired the law there."

They called that little town Dundas, on the Cannon River, three, four miles south of Northfield, and, sure as hell, if them damyankees in Northfield had any sense they would have keyed off a telegraph in a hurry, and we'd be riding into a posse, us having forgotten to cut the wires on our way out of town.

Well, we hadn't forgotten. Didn't have time.

We rode.

Bill Stiles had told us he knew a few crossings, but the water roiled from recent storms, and Stiles was deader than Brutus. Only crossing that we knew of was the bridge at Dundas. We rode.

"Damn it all to hell, Dingus," Cole said, "we got to stop. Now."

Jesse listened, changed his mind, and we eased our horses off the road near the bridge and rode down to the Cannon River. Bob Younger practically fell off the horse, and Cole hobbled over beside him.

"Better reload your guns, boys," Jesse said. "We'll have soldiering to do. That posse will be waiting for sure now that we've stopped."

"Go to hell, Dingus!" Jim Younger bit back.

Mightily I wanted to slide down off the saddle on the big dun horse, pour some cool river water over my bleeding leg, but didn't feel overly confident I'd be able to climb back in the saddle again, so I just watched, tied a bandanna over the gash above my knee, keeping my eyes on the road. That's how come I saw the man coming from Dundas in his wagon — a team of grays in harness — coming casual as you please, and it struck me that, since town lay just up the road and this man didn't have a care in the world, maybe those dumb Yankees hadn't thought to telegraph the first town. (Turns out I was wrong, that the Yanks weren't all as dumb as they looked, and they had got the wires humming, but the fool operator in Dundas was having his afternoon sit-down in the privy.)

"Jesse." Thumbing back the Remington's

hammer, I pointed the long barrel at the rider, who hadn't spotted us.

My brother grinned. "The Lord giveth. Looks like we got that horse for you, Bob," he said, and Jesse and I rode up to the road, meeting the fellow just as he crossed the bridge.

"We'll be borrowing one of your horses," I informed the man, showing him the business end of my .44.

"What's the meaning of . . . ?"

"Just shut the hell up, you little son-of-a-bitch, and cut one of those grays from the harness," Jesse said. "Sass me, and I'll blow your damned head off."

He was hauling rails, and he got right to work on the horse, after Jesse split his scalp with his Schofield, realizing the seriousness of our moods. She was a right solid little mare. Lucky, Bob was, and we had the gray about rigged up for him when Charlie Pitts, now watching our back door, spotted two men riding down the road, riding, it looked like, on Clell Miller's and Bill Stiles's horses.

"Keep back, you damned curs!" Charlie shouted at them, and the spineless bastards did as they were told, respectful of us.

Cole and Jim, though both still hurting, helped Bob, his arm busted from that shot, onto the gray, then mounted their own

204

horses. We rode through town, spurring our mounts, raising dust.

Dundas, thank God, was quiet, but we needed to put some miles between us and Northfield, and those two cowards trailing us. One drummer in a sack suit pointed at us when we galloped along, saying in his Yankee voice: "Friends, you ride like a cavalry regiment. But if Sitting Bull were after you, I warrant you might even ride faster."

Jesse aimed his Schofield. "Get inside, you son-of-a-bitch!"

The drummer got inside in a hurry.

We had to show a couple other gents our guns, which irked one of the bastards idling away his afternoon in front of some store. He took offense, telling Charlie: "Get off that horse and I'll whip you. I can whip any man points a revolver at me."

Charlie would have bashed that son-of-a-bitch's face in, but we had no time for fisticuffs.

We rode.

Now, Bob rode the gray bareback, and, with his arm so bad, we had to get him a saddle, so we appropriated one off some dumb farmer, telling him we were Rice County sheriff's deputies and chasing horse thieves. The man didn't say nothing, just bobbed his head and chewed a straw. Doubt if he believed us. Actually I don't rightly give a damn.

Our next stop came at another farm because Bob had started begging for water. I had a powerful thirst, too, and this time I eased my bad leg out of the saddle, once the farmer — man named Donaldson — said to help ourselves after Jesse told him that Cole had taken a spill from his horse and broke his leg.

"Bring him inside," Donaldson said.

"Oh, no, we'll just get him home."

Donaldson sprayed the ground with tobacco juice, his black eyes focusing on Jim as he helped Bob take a drink of cool well water.

"What happened to that fellow's arm?" he asked.

"Shot," Jesse said. "A blackleg shot him after we had this row in Northfield. We killed him."

Donaldson switched the chaw from one cheek to the other.

I pulled myself in the saddle, rubbing my leg, and thanked the farmer for his hospitality. As we eased our horses toward the Old Dodd Road, the farmer called out to our backs: "What was the name of that gambler you killed?"

"Stiles," Jesse answered with a grin before spurring his horse into a lope.

That's how things went pretty much that first day. We'd stop at a farm here and there to bath our wounds, look at some horses that we might steal, but nothing caught our fancy. We met up with a score of folks, farmers mostly, and they'd suspicion us considerable, but, hell, we told them we were chasing horse thieves or hauling a thief to jail.

One farmer told us we were taking the wrong road if we were heading for this-and-such town, but Jesse, still in jovial spirits, said: "Oh, no, we're taking the right road."

We wound up relieving one sodbuster of his horse a mile or so out of Millersburg, and Cole took the farmer's hat to replace the one he'd lost. Later we stole another saddle, kept riding. Long about dusk, the saddle girth snapped and sent Bob sailing into the ditch. The horse run off back toward Millersburg, and Jim and Charlie gave it a chase, but it was no use. Both of them boys had been shot in the shoulder — Jim's wound looked the worser — and our horses were pretty much played out. Cole knelt over his brother, who wailed in pain, but Cole gave Bob a stick to bite on, tightened the bandage on his busted arm, helped young Bob onto the back of his horse.

We rode.

That night, we camped in the woods. Cole took off his undergarments, which we tore into strips and used for bandages. No coffee, not even a campfire that night. No interesting debates with Cole. No fiddle playing by Jim. No sermons from Jesse. We licked our wounds.

I sat beside Cole, thinking maybe we should compare our leg wounds, but figured Cole would find no humor in this at the moment, but Charlie Pitts inquired about the money, and so I emptied my pockets.

"Where's that sack you took, Bob?" I asked. "From the till?"

"It's on the street," Bob answered with unusual bitterness when addressing Jesse or me (now his brothers . . . that was another matter). "Want to go back and fetch it?"

"Maybe they'll forward it to us," Jesse chimed in.

"Charlie?" I asked.

Pitts shook his head. "I didn't get none."

"Christ A'mighty," Cole said, and carved off some chawing tobacco from a twist one of the farmers had given him that afternoon.

Robbery is an interesting profession. From what all has been printed, a body would think the James and Younger boys lived high on the hog, eating off the best china, sipping Madeira from crystal wine glasses, richer and merrier than Robin Hood. Truth be told, most of the banks we chose were as poor as the rest of Missouri. Lots of time we didn't get enough for our troubles. Rich? Not hardly. And all that wealth Bill Stiles had promised . . . ?

As I tossed a two-cent penny onto the pile, I announced: "Twenty-six dollars and forty cents."

Jesse laughed. "You can have my share, Bob," he said, and pulled his dirty duster over him like a sheet, adjusted his hat, and, gripping his Colt, his Schofield and Smith & Wesson close by, went to sleep.

Things got quiet. Charlie Pitts announced that he'd take first watch, asked Jim to spell him in three hours, and he walked off into the woods and found a spot. Jim started snoring softly, and Bob tossed about in a fitful sleep.

Cole spit. "What happened in the bank, Buck?"

I shrugged, packing my leg wound with finely ground gunpowder and tightening the bandanna around it, then stretched out and asked to partake of Cole's twist.

When I had the tobacco good and moist and comfortable, I got around to answering Cole's question. "We were trying to make the cashier open the safe. One of the other bankers took off running out the back door. Charlie give him chase, but he got away, though Charlie said he hit the son-of-a-bitch. Anyway, it was no good from the get-go."

"Damn' right, Buck," Cole said. "You saw how crowded town was. Never should have gone in the bank in the first place."

" 'If the blind lead the blind, both shall fall in the ditch,' " I said.

Cole spit. "Guess we all fell in the ditch."

"Least we climbed out. For now. All except Stiles and Clell."

"What else happened in there?"

"I killed the cashier. Shot him as I took my leave." There, I'd said it.

"God, Buck, God. I told you-all in the woods that there wasn't to be no killing. Why'd you kill him? Think he was going for a gun?"

I couldn't answer that. Still can't. I don't have one notion as to why I shot that bastard. Rage? Did I think he was a threat? Just my plain old cussedness? Maybe Cole had the answer.

"Just how drunk were you?" he asked.

I spit, turned to face my old friend. "How drunk was you, Bud, when you shot that unarmed fellow out on the street?"

Cole didn't have an answer, either, and I felt bad for him, knowing how much he had wanted to avoid killing. So I said: "Maybe you just give him a headache. Doubt if that little Thirty-Two would have killed him. I bet he'll just have a scar and a story to tell his grandkids."

"Maybe," Cole said hopefully.

We didn't say much after that, finished our chaws in silence, tried to catch some sleep in the woods, figuring the next day would be a hell of a time.

It rained that Friday. A cold, mean, soaking rain that had some blessing, as it cooled off the fever Bob had taken during the night, and it made tracking us a damned sight harder for any posse that might be out sloshing through southern Minnesota. We met the first posse at the Little Cannon. Well, it was more of a picket than a posse, and I had to give the Minnesota laws some credit. They had a bunch of men chasing us, and guarding the fords of the creeks and rivers was a good chess move. Might have worked if even a quarter of the men they had on our trail was worth snuff.

These three idiots fired at us without so much as a warning. Raining like it was, coming down in sheets at the time, we could have been the Rice County sheriff and Governor Ames himself. They couldn't shoot worth a damn, either, so we just turned back, waited in the woods. A few minutes later, those three heroes of Minnesota give us chase, only they rode right past us. We waited a couple of minutes, returned to the road, and forded the river without any trouble.

Word was out by then, all across Minnesota, about the Northfield robbery and murders, and already they laid the blame on the James-Younger Gang. This we learned from a farmer who had heard the news in Janesville.

"You are ubiquitous," I told Jesse, a little running joke betwixt us. My brother liked to say that himself, vainglory being one of his foibles.

"Who else would have the gumption to rob a Yankee bank in Minnesota," Jesse said, defending himself.

We rode.

"Hell, we can't see shit in this rain," Charlie Pitts snapped later that day. "We need us a damned guide."

Which is how come Jesse borrowed the first kid from the farm. The kid got us past Janesville, where we turned him loose and gave him a dollar from our Northfield plunder for his trouble. At the next farm, we borrowed two more little yellow-haired boys, and they got us to the swamps just shy of Elysian. Those kids we paid a dollar each, too, then wound up borrowing some horses from the next two farms we come across.

"Hell, Dingus," Jim said. "We keep kidnapping little kids and stealing horses, rain or no rain, we'll be leaving a trail any fool can follow."

"You got a better idea? You know where we are? You know how to get us home, James Younger?"

"West and southwest," Cole said, acting the peacekeeper for once. "The posse ain't gonna be able to follow us worth a damn through these swamps."

So we made camp that night in the thickets between Elysian and what one of them tots said was German Lake.

That's where we got the notion to leave all of our horses. Jim Younger was right. If we kept stealing horses and borrowing youthful guides, the laws would find us certain sure, but it also came to Jesse that the posse would be chasing six men on horses. One of the horses we had borrowed was a fancy bright gelding. "Yaller horse," Charlie called it, and it was sure to attract attention. 'Course, we could have simply left that horse, but we figured on making better time afoot in the brambles and sloughs and woods. We'd sneak on past the posses.

That's what we done.

This is the life of an outlaw, worse than being chased by Pinkertons or Redlegs, worse than anything I'd experienced in Missouri during our war for liberty. We made four miles the first day afoot. When the rain stopped, the mosquitoes came out, and Jim's shoulder wound started festering. I figured Bob — in fever, delirious, breaking sticks in his mouth the pain was so fierce — would wind up losing that arm, or the rot would set in and kill him. After the mosquitoes had damned near sucked us dry, the rains would start again, damned torrents.

We ate watermelons till we grew sick of them. Green corn that laid some of us low with bowel complaints. I cussed Jesse and his idea to abandon the horses, not so much for not having anything to ride, but I figured I could always cut a sliver off the saddle strings and chew on it like jerky.

We walked, trudging along through mud, fording sloughs when we had to, soaked to the skin, about to catch our deaths.

The worst came after Jesse and Charlie

snuck up to this farm, and caught us chickens and a turkey and, after wringing their necks, brought us back supper. Fresh meat at last. Charlie even had some lucifers that wasn't soaked and ruined, and we decided to risk a fire. Cole and I rigged up Bob's blanket over a tree branch, hoping that would catch most of the smoke and keep the rain off our cook fire. Jim cleaned the turkey while Charlie and Jesse plucked the chickens, and soon we had them birds roasting over our small fire.

Hell, I was so starved, I could have eaten them all raw.

Which is what maybe we should have done.

When you look back, it was a damned poor idea, because, sure enough, somebody either smelled the smoke or seen it or smelled the fowls cooking, 'cause here came some Minnesota sons-of-bitches sloshing through the woods, making more noise than a regiment of Yankee cavalry.

We had to run, leaving behind those birds, still roasting under the soaked blanket. Painful. What a tragic waste.

Next day was Wednesday. Almost one week since we'd robbed the damned bank in Northfield, and what did we have to show for it? Starving bellies. Ruined clothes,

boots, hats. Two infecting wounds tormenting Jim and Bob, and the rest of us shot up
and ailing considerable. Even Jesse had
caught a flesh wound back in Northfield,
though, Jesse being Jesse, he never let on till
I spied it one evening when he was trying to
doctor himself with a strip of his own
underwear. Almost a week, and, damn it all
to hell, we were still in Minnesota. Not even
to Mankato.

"We got to find us a guide," I finally said.

"We've discussed that," Cole began. "The
risk. . . ."

"The hell with the risk, Bud!" I was wet,
cold, hurting from a bullet that had torn my
leg up bad. I missed my mother and my
wife, and I just wanted to get out of these
damned woods, get out of the rain. Noose
or a bullet looked a far sight prettier than
rooting in them wilds like some feral hog.
"They got a thousand men chasing us, if
you believe that farmer Charlie saw the
other day when he was scavenging."

"But they haven't caught us," Cole argued.

"Yet. They will. Look at that damned tree
over yonder, Bud. You see it? You remember
it? You should, with that double fork and
the deer's skull at the base. Ain't likely to
be another like that from here to Eden. But
that's the third damned time I've seen it."

"Lord have mercy," Jesse said. "We're going in circles."

Thunder rolled. The wind picked up. They all stared at me as I hadn't finished my stumping.

"We have to get past Mankato. Then Madelia. I think if we can make it to the Dakotas, we can get out of here alive. But we're on foot, and Mankato's a big town, and we sure as hell are lost."

"So we borrow another guide?" Jim asked.

"Damn' right. Just to get us to the other side of Mankato, maybe near Madelia."

"And what happens to us after he tells the law, Buck?" Cole asked.

"He don't tell nobody nothing," I said, "if we bury the son-of-a-bitch."

CHAPTER SIXTEEN:

THOMAS JEFFERSON DUNNING

Tell me you wouldn't have done the same thing I done. You tell me that if a man pointed a cannon in your face and said to do as he'd say or he'd kill you, you tell me you'd be brave as Achilles. Tell me you wouldn't be shaking in your brogans if you got shanghaied by the notorious James-Younger band of murderers.

I didn't wet my britches. I didn't cry or beg — well, not then, not till later — and you'd have done the same, damn it. I didn't do nothing but do as I was told. Does that make me yellow? I don't think so. Tell me you'd have done different.

Hell, I ain't no gunman. Ain't no lawman. Ain't Wild Bill Hickok or some other dime novel hero. I'm a farmer. Don't even work my own homestead. Just a working man. Field hand. Farm manager. Rich man's white nigger. What was I supposed to do?

Name's Thomas Jefferson Dunning, but I

answer to Jeff, and I work for Mr. Henry Shaubut, one of the richest by-God farmers in Le Sueur County. All them Shaubuts in these parts is rich. Mr. Shaubut's a good man, though, treats me decent, pays me decent, goes to church regular, and I don't think he'd've done no different than I did.

That morning, Wednesday, September 13th, found me in the field, herding some cows afoot, maybe 6 o'clock or thereabouts, when I spotted six men walking straight toward me. They was all dressed practically in rags, sickly looking, and at first I thought they might be part of the hordes of damned fools chasing the killers who raided Northfield the week previous. Chasing ghosts, if you'd asked me then. By that time, I figured those killers had long escaped Minnesota law, was likely back in Missouri, laughing at our peacekeepers and bounty men. So did Mr. Shaubut. Reckon lots of folks now thought the same as we did. The Jameses and Youngers was long gone, and the posses still out in the Big Woods and such was chasing themselves. Only it come to me that these men coming toward me, if they was part of the pursuers, they wouldn't likely be walking, limping mostly. By jacks, I think the rewards posted for those killers brought out more fools than a keg of forty-rod whiskey.

" 'Morning," one of them said with a smile, and he leaned on this cane he had made himself (I could tell). His left hip was wrapped tightly with a dirty strip of cloth, and he'd been bleeding a mite. "We've kind of lost our way. Wonder if you might help us?"

Well, right then I knew those six men was the very same killers half the country wanted, and right then those six men knew what I knew because the one with the beard that wasn't from a lack of shaving, he drew a wicked revolver, earring back the hammer before it ever left the holster, and stuck it under my nose.

"To hell with good manners, Bud," the man said to his friend, then told me: "We need food. Clean clothes. And we need to get the hell out of this damned state. This your farm? Answer me, you son-of-a-bitch! Is this your farm?"

"I just work here," I said.

"Where's the house?"

I pointed past the pasture. "Just beyond that tree line."

"Anybody home? And don't lie, you miserable bastard, because, if you lie, we won't just cut your throat before we blow your brains out. We'll kill everyone in the damned house. Every man. Every woman. Every kid, dog, chicken, and pig."

"Nobody. Mister Shaubut went to Mankato for a few days. I'm alone."

"You know who we are?"

"I got a strong notion."

"You know where we're from?"

"Missouri," I said, nodding. I'd read about it in the *Record.*

"We're a damned long way from Missouri. But you're going to help us get there. Savvy?"

My head signaled yes.

"We need to get through Mankato. How well do you know this country?"

"Not well at all. . . ."

The tall man struck me with the butt of that revolver, and down I went, rolling in the mud, tears streaming down my face. Damn, that hurt, hurt like a son-of-a-bitch.

"Don't you lie to me!"

"I ain't lyin'. . . ."

He kicked me in the ribs, but I must have known what he planned, because I rolled away from his boot and his toe just glanced my ribs. Only one of the other men stood behind me — ain't got the foggiest how he got there — and booted me hard in the back, and I gasped and groaned, but before

I could even get my lungs to work again, another mean-looking man jerked me up by my hair and back, pinned my arms till I thought they'd bust.

"How well do you know this country?" I was asked again.

"I wasn't . . . lyin' . . . I. . . ." I had to catch my breath, though I figured the outlaw would kill me before I had the chance to explain. Somehow, he didn't shoot me, or slit my throat, just waited. Maybe he believed me.

"How well?"

"I just hired out here . . . late summer. Ain't even from . . . this area."

"Well, you know it better than we do. Savvy? You know who we are. You know we killed that banker in Northfield?"

"And the Swede," I said.

"What?" This came from the fellow leaning on the cane, the one who had acted polite at first. The Indian-looking man about to break my arms suddenly released me.

"What?" repeated the one on the cane, the one called Bud.

"Swede," I said. "Or some foreigner. The one shot . . . in the street. He died . . . day or so ago. Mister Shaubut told me."

Sighing, the man sagged against his cane.

"You all right, Capt'n?" the one behind me asked.

"Hell." He sighed again.

The bearded man tapped the pistol barrel on the side of my head that he hadn't clubbed. "The banker wouldn't open the safe for us. That's why he died. He would be alive if he had done as directed. So we scattered his brains across the wall. So you know what I reckon . . . ? I didn't catch your name. . . ."

"Jeff. Jeff Dunning."

"Well, Jeff Dunning, I reckon the next time we rob a bank, the cashier won't be so damned stubborn. Won't play the hero or play the fool. He'll be thinking about that dead man in Northfield. You reckon that's right, Jeff Dunning?"

"Yes, sir."

"So if you don't get us to Mankato and across the river, then I guess we'll blow your brains out so the next fool we come across won't be after no reward. But if you do as we say. . . ." He lowered the hammer slowly, his eyes never leaving mine, and slammed the revolver in his holster.

"Now let's go to the farm. And remember what I said, Jeff Dunning. Remember it well."

■ ■ ■ ■

They wolfed down the corn pone and potatoes in Mr. Shaubut's home, looked around for powder and ball, or even a weapon, but Mr. Shaubut didn't own nothing but an old muzzleloading shotgun and he had taken that with him to town. They did find Mr. Shaubut's brown clay jug, which he kept hidden under his bed, but didn't drink it, not then. They made me milk the heifer, and they gulped it down, relishing it like they was eating in some fancy restaurant in St. Paul, only making a big mess. They washed their wounds — I think every damned one of them had a bullet hole in him, if not more — and then the big mean one who hadn't said a word but looked like a red nigger, only one with a mustache and beard stubble, he forced me outside and had me dig a hole. First I thought it was my grave, yet soon I realized they was just burying the bloody rags they had been using for bandages.

Once they was all filled and refreshed, the bearded one with the big pistol said: "Jeff Dunning . . . 'A hundred thousand welcomes. I could weep, and I could laugh. I am light and heavy. Welcome.' " That ain't no stretcher. That's what he said, and he was smiling when he spoke them words. Reckon food and shelter will do that to a body that has been suffering so. Ain't got the slightest notion what he meant.

Groaning, the tall man stood up, and put his right hand on the butt of the revolver, the friendliness gone from his eyes. "Which way?" he asked.

"Bluff Road, I reckon," I said.

"Lead the way."

When we got near town, they decided to have a little parley in the woods. I trembled as I walked, fearing this was their pretense, that they'd kill me here and leave me to the worms, but they all sat down and passed the jug of sipping liquor they had stole from Mr. Shaubut.

"Can we swim the river, Jeff Dunning?" another one asked. If you was to question me on the subject, I'd say he looked like the bearded man's brother, only shorter, but both had them same cold eyes, and this one packed three big-caliber pistols on his belt, showing them off cavalierly. He struck me as a peacock, only peacocks never killed no man in cold blood.

"No," I said, which was the Lord's truth. "Water's too high. Minnesota and the Blue

Earth, both. Current's mighty swift. You fellows would all drown, in your condition."

"How about stealing a boat?"

"I reckon that's a good notion," I said. "Only I don't know where we'd find one."

"Where else can we cross?"

"Dingus," the man with the cane said, "this ain't worth a tinker's damn."

"What do you mean?"

"Turn this farmer loose. He got us to Mankato. We can find a way through town, sneak in after dark."

"The idea, Bud," the man called Dingus said haughtily, "was to find a guide to get us past Mankato. Over the river. Maybe to. . . ." He shut up, and cast me a cold, disdainful eye.

"The idea," the one known as Bud said, "was we'd be richer than Midas, the way you and Stiles talked, but it didn't turn out that way. The farmer got us this far. I think we can go the rest without him."

"That's fine," said Dingus's brother, hand on his weapon.

My mouth went drier than a Mormon's icebox.

"You going soft because of that Swede?" Dingus asked Bud.

Bud looked riled, and his grip tightened on the cane, but he spoke calm. "We can turn him loose, give him a chance to get back to his farm before his boss. That way they'll be no suspicion, and I got a strong feeling this lad'll keep his trap shut. Ain't that right, Jeff?"

"Yes, sir." Those words flied out of my throat.

"Maybe so," Dingus's brother said, "but I have a recollection of us deciding on another way to keep his trap shut." He drew his revolver, already cocked.

Right then and there, I fell to the ground, right on my knees, clasping my hands in front of my chest. Almost at that moment, rain started drizzling, and I won't lie to you. I cried. I begged. I didn't want to die, especially not here alone, not now. Do that make me a coward? I don't think so. You tell me how you'd just stand up and face a killer like that and tell him to shoot and shoot true. Tell me. Tell me that to my face and I'll call you a damned liar or a damned fool or both.

"Shut up!" Dingus snapped at me, kicked at me. "Buck up there, boy. Be a man, damn you."

"I don't want to die. Oh, please, God, please don't kill me. I won't tell a soul. I promise. I swear on my dead mama's grave. Just please, please let me live." I couldn't shut up, probably wouldn't have never shut up if Dingus hadn't buffaloed me with one of his pistols.

Down I went, aching but still living. I prayed, prayed with the rain coming down harder, drenching my face, mixing with the blood and mud and leaves in my hair, prayed — and I hadn't prayed in so long. Prayed while killers debated over my life.

"Killing him won't help us," the decent one named Bud said. Well, I'm calling him decent since he hadn't hit my head or abused me none and was arguing for my life.

"And letting him live will?" Dingus said. "We let this yellow bastard go and every man jack son-of-a-bitch in Mankato and beyond will be on our ass. Kill him!"

Dingus's brother leveled his pistol. I closed my eyes, expecting to hear the gunshot — if I heard anything at all — but instead Bud's voice reached my ears.

"No, we will not kill him."

"Like hell, Bud. It's the only way."

"It's no good. We let him go, he keeps quiet, and he will, or we'll come back and slit the son-of-a-bitch's throat from ear to ear. You hear me, Jeff?" I opened my eyes, saw Bud's face inches from my own. Dirty water dripped from his reddish-colored mustache and goatee. "You won't say a word, will you?"

I sputtered out something. Reckon I agreed to what he was saying.

"Well. . . ." I don't know which one said that. My eyes was blinded again by tears and rain, but some men jerked me to my feet and shoved me against a tree.

Dingus's brother holstered his revolver, shaking his head as he said: "We are at a crossroads. The Rubicon. I say this, let Bob decide this bloke's fate. Bob's hurt the worst amongst us."

Bob stepped forward, sweating, or maybe that was just the rain water, holding his right arm close to his chest. Dingus's brother wasn't lying none, that boy was hurting. Hurting bad.

"You're the judge, dear Brother," Bud said, and we waited.

I figured I was dead for sure, but Bob shook his head, finally hung it, and muttered something that I could just barely make out. "If he joins pursuit, there'll be time enough for shooting. I say . . . I say, hell, I'd rather be shot dead than to have that man killed for fear he might put a hundred men after us."

"Amen," the Indian-looking savage said, which surprised me. "What's another hundred when they got a thousand chasing us already?"

The kind man shoved me past the tree, toward the road, right into Dingus's brother's arms, and I started blubbering again, bawling like a newborn baby, knowing they was bound to murder me no matter what Bob and Bud and the mean-looking one said. Sure enough, Dingus's brother rammed the barrel of his revolver into my Adam's apple.

" 'Luck is a mighty queer thing. All you know about it for certain is that it's bound to change.' You know who wrote that, Jeff Dunning?"

"Shakespeare? Jesus Christ?"

"Bret Harte, you ignorant son-of-a-bitch. Now get back to Mister Shitbutt's farm, and, remember, if you sell us up the river, I'll be back. If I get killed, I'll send one of my pals, and we got many, many pals. We'll slit your throat in your own damned bed, but, before you die, we'll cut off your pecker and shove it down your throat. Remember that, Jeff Dunning. Remember it well."

He pushed me toward the road. Then the clouds burst.

I swear to God, I had no intention of telling nobody what had happened. That's right. I was scared. I run all the way back to Mr. Shaubut's farm, and I was there in my little room beside the barn when he come home the following morn. He come charging inside, yelling that I was a lying, worthless little weasel, that the cow hadn't been milked, his house was a shambles, the eggs hadn't been gathered, his corn whiskey was stole, and the cattle not been moved to the pasture.

He seen me just shivering, just praying. Every damned time I closed my eyes, I seen Dingus's brother, smiling, quoting Scripture or whatever he was reciting, him or his brother splitting my head open with their pistols, and I seen him in my dreams, with a big knife, cutting me, seen me gurgling on my own blood and that knife going down low in my britches. Hell, when Mr. Shaubut come charging in there, I fell to my knees, begging him — on account I thought he was one of those brigands — to spare my miserable life.

Suddenly Mr. Shaubut was holding me, good man that he is, comforting me, begging me to tell him what had happened. So I broke my vow to those outlaws. Is a word to a killer worth a damn? Tell me you'd do otherwise. Tell me.

I told Mr. Shaubut that I had been taken

by Jesse James and his black-hearts. I told him that those boys wasn't out of the state, not by a damned sight, told him they was past Mankato by now, heading toward Dakota.

Felt better once I'd confessed, too, but I'll be drawing my time from Mr. Shaubut and lighting a shuck for somewhere else just as fast as I can.

CHAPTER SEVENTEEN:

JESSE JAMES

Personally I would have killed the yellow bastard, but Frank was right to leave his fate in Bob Younger's hands, and Bob granted the sodbuster a stay of execution, a pardon, so we sent him on his merry way. Not that we believed he'd keep his mouth shut. Our only hope was that the son-of-a-bitch ran back to his farm, not to the nearest law in Mankato. Trust him? Hell, I trust in the mercy of God.

God has been merciful. Waiting in the pouring rain that evening, waiting in the mud and muck, trying to determine our chances of sneaking through that city, I heard the train whistle in the distance. I wondered what would have happened had we robbed the bank here, instead of the one in Northfield. Well, we cannot change history. The train sang out its night song again.

"Mercy," I said softly. "A train."

"You want to take the train back home,

Dingus?" said Jim, in one of his moods. "Or rob it?"

"Trains can't swim the river. There's gotta be a bridge down yonder somewhere."

Jim leaned forward, suddenly ashamed of mouthing me so. "There'll be guards."

"Not as many as we're liable to meet up with in Mankato."

So we started walking, moving south a bit, skirting around the city, and then along the banks of the Blue Earth River, which hooked up with the big Minnesota River just a ways from us. And, sure enough, long about two in the morning, we come to the bridge.

Sentries had been posted, all right, two men and a teen-age boy, all of whom looked as miserable as we did, so we walked right up to them, hallooing the camp, where they had coffee brewing over a stove that had been made out of a rusty old barrel.

"We're from Freeborn County," I lied. "Been chasing those killers from Northfield. Coffee smells inviting."

"Help yourself," said a fat man with a handlebar mustache.

Didn't have to tell us twice.

"You come a long way," the boy said as we gulped down coffee and warmed ourselves by the fire.

"That we have."

"Where's your horses?"

"Livery."

"You walked that far?"

"Mind your manners, Lars," the mustached man scolded the boy, but I caught him looking for his shotgun, which stood leaning against a tree out of the rain.

"I'd sure like to get a gander at them outlaws," the boy said.

I showed him my Schofield. "You're looking at them now," I said.

"When's the next train due?" Cole asked the leader, and, when we learned not until dawn or thereabouts, we tied the two men up and the boy, finished our coffee, hating to leave the fire, and crossed the railroad bridge over the Blue Earth River.

Didn't matter now that we had let the spineless sodbuster go. Whether or not he opened his trap, these three guards would sound the alarm once they were freed or found. Such is fate.

Yet God blessed us again when Charlie and Frank caught some chickens at a farm on the far side of the Blue Earth, and this time we managed to cook and eat them before some law dogs came to chase us away. Morning found us on the north bank of Rush Lake, and we rested again.

"Lord, show me the way," I whispered. Earlier, Frank had said we had come to the Rubicon, but I thought now we faced that figurative river, that now we had to make a decision, one that would affect our lives, perhaps decide which among us would live and which would die. Jim's shoulder had taken a bad turn, and Bob had never been much good, though always game as a rooster, with his arm busted and shot to pieces. While the two desperately wounded brothers tossed about, delirious, fevers high, I poured the last of the corn liquor we had stolen from the Shaubut farm over their wounds, allowing Charlie Pitts to go to work with his knife and drain the pus and blood, rid some of the infection.

As Charlie commenced with his doctoring, I took a few steps back, and turned my head. The sight of blood often sickens me.

"It's no good," Frank told me.

Cole came over to join our parley. Cole Younger never cared much for me, and I can't say I liked him much, but he was a good man, damned fine pistol fighter, and we'd been together for years. I hated for things to end this way, but the Lord had whispered the way in my ears. The only way.

"By now," Frank said, "that farm hand and those inept guards at the railroad trestle have spilled their guts."

"Most likely," Cole said.

I loved Bob Younger as if he were my own brother, and wanted Jim at my side in a fight. We Missouri bushwhackers do not kill our own, and we damned sure don't leave them to die, lessen we have to.

"I'm thinking the best deal for us is to split up," I said. "We'll steal horses, but that farm we passed down the pike didn't have but two. Those on horses can ride like hell for the Dakotas. I'm betting the laws'll take notice of them. That'll make it easier for the ones afoot to sneak out of Minnesota."

"I suspect you're right, Jesse," Cole said, and he never called me Jesse. Always Dingus.

"Can you ride, Cole?" I always called him Bud.

"No, you put somebody else on a horse. My leg's swole up. Hard enough for me to walk, but I got a good cane. I'll stay."

Charlie Pitts had joined us, wiping his knife blade against his thigh.

"I'll stay, too," he said.

"Ain't no need," Cole began, but Charlie shook his head.

"Mind's made up, Capt'n. If you stay, I'll play out my hand with you."

Charlie Pitts walked back to Bob and Jim,

now awake, sitting up, faces ashen and weak.

"Then it's settled," I said. "Frank and Bob will take the horses. I'll stay with you-all."

I turned to embrace my brother, but Cole put his hand on my shoulder, and I looked back at him.

"Appreciate the offer, but Bob can't sit a saddle. Jim . . . I don't reckon he's in no condition to ride right now, neither. No, you ride with your brother. Maybe you're right. Maybe the posses will take after y'all."

I half expected my brother to quote something from the bard — "parting is such sweet sorrow" — that kind of thing, but he just hung his head, shuffled his feet in the mud, and I shook Thomas Coleman Younger's hand and walked over to his brothers. I didn't have to tell them the plan. I could tell they knew this was good bye. Charlie stood up and made room for me, and I knelt beside those solid soldiers of the Lord, took off my hat, pulled them close, and, as we embraced for that final time, I began:

" 'The Lord is my shepherd; I shall not want. He maketh me to lie down in green pastures; he leadeth me beside the still waters. . . .' "

Afterward, I kissed Bob's cheeks, shook Jim's feeble hand, and, wiping tears from my eyes, I followed my brother out of the woods.

Jim Younger called out to our backs: "Die game, boys!"

Frank started to speak, but, for once, my brother could find no words, none to recite, none to create.

The next time we'd meet up with the Youngers and loyal Charlie Pitts, one way or the other, would be on the streets of Glory.

Our journey home would not be pretty. We stole a horse from the farm we had spied — the other damned nag was lame — and rode double. Almost didn't make it through that night because somehow we rode right close to one of the picket camps at this bridge around this place called Lake Crystal. Foul luck. All the guards had fallen asleep except one.

"Who are you?" he yelled. "Halt and identify yourselves!"

"Go to hell," I said, but damned if that son-of-a-bitch almost didn't send me in that direction.

The rifle bullet tore off my hat, sending that worthless farm horse into a buck that spilled Frank and me into the soaking ground. By the time we scrambled to our feet, the horse had bolted down the road, and we hightailed it into the woods, Frank limping so bad now that I had to all but drag him.

Yet we did not stay afoot for long, because soon God showed us the light, the light of a cabin, and by the cabin stood a barn, and inside the barn we found a fine pair of grays. No saddles, but Maw had us riding bareback before we were out of diapers.

Onward we traveled. I bought a hat off a buck nigger along the Des Moines River — hated to wear a hat that had been on a damned darky's head, but, hell, it was still raining. Hated to give money to some darky, but the boy was bound for church, and I figured the dollar would serve as my tithing.

When we wore out the grays, Frank stole a pair of black horses, and, as we made our way nearer the Dakotas, I had a good laugh at my brother's judgment of horseflesh.

"You look well suited, Frank," I told him.

"I love a black horse," he said.

"As do I. You know your horse is blind in one eye."

"Lucky is all."

"How so?"

"Yours is blind in both."

Thus Frank had the last laugh, as older brothers tend to get. One horse blinded in one eye, another blinded in both. How well the James boys traveled!

On Monday morning, we stole yet another pair of grays — Minnesota farmers must sure love gray horses, but for an old Confederate, they suited me — and sometime that day, we crossed into the Dakota Territory. God sent us a sign, I believe, for the sun burst through the gray clouds, which soon cleared, and bathed us in refreshing sunlight, drying our ruined clothes.

We rode to a farm around noon, and asked the farmer if we might partake of his well.

"Help yourself," the man said.

"Where are we?" I asked. "We seem to have lost our bearings."

"Valley Springs is the closest settlement."

Before I could drink, my horse nudged me out of the way and slaked his own thirst from the bucket I had drawn. I let him finish, as he had a long way to travel before we could find some fresh mounts. As I reached for the bucket, still holding enough water for a man, the farmer cried out: "Hear! Hear! Let me get you a fresh bucket, mister."

The bitterness hit me hard then, as I thought of that treacherous Bill Stiles, a man I had befriended, a man who had the gall to get himself killed, leaving us lost and stranded in Yankee country. I thought of those bastards in the bank, who refused to open the safe, and the men in town shooting at us from all sides, boys hurtling sticks, stones, and insults in our directions. I thought of all the Yankee sons-of-bitches who had slandered, shamed, or slaughtered my family. And I thought of this cock-of-the-walk farmer in the middle of nowhere, looking at me as if I were trash.

"I'd rather drink out of a pail used by a horse than by some men I know," I said, and let the cool water slide down my throat.

Safety is fleeting, as is good fortune, and, before the day had passed, we came across more posses. By then, word had spread that the James brothers, or some of the Northfield bandits, had escaped into Dakota. For a couple of days we hid in a cave, resting, but hunger drives a man. So does the thought of home, of a wife and mother and a year-old son.

We left the cave, slowly rode south.

Dakota is a miserable expanse of bad grass and treacherous ravines and rocks, of which we stumbled over many, and Indians, of which we saw none.

"Country can swallow up a man," Frank said.

"Yes," I agreed.

We had entered a badlands of pink and red cliffs and spires climbing perhaps fifty feet high as we entered a stream aptly named, as we had learned from a farmer upon asking directions, the Palisades.

"I think it's best if we split up," Frank said.

Again, I agreed with my brother.

He rode left, and I turned right, and for the longest time, after Frank had been swallowed up, I heard nothing but the hard *clops* of my gray's hoofs on the rugged ground. The sound almost lulled me to sleep, and I dreamed of a twist of tobacco to chew. I glanced at the blue water rushing fifty feet beneath me, cutting a wide gap that separated me and my brother, somewhere on the opposite side. Some might call this beautiful, but I longed for Clay County.

Clop. Clop. Clop.

Heavy grew my eyelids.

Clop. Clop. Clop.

Soon, I slumbered in the saddle.

The gunshot woke me, or perhaps some instinct took over, and my eyes flew open a mere second before the rifle roared. I whirled in the saddle, drawing the Colt, preferring it in the saddle over the Schofield and Smith & Wesson. Giving the gray plenty of rein, I spurred the gelding ruthlessly.

Quickly I counted a dozen men behind me, saw the puff of a rifle shot, heard one of the men yelling at me, calling out to surrender, that I had nowhere to go.

Except hell.

I kept the gray running close to the cañon's edge, estimating the depth now to the river at perhaps 100 feet, yet the width between the cañon's high, hard walls lessened. Although tired, the horse underneath me was not blind, not lame, perhaps as grand a mount as any we had liberated in Minnesota, so I wheeled around and charged the posse coming straight at me, twice firing the Colt.

That caused those Yankee cowards to reconsider. Two reined up. Another galloped in retreat.

Just as quickly as I had begun my charge, I sent off another round, reined the gray around, and galloped for the cañon. Behind me came the report of a rifle, then another, followed by a lawman's stupid shout: "Stop, you damned fool! You'll be killed!"

One way or the other, I thought. I pitched the Colt to the ground. Every bit of weight would count. The darky's hat sailed off my head as the gray found its feet, leaped, soared. The wind battered my face, my heart pounded against my ribs, the gelding snorted as if summoning some extra effort, and the far red wall neared.

One way or the other, those sons-of-bitches chasing me would remember this moment forever, would remember Jesse James.

Forever.

CHAPTER EIGHTEEN:
A. O. SORBEL

Boy howdy, you never seen such a commotion as what grabbed hold of Minnesota — folks riding here and there, to and fro, searching barns, guarding bridges and crossroads, chasing each other most of the time, it seemed to me. I even heard tell that some Dutchy congregation around Millersburg had gathered at some farm, scared out of their wits, and fired the one shotgun amongst them on the hour to frighten away those border ruffians. *Outlaws* was on the lips of every man, woman, and child. There was a right heap of a reward put up for the capture of the raiders who had robbed the bank and killed two people in Northfield. The newspapers and preachers all said the culprits was Jesse and Frank James and Cole Younger and his brothers.

About two weeks had passed, and things still hadn't settled down.

Some of our cows wandered off, wandering being in their nature, especially after all that rain we'd had. I had to go round them up and herd them back home, and, when I come over the bridge on the Madelia road, I spotted two men hiding in the woods.

"What are you fellows doin' yonder?" I called out, because Ma says I'm as curious as a cat, while Pa says I can be as forgetful as a turkey. Guess I was both on that day, because it never occurred to me that those two fellows could have been outlaws.

"Go on with your cows, son," one of the men said.

"Well, what are you doin' there? It's a poor place for huntin'."

"Depends on the game, perhaps," said one of them, and he stuck his head up so I could better see him. He carried a big rifle, and I spied a little pistol shoved in his waistband. He had a big, black mustache and a bowler hat, dressed in store-bought duds, too nice to be hunting and hiding in the wet woods. "Do you know who I am?"

My head bobbed. "I think I've seen you in Madelia a time or two."

"I am Colonel Thomas Vought, son," he said. "I own the Flanders Hotel. Now, be gone."

"Not till you tell me why you're hidin' in them woods. For all I know you might plan on robbin' some traveler."

"Quite the opposite. We hope to bag some robbers."

The colonel — wonder if he was a real colonel — went on to say that a while back, before the big shooting match in Northfield, two men had visited his hotel. He'd thought nothing of it until after the bank robbery, then when he read descriptions of the men who had escaped, he began to wonder about those visitors. They'd said they had been looking for farms to purchase, but no farmers had since been approached, and those strangers had been quite inquisitive about the lay of the land, especially around here.

"If those two men were a party to that crime," Colonel Vought said, "I think they might be headed this way."

"Fits," said the other fellow, who hadn't given his name or gotten up so I could get a good look at him. "They were last seen crossing the Blue Earth River at Mankato and, perhaps, at the Lake Crystal bridge."

Said the colonel: "So, that is our purpose. Now move your cows along, son, so you do not reveal our hiding place or agenda to those desperadoes."

"Outlaws!" Now this really excited me. "Gee! I'd love to take a shot at those fellows with Dad's old gun."

The colonel grinned before sinking back behind the brush, and I hurried away to catch up with my cows, but he called out after me, and I turned around.

"Keep your eyes and ears open, son," he said.

I sure planned on doing that.

I had turned seventeen that March, all of those years spent in Brown County, most of 'em on Pa's farm near Lake Linden. All those years, nothing like this had ever happened. Oh, sure, the war came, but that had been fought down South, when I was just a kid, and the Santee Sioux rose up in Minnesota during that time — they hanged a slew of them in Mankato — but I couldn't remember a thing about that.

Outlaws, and not just outlaws and murderers and bank robbers, but, boy howdy, Jesse James and his gang. Now that was something. To me, anyway. When I told Pa about the men I'd spied in the woods, about what they had planned and how they had warned me, he just let out a grunt and reminded me of the chores to be done. Ma, she didn't have any interest in Jesse James or Colonel Vought, either. Pa and Ma hailed from Norway, came to Minnesota to farm. Nothing interested them much, excepting the weather and the cows and the corn.

Next day, I got up before the sun rose, pulled on my britches, boots, and homespun shirt, and walked outside to start my day. I found the cows in the road, but that's where they were supposed to be. For the past two weeks it had done nothing but rain, and the mud in the pens would have sucked down all the cows, and me, too, into the bowels of the earth had we left them there.

Pa had woke me up, as was his nature, and he stood by the gate, considering the cows while tamping tobacco down in his pipe, marveling at what a sight it was to behold, seeing that sun and nary a cloud in the sky, and finally stuck his pipe, unlit, in his shirt pocket, picked up the pail, and went to milking Henrietta.

As I walked toward him, two men came down the road, and I stopped, startled, then resumed, never taking my eyes off them fellows.

"Good morning," one of them said, and, remembering Colonel Vought's instructions, I hurried to the gate, and looked the two men over. Just two. I'd heard there was something like forty men who had robbed the Northfield bank. They stood on either side of Pa, the cow between them.

Well, those fellows didn't look like forty

men, and sure didn't look like robbers. Looked like nothing, if you were to ask me, but the most miserable varmints that ever walked on two legs. Both stood fairly tall, one with a thick mustache and several days of stubble over the rest of his face, along with an under-lip beard, the kind Ma despised on a man. The other was much slimmer, almost pale, with big ears, shorter hair and several days' growth of beard, lighter hair, down his cheeks and chin, though not much for a mustache. Maybe he couldn't grow a mustache. I couldn't, and I'd been trying for five years.

"Good morning," Pa answered, looking up, still milking. "I'd say a great morning. Looks to be a fine day in the making."

"Appears like," said the slimmer one.

He kept petting Henrietta's back, but, while he addressed Pa, he was looking at me, though only briefly. He took in our house, the road, the barn, and pens, wet his lips, and winced. His eyes were blue, also sickly looking, and he walked away, calling at us to have a nice day, gently rubbing his shoulder, followed by the bigger, darker man. Man alive, their clothes were ruined, nothing more than rags, and with me being downwind of those two, they both stank to high heaven. Suspicious, I watched them go, but they kept walking, disappeared around the bend, and I told Pa: "That was the robbers."

"No," Pa said as he rose, his knees popping. "They was nice men. Said 'good morning' and all. Nice men."

Well, good manners didn't convince me of anything, so I dodged the cows and walked till I found some good footprints those strangers had left in the muddy road. "I'll show you how nice the men was," I said, squatting by the tracks.

Now, the Army isn't going to come knocking at my door and asking me to join up as a civilian scout and go after those Sioux and Cheyennes causing a stir in Montana, but I know a thing or two about reading sign. You spend a healthy portion of your years chasing heifers that had wandered all over the tarnal county, you'll learn to track some, too. Those men's boots had been so worn, I pressed my fingers slightly on toe prints in the mud.

"Come here, Pa," I said, loud enough for him to hear but not so loud as those two men might.

"Never mind that," Pa told me. "Come finish the milking. I'll see about breakfast."

I let out a little sigh of disgust, not loud enough so that Pa would hear, and walked back to Henrietta and got to choring. The milk sprayed in the pail, and I tried to concentrate, but, well, it got hard because my excitement kept building, and so did the notion that those worn-out skeletons were outlaws on the run.

Henrietta ridded herself of gas, and that just about made up my mind for me. I glanced over my shoulder, couldn't see Pa, set the milk pail on the other side of the gate, and went following the tracks the two strangers had left. It was just my luck, though, that Pa came outside and spotted me before I had reached the turn.

"Asle Oscar Sorbel!" he called out, but I hurried my steps. "If they is outlaws, boy, they'll shoot you!"

I didn't turn back, couldn't. I just had to learn for myself. My figuring was that I was too old and too big for Pa to hide any more, and I'd milked the cow, could go without breakfast, and catch up on my chores when I got back home.

If the outlaws don't shoot me, that is.

About eighty rods up the road, after the curve, they had cut into the timber, and then I told myself . . . they got to be outlaws! I didn't see them, but I could tell from the tracks that they had crossed the creek. This being Mads Ouren's property, I paid him a visit, but he hadn't seen a thing, and I couldn't find any tracks. Next I went over to Gutterson Grove's place, and Mrs. Grove let me climb up on her roof to get a good look-see, but I didn't glimpse a thing there, either. It looked like those outlaws had vanished, if they were outlaws. I ran up the hill, a mighty good perch to keep an eye on the Madelia, Lockstock, and New Ulm roads, only to find those roads empty as my heart.

My convincement had started to fade a mite.

So I went home.

Pa was in the barn, and now I had worked up an appetite and started regretting that perhaps I had missed a chance at breakfast — Ma being a real fine cook — so I went inside, pulled off my boots, and called out to my mother.

"We didn't know where you took off to, A.O.," she said.

"Can I eat?" I asked.

"You're lucky." Her head tilted toward a platter of eggs and bacon. "Some hunters passed by while you were gone, asked if they could buy breakfast, but it wasn't ready yet, and they said they couldn't wait, so I just gave them yesterday's bread and a bit of butter. Next time you'll. . . ."

"What hunters?" My convincement had returned.

"Two strangers," she said.

"Same fellows who come here earlier?"

Pa had just walked inside, and he answered: "No, two other men. One man on a cane. The other had his right arm hanging in a bandanna sling. I doesn't think they was hunters."

"The robbers!" I no longer felt so hungry.

"I suspect you're right, Son," Pa said, and it felt mighty good to see him come around to my way of thinking. "They walked down the road, same way those other two men had gone."

"I'd best go tell Mister Ouren and the others. Tell 'em there are four outlaws, not just two."

Pa shook his head. "No, A.O. They'll kill you if they're them men from Northfield."

"Well, we got to warn 'em, Pa!"

Ma agreed, and we sent my sister, figuring the outlaws wouldn't suspect her, and even if they did, they weren't likely to harm a girl.

"Can I take the horse, Pa?" I begged. "Ride to town. Give the warnin' that the outlaws is around?"

"No. You might be hurt."

"Pa! These are outlaws. The men who

killed them two fellows in Northfield."

"And we won't have them killing you, Son," Ma said.

"But, Ma, Pa, we got to give the warnin'. There's a reward out for those men, and we got to let that colonel and the others in Madelia know."

Pa found his pipe, tapped it nervously on the kitchen table, and at last he nodded. "But," he said as I leaped toward the door, "you take the east road, so them fellows won't see you. And you ride to Madelia, tell the sheriff, then you stay put!"

I was halfway out the door before he finished.

Pa had hitched the horses to the wagon, but I took off the harness, tossed a blanket over Nutmeg's back — we didn't have a saddle — fixed a hackamore up, and leaped aboard, riding through our muddy fields and down the little game trail to the woods, then took off down the little woods road, keeping the timber between me and the main road. It was seven miles to Madelia, and I held Nutmeg at a good lope.

It was some ride, and I felt like a bona-fide hero till Nutmeg slipped in the mud and sent me over his neck and into a puddle. Luckily nobody saw my wreck, and Nutmeg wasn't the type of horse who would wander off without me. I caught up with him, wanted to cuss him, but just wiped the thick slime off my face and hands, pulled myself back onto the buckskin's back. Two miles later, I struck town, pulling the hackamore to stop my horse in front of the first man I saw.

"Robbers!" I cried out. "I've seen the Northfield robbers!"

The townsman looked at me from underneath his spectacles, chewing on a toothpick. Guess I didn't meet his expectations of a real sentry, what with me on a farm horse, muddy blanket for a saddle, hackamore instead of headstall, bit, and reins, and me in my farm clothes now caked with mud.

"Boy, I got no time for your foolishness." He turned to go, but I yelled that I was telling the truth.

"How many?" he asked, still unconvinced.

"Four," I said.

"Newspapers and Sheriff Glispin say eight or nine men are on the dodge."

"Well, all I saw was four."

"If you're fibbing, I'll whup you even before your pa does."

"I ain't lyin'!"

"You know anybody in town? Anybody

who can vouch for you?"

"John Owen knows my Pa," I told him.

"You wait here," he said, but took his time making his way to Mr. Owen's store.

That's when I spied the Flanders Hotel, and, remembering Colonel Vought, I kicked a worn-out Nutmeg into a walk down Buck Street, slid off the blanket, and tethered my horse to one of the skinny trees in front of the porch. The way my luck had started to turn, I figured the colonel would still be hiding in the woods by the bridge over toward our farm, but my heart about leaped into my throat when I saw him eating breakfast with another man.

I ran up to his table. "I found them bandits!" I cried out.

He looked up, chewing his ham, winked at his companion, and said to me: "What did you do with them?"

He didn't believe me, neither, darn him. "They're still there. Four of 'em. Came by my house this mornin'."

"That's a big haul." He winked again, which I found mighty bothersome, and reached for his coffee. "Have you had breakfast, son?"

CHAPTER NINETEEN:
SHERIFF JAMES GLISPIN

To me way of thinking, the James and
Younger boys, or whoever had robbed the
Northfield bank, had escaped. Sweet Mary,
but I hoped they had, or at least out of Watowan County they'd stay. The year 1876
found me in me third term as county sheriff,
and in me jurisdiction, I liked things quiet.
A six-shooter I carried, the county bought
me a couple of shotguns, a Henry .44 and
Spencer carbine, and above the door at me
home hung the Springfield rifle I'd shoul-
dered during the war. But I didn't want to
use them in the line of duty, not ever.

In the war, I'd seen enough killing, whole-
sale slaughter. Death eats at a man's soul,
and a horrible amount I'd seen during those
awful four years, seen me friends die by the
score, and had lost count of the number of
brave Southern boys who'd fallen at me
hand.

Enough I'd seen in the East, so West I

came, settling here in Watowan County. 'Tis quieter than Massachusetts. Nothing but lads of the soil and real nice colleens. As a lawman, I'd have to break up fisticuffs once in a blue moon, but most of me such noble duties involved hauling off dead animals and collecting taxes. That changed after the 7th of September.

For two weeks, I'd ridden all over the county, chasing rumors and fairies, chasing the wind, looking for those desperate men who'd robbed the Northfield bank. For two weeks, I'd ridden in the rain till a tadpole I felt I'd become. Now that the sun had come out, I hoped to dry out and rest, prayed those bad men were long past me county.

'Twas the 21st of September, and I'd just finished breakfast and started making me way down the boardwalk to the livery by the Flanders Hotel, when Colonel Vought stepped outside, holding his rifle, followed by a corn-fed boy covered in dried mud.

"Jim," the colonel said, "this boy says four men came by his farm this morning. He thinks they're the Northfield bandits."

A good look-see I gave the child. "What's ye name, boy?"

"A.O. Sorbel. Well, Asle Oscar, but most folks call me A.O."

"Ye be Ole and Guri's boy, aren't ye?"

"Yes, sir. I rode my horse all the way from the farm," he continued. "Two men were walking down the road while Pa was milking Henrietta. They were filthy, in rags, and I looked at their boot prints after they walked on. Boots were worn to a frazzle, Sheriff. I could see the toes prints they was so bad off."

"Two men?" I asked.

"That's right. But while I was gone trailing them, two others come by the farm, said they was hunters, but one had to walk on a cane and the other had a bum right arm. That's what Pa and Ma told me. They asked to pay for breakfast, but when Ma told them they'd have to wait, they said they needed to get along, so Ma gave them some bread."

Colonel Vought added: "I had my doubts, but the boy's persuaded me that these men are the fiends we seek."

"Just four men?" I asked.

"That's all we saw."

Well, fine Christian folks were Guri and Ole Sorbel, tillers of the soil, like me own father had been back in County Cork, and I don't think their son would ride all the way to town to tell some stretcher. Now, the Sorbel farm lay over in Brown County, not officially me jurisdiction, but I decided the devil with boundaries. They were close

261

enough to Watowan County. To St. James I ordered me deputy, told him to send as many riders as he could round up to the Sorbel farm, then asked another lad to warn all the crews working the threshing machines, to tell them to unhitch their teams and make for open country. The last thing I wanted was innocent people getting shot, and I figured those outlaws would be desperate for horses, especially when they found out we were after them.

By then, Cap Murphy had ridden up in his buckboard with his little boy, probably coming for breakfast, and I'd sure want Cap along in a fight, even though I prayed it wouldn't come to that. I'd want Colonel Vought along, too.

Cap told his boy to wait in the hotel, and then we went running everywhere, to saddle our horses, to fetch our guns. Young Sorbel told Doc Overholt that he could ride his horse, and the kid and Cap Murphy climbed into the wagon. To the farm we dashed, me, Colonel Vought, Cap Murphy, the Sorbel boy, Doc Overholt, Will Estes, and Big Jim Severson.

By the time we reached Ole Sorbel's place, his cows had practically wiped out all the sign, but A.O. said he knew which way the strangers had gone. His mother didn't want the lad to come along with us, but I promised to keep him safe, that he'd do nothing more than lead our way and hold our horses if to a fight it came. That didn't settle Guri's nerves anyway, and she went inside, wailing like a banshee.

Not long after that, Charles Pomeroy, Jr. and George Bradford rode in from Madelia, and Ben Rice and G.S. Thompson, both of St. James, met up with us, too. We left the farm, letting young A.O. Sorbel show us the way. If Sorbel wasn't mistaken, the four men were traveling southwest.

The alarm had spread, and another bunch of riders from Madelia and St. James we met. Mayor Strait of St. Peter also rode up with news that the Army had practically a company in the field after the outlaws. Our own army on the Madelia road kept growing.

We split up, Mayor Strait taking his party one way, and me leading mine toward Lake Hanska. Me heart pounded, and I found meself sweating like a man laid up with fever. I wanted to make sure these four men didn't slip from our grasp, so that meant catching them before sundown would be our best hope. More importantly, I didn't want to wind up killing or wounding four innocent tramps.

Enough innocent blood had been shed in Minnesota that month.

Across the fields we galloped, over roads, through fields and forests, and, as we neared the Watowan River country, I saw them. Four men, working their way across Hanska Slough.

"Hold up there!" I shouted.

They made it across, climbed out of the water, and toward the woods they bolted, though they did not make good time. Tired, I'd say they were, exhausted, limping badly the lot of them.

Severson and Doc Overholt opened fire.

"They're out of range!" I shouted.

Doc didn't listen, got off the Sorbel horse, handing young A.O. the hackamore, and squatted in the mud. He carried a Sharps rifle, one of those weapons the snakes-in-the-grass used during the war, now popular among the buffalo hiders, and squeezed off a round. By thunder if his bullet didn't snap the cane one of the fugitives was using, spilling the man with a curse. Another helped him up, practically carrying him to the woods.

"Stop and surrender!" I yelled. "I'm sheriff of Watowan County!"

This time, they fired back before into the thicket they vanished.

Woods around Hanska be thick, daunting, providing plenty of cover, and a tough time we'd have getting through all those bogs and streams.

"We must go slowly," Cap Murphy said from his wagon seat, "but with resolve."

"And keep them afoot," I said. "Don't let them take any horses. Kill the horse if ye must."

I'd rather see a horse dead than another man.

Four farmers, armed with shotguns, joined us, and glad I was to have them. Other groups rendezvoused with us till our number totaled sixteen. Sixteen against four, but those four, if indeed the guilty party, were killers, veterans at this kind of fight. I had a posse of store clerks and farmers, mostly, though some veterans of the war, including Cap Murphy.

Yet soon I spied other mounted men in the distance, and I dispatched Doc Overholt to intercept those troopers, to have them surround the thicket in which the lads hid.

Cautiously we closed in on our prey.

"What do you want?" called a ragged voice from the brambles.

"Throw up ye hands and surrender," I

replied, ducking as the bandit sent a shot in me direction. Not even aiming me Henry, I fired back, levered another round into the chamber, and the battle commenced.

Too hot for us out in the clearing, I directed our men to retreat and take shelter in the woods. There we gathered, regrouping, ready to formulate a final battle plan.

By now, I had no doubts that these four men were part of the Northfield gang.

Nor did Cap Murphy, who leaped down from his wagon, with A.O. Sorbel right behind him, taking cover in the sumac and ash. Taking charge Murphy did, and I let him. At this kind of thing, Cap Murphy had a lot more experience than me.

"Let's go get 'em," Murphy said. "Aim low, but shoot to kill for they'll kill you if they can."

"We've got them practically surrounded," Willis Bundy said. "Why not keep them here, have a siege? Starve them out?"

"I have no patience for that," Murphy said. "I'm walkin' right in there. Who's coming with me?"

During the war, charges I'd seen, took part in me share, but let me tell ye something . . . what Cap Murphy suggested would turn even the bravest lad's stomach.

266

This wasn't open ground we'd be charging through. We'd fight our way through brambles and briars and brush thicker than Cap Murphy's beard — against well-hidden man-killers facing a noose if captured alive.

I'm an Irishman, a Massachusetts man by birth, who sold farming equipment before pinning on a badge. I'd rather fight with me fists than with me gun, and I sure had no longing to commit suicide, but these farmers and merchants and friends had elected me sheriff, and though enough killing I'd seen, knew me duty I did. I stepped forward.

A.O. Sorbel, bless his heart, volunteered next, grabbing Ben Rice's Winchester, but Rice, a Southerner by birth who'd spent most of his years in Minnesota, and had won more turkey shooting contests than anyone in St. James, pulled the gun away from the kid and tousled Sorbel's dirty hair. "Brave boy, but mind your business and hold the horses," Rice said, "like we promised your mother you'd do."

"Dang it," A.O. started, but I told the boy to hush and do as he was told.

Charles Pomeroy, a New Yorker who'd fought in the Sioux scare back in '62, and George Bradford, who taught school in the winter and farmed during the summer, said they'd go. So did short, fat Jim Severson, who clerked in town when he wasn't court- ing some lady or making a joke. Big Jim cocked his rifle and said: "This should make Miss Hildegard take a shine to me."

We waited for others, but none of the ten stepped forward.

"Six," Cap Murphy said, "should be enough."

"Seven's better," Colonel Vought said at last, and stepped into the clearing, heading to the thicket.

Cap Murphy called out directions as he thumbed back the hammer on his rifle. "Keep fifteen feet apart," he said, "just keep walkin' right at 'em. When you see 'em, hol- ler at 'em to surrender. If they shoot, shoot 'em. Shoot to kill, boys, and keep on shoot- in' till they surrender or are all dead. Or we are."

Our rifle barrels became machetes as we slashed our way through the brush, drown- ing out the noise of the bubbling water, of the singing birds, and I cringed at the noise we made approaching four bad men.

Sweat streaked down me face, and breath- ing became difficult. Fear? Certainly. Dur- ing the war, never had I entered a battle when fear had not practically consumed me, but I understood that once the first shot was fired, instincts would take over, a will to survive, a duty, a knowledge of the job at hand.

We have them surrounded, I kept telling meself. Perhaps they will surrender.

I knew they wouldn't. A fight unto the death this would become.

At that instant, a bearded man leaped just a few rods ahead of me, a snarl on his lips and six-shooter in his hand, pointed at me head. Out of the revolver's cavernous bore belched smoke and flame.

CHAPTER TWENTY:

BOB YOUNGER

"This is all my fault," I told my brothers, tears cascading, unashamedly, down my cheeks.

I'd wind up getting Jim and Cole killed, Jim and Cole, the best older brothers a man could want. They had tried to talk me out of riding north with Jesse, but I hadn't listened. I'd been the fool, forgetting my family, forgetting how wise older brothers are. Now, it had come to this.

Jim and Cole, and Charlie Pitts, would die. Die like animals trapped in a thick forest. Die in a damned Northern state. Die because of me.

I'd die, too. Far from Maggie, my girl, and her son, who I'd prayed I'd soon raise as my own. Far from my sisters, far from Lee's Summit, Missouri. I'd die for nothing, too. For $26 and 40¢. Die because of my own damned arrogance.

"Hush up," said Cole, squatting beside

me. "This ain't your fault, Bob. Ain't nobody's . . . 'cept mine." The last two words came out as a whisper. "How you holdin' up, Bob?" he asked again, and tried to smile.

"Arm still hurts like blazes," I said. "But you give me a gun and I'll fight alongside you, Cole."

"You'd do us better was you to reload for us. Think you can handle that chore, Bob?" My head bobbed slightly, and my brother dumped some cartridges between my legs, along with a pair of pistols. We started reloading together, while Brother Jim and Charlie Pitts crawled about to scout out our situation.

I already knew our situation.

Hopeless.

I thought about what had brought me here. It was all for Maggie. She was a Yankee, and a widow, having moved from New England after her husband passed away from fever, and took up farming just over the Jackson County line. The most beautiful woman I ever met, and, Yankee blood or no, she captured my heart, which hadn't put up much of a fight. She helped me get through the hard times when those damned detectives shot Brother John dead back in '74. Her boy, Jeremy, he was a strapping young fellow, and me and him got along just fine. Yes, Maggie was always there for me, and she said she'd marry me if I'd quit being an outlaw.

Which had always been my intention. Truth be told, I really wasn't an outlaw, not in my eye, when I first fell in love with Maggie. I was a farmer, an honest one, who just happened to be named Younger. Now Jim, he loved being a cowboy, and Cole liked debating religion and politics or dancing and having a good time, and working cattle, too, but I guess I had more of Pa in me than anything else. Farming. That's all I really wanted to do, and it's what I would have done if those Yankees had left me alone, if they hadn't killed my father, drove my ma to her grave, and murdered John.

We were Youngers, and the law would hunt us down just because of our name. They didn't give a tinker's damn if I was a farmer, if I'd never popped a cap on anyone, if I'd never robbed a bank or train, if I'd done nothing except live a honest life, which I had, at first. They'd never let me be, so that's why I joined up with Jesse. That's why I became an outlaw. That's why I robbed the train in Muncie, Kansas, with Frank and Jesse, Cole and Clell. Maybe, I figured, if I could get that farm up and running, get myself out of debt, maybe that would make things easier, make Maggie understand. She'd become my wife.

After the Muncie case, I had leased farmland down around Greenwood — had to make up a name to do it — but things remained hard, and wasn't long before I needed more cash, which was a hard crop to raise in Missouri after the war. Maybe if I could haul in enough cash, I could buy that farm, be my own man, even if I had to use another fellow's name. I needed money again, for me, and Maggie and Jeremy. So I started paying Jesse these visits, and, well, to hear Jesse and Bill Chadwell — no, Stiles was his real name, Bill Stiles — talk, the streets of Minnesota were paved with gold. Greed, I guess, greed and love had brought me here.

Brought me here to die.

Charlie Pitts came back, shaking his head. "Capt'n," he told Cole, who busied himself thumbing shells into his Smith & Wesson, "they got us entirely surrounded. Best surrender. Ain't no way out."

My brother didn't look up. "Charlie," he said, "this is where Cole Younger dies."

I'll never forget the look on Cole's face, the tears that welled in his eyes, when Charlie said: "All right, Capt'n. I can die as game as you can. Let's get it done." Ducking, Charlie Pitts headed to some tree and brush, thumbed back his hammer, and waited.

Jim came to us, picked up a revolver I'd just finished loading, and shook his head. "A bunch of them are coming right for us, Cole," he said. "Ten, fifteen feet apart, I'm thinking six or seven."

"Brave sons-of-bitches," Cole said.

"Yeah."

Waiting.

I was twenty-one years old. Today, I felt like as though I were sixty-one.

The Yankees drew nearer, making a terrible racket in those woods. Then Charlie Pitts jumped up and fired at a mustached man wearing a badge. Charlie had always been a mighty fine shot, but he missed — don't ask me how; maybe it was just how bad our luck kept turning — and the man with the badge dropped to a knee, brought his rifle up, and pulled the trigger.

Charlie Pitts died game. Things happened slowly, it seemed, Charlie staggering back with a bullet plumb center in his chest, then the rest of the posse opened up, and more bullets slammed into that brave comrade, driving him against a tree and, finally, to the wet ground.

Cole charged forward, leaving me and Jim, firing his Smith & Wesson, until reaching Charlie. He swore savagely, tossed his empty pistol aside, and pried Charlie's Colt from his dead fingers, drew the Smith & Wesson from Charlie's holster. A bullet clipped the Colt as Cole brought it up in his right hand, tearing off the extractor, but Cole acted like nothing had happened. The Colt roared back. Then he was standing and ducking, snapping shots, as bullets flew all around us.

My big brother is quiet by nature, but in a battle he is consumed with rage, like he's a totally different person. I reckon he learned that riding with the boys during the war. I reckon the war made him that way.

"Make for the horses, boys!" Cole called out, emptying Charlie's Colt, dropping it while tossing the Smith & Wesson to his right hand. "Ain't no use stopping to pick up a comrade here, for we can't get him through the line. Just charge 'em. Make it if we can!"

We were about to charge, and I was ready to follow Cole. I'd be like Charlie Pitts. I could die as game as my brother.

From the Yankee line back in the woods, I heard one of the laws shout in his Irish brogue: "Stand firm, laddies! Stand firm!"

They stood firm, and cut loose with a cannonade of rifle fire.

Cole, who I always considered invincible, fell to his knees, blood pouring from his nose and mouth.

"Cole!" I cried out. "Cole! Cole! Cole!"

All during this time I had been reloading Jim's pistol, but now I stood, watching as Jim raced by me, firing his Colts, screaming a Rebel yell. One of the Yankees doubled over, and I thought he would fall, killed, but he straightened, raised his rifle. His face disappeared in the gunsmoke.

"Come on, Bob!" Jim yelled to me.

An instant later, a bullet slammed into Jim's mouth, blowing out teeth and jaw bone and blood, spraying a tree trunk with blood. He fell hard, and did not stir.

I leaped forward, trying to reach him, but bullets drove me back, clipping branches off the trees, and I fell down, exhausted, pain shooting all up and down my right arm. I looked for a pistol, a rock to throw, anything, and hugged the ground tightly, looking up.

Jim I couldn't see from my position, and I figured he had to be dead, figured they were both crossing over the River Jordan, but Cole had pulled himself up.

"Come on, you Yankee bastards. I'll kill ever' one of you yellow sons-of-bitches. Come on!"

Buckshot slammed into his back, but Cole laughed, turning, firing toward the shotgun blast. "Is that the best you can do?"

"Cole!" I cried out over the deafening roar of musketry. "Cole!"

He didn't hear me. I don't think he heard anything in those final moments. I don't even think he knew he was in Minnesota. "Muster 'em out, Arch! Make 'em pay for my daddy! . . . Come on, Buck, it's time to light a shuck. . . . Hell's fire, it's Charlie Hart, look at that brave man ride!"

Another bullet drove him backward, but he still stood, lifted another revolver, squeezed the trigger.

"Birds belong caged, don't you know that? So let's step inside the vault, fellows."

He fired again. My ears rang. I think he took another hit, but, stubborn as all us Youngers, he just wouldn't fall. Wouldn't quit. Wouldn't die.

"Ride out! Save yourselves!"

The hammer struck an empty chamber, but Cole didn't notice. He thumbed it back, pulled the trigger. Another click.

"Ride out, damn you. You ain't leaving nobody!"

Tears blinded me.

"For God's sake, boys, hurry up! They're shooting us all to pieces!"

I wiped my eyes, cleared my vision, tried to pull myself up as the bullet slammed into Cole's head, and he sank into the brush and lay still, silent.

Down I fell, crying softly, unable to do anything, hating myself, trying to shake the image of seeing my brave brothers, and a great pard like Charlie Pitts, cut down before my very eyes. A few more shots sang out, and I just tucked myself into a ball and rocked back and forth, back and forth.

My fault. All my fault.

"Hold ye fire!" a voice bellowed. "Hold ye fire!"

Silence. The ringing left my ears, and sounds from the thicket drifted to me, of the bubbling water, of the wind rustling through the trees, but no birds singing. Not any more.

"Is anyone still alive? Speak up. Speak up and surrender!"

I made myself stop bawling. Hell, I was a man, a Younger, and no Yankee bastard was going to see me cry. I pulled a dirty handkerchief from my pocket, lifted myself to my feet, and walked toward the posse, waving the handkerchief over my head in my left arm.

"I surrender," I said. "They're all down but me."

The man with the badge stepped forward, a taller man with a thick mustache and beard (but no side whiskers) beside him wearing boots tucked inside his striped britches, and a battered bowler hat. He didn't look much like a fighter with his triangular face and the biggest dad-blasted ears I'd ever seen, and he had no badge pinned on his vest, but I figured him to be the man in charge.

"Put both of your hands up," he told me.

"I can't. The right one's broken."

"Then come on toward us, but walk slowly, and keep your left hand raised."

"It's over, Cap," the Irishman with the badge told Mr. Big Ears.

I kept walking. That's what I was doing when somebody on the bluff behind them shot me in the chest.

At first I didn't know what to think, couldn't even believe they'd shoot me while I was giving up, holding a flag of truce. Yet when my left hand dropped the handkerchief and reached over to my side, it felt sticky with blood, my knees buckled, a wave of dizziness consumed me, and slowly I sank to the ground, thinking: You lying Yankee sons-of-bitches.

CHAPTER TWENTY-ONE:

WILLIAM WALLACE MURPHY

"If any of you jackasses fire again, I'll shoot you myself!" I yelled, and, ripping off my bowler and turning in disgust, I screamed at the men behind me, the cowardly bastards who lacked courage to walk into this thicket with me and these six others. Yet one of them had shot down a young man while he was trying to surrender.

"Who fired that shot? Damn it, I said who fired?"

"I did, Captain Murphy." I could just hear him from the bluff. He waved his straw hat like a fool. "Me. Willis Bundy. I didn't know. . . ."

"Put your rifle down, Bundy! I might have you hanged. . . ."

"He's alive, Cap," James Glispin said, and I swallowed down the bile, and approached the bandit Bundy had shot down. Shock masked his face, drained of all color, and he just sat there, holding the side of his chest where Bundy's round had hit him. Well, even outlaws have their angels, for the wound did not appear mortal.

"I was surrendering," he said, his voice a stunned whisper. "Somebody shot me while I was surrendering."

I nodded, but had no remorse for this boy, no matter what threats I had hurled at Willis Bundy. He had been shot while surrendering. So be it. What of those two dead men, unarmed men, buried now in Northfield?

I have no tolerance for lawbreakers, whether they are damned secessionists in Virginia or claim-jumpers in California. I have fought them all.

In Westmoreland County, Pennsylvania I was born, of sound Scot and Dutch stock, but took off for the California gold fields after turning sixteen. Nigh seven years I spent there, and, while I never made it rich, well not as rich as some, I did learn some important lessons. Such as how do deal with vermin. You exterminate them.

By the spring of '61, I had returned to Pennsylvania, making my home now in Pittsburgh, and, when the call came for volunteers to save the Union, I raised a company for the 14th Pennsylvania and entered the war.

I had the honor of serving under General Phil Sheridan, the honor of receiving wounds from Rebel sabers and muskets, at Lexington and Piedmont, and the dishonor of spending three and a half months in the miserable confines of Libby Prison after being captured at Mimms Flat. I despised being out of the fight, but that brief period in that horrible dungeon taught me another important lesson about vermin. Fellow officers wouldn't let me exterminate the traitors amongst us, but we could brand those callous fiends, and that we did, carving a T on their turncoat foreheads.

Freed from prison after the surrender of General Lee — they should have hanged him, too, and Jefferson Davis and all those mutineers, seditionists — I had hoped to continue the fight in Texas, where Company D was ordered, but, alas, the Rebs there surrendered while we marched to Fort Leavenworth in Kansas. Deprived of further glory, one good thing came out of the march. In Kansas I met my lovely bride, Inez, married her, and moved here to Madelia after being mustered out of the service of my country.

Since then, my fights had been confined to the state legislature, to which I had been elected in '71, but when I by chance found

Sheriff Glispin in need of volunteers to track down and capture the Northfield plunderers, I was more than ready.

It is little wonder that I took command when we had our prey snared. The only thing that surprised me was the fact that only six, and not all, of my troops had the courage to march against brigands with me, and that one had the audacity to shoot a man while he showed the flag of truce.

So be it.

"I think you'll live," I told the boy, then took in the scene of battle. Three bodies lay spread in the thick brush, their bodies riddled with bullets, and relief washed over my face at the sight of the six members of my volunteers standing before me.

"Is anyone injured?" I inquired.

Colonel Vought let out a nervous little laugh, reached into his vest pocket, and withdrew a chunk of his large rosewood pipe, now shattered by a ball. "I found the piece of lead in my cartridge belt," he said, shaking his head.

"God looks after you," I told him.

Vought said nothing, looking away as if ashamed. 'Twas a good thing he had not been smoking the pipe, else the bullet might have killed him.

284

"You ought to have a watch fob made out of that," Ben Rice said, "for luck."

The colonel's head bobbed fretfully. He shuffled his feet.

"You're bleeding," I told George Bradford, who clutched his wrist.

"Scratch is all, Cap," Bradford told me. "Ruint my aim, though. I'll be fine."

Yes, I thought, God has looked after us all.

"Come in!" I shouted to the rest of the posse. By now the slough was surrounded by scores upon scores of men who had taken up arms to rid this county of vermin, or men who'd come along as damnable tourists, hoping to pick up souvenirs and touch the bodies of the dead. "It's all over!" I cared not a whit to be in the company of cowards, but I needed pallbearers for the slain and Doc Overholt to tend to Bradford's scratch and the living border man's mangled arm and other wounds.

"Come in! The bandits are all dead, except one, and he has surrendered and is wounded!"

As soon as I had spoken those words, one of the outlaws I thought dead climbed to his feet, and I swear Big Jim Severson leaped as if he had stepped on a nest of rattlers or seen a ghost.

"Cole!" the young outlaw beside me said, and rushed toward the man I now knew must be the nefarious Cole Younger of Missouri. The reports had not been in err. The James and Younger brothers had been the bushwhackers behind the Northfield raid.

"Come on, you Yankee sons-of-bitches," the gravely wounded Cole Younger said, his voice slurred but his spirit strong. He spit out blood, mouth frothing like a hydrophoby wolf. Blood leaked from his nose and countless other wounds. "I'll fight your two best men at the same time. I can lick all you sons-of-bitches."

Waving a little pocket pistol in his right hand, one I knew was empty, having heard the metallic clicks as he pulled the trigger before we downed this haughty lion, Cole Younger kept on challenging us.

"Cole," the other one said. "It's me, Bob. Come on, Cole. Come on. Come, or we'll all be hanged."

"Let'm hang me. Let'm try!" He coughed, spit out more blood and saliva, and the slim one threw his brother's arm over his chest and helped lead him toward me. "I'd as soon be hung today as tomorrow," Cole Younger said. "Come on. . . ."

They collapsed in a little sinkhole, and

young Bob examined his brother's wounds.

Cole Younger had been hit several times by buckshot and ball, including a slug that had slammed into his head, swelling one eye shut. Yet his brain must have cleared, because he let out a little sigh, and realized the fight had ended, that he, as all outlaws must eventually realize, had lost to the arm of the law, the arm of righteousness.

Answered, I thought with pride, to Cap Murphy's law.

Studying the rimfire pistol as if it were foreign to him, Cole Younger suddenly grinned — how a man like that, in that condition, can grin is foreign to me — and whirled it around, offering it, butt forward, to Sheriff Glispin.

"Sheriff, I had the sure bead on you, but you was too quick for me. You're Irish for sure. It's all right." I think he addressed the last sentence to his brother Bob.

Seconds later, to my surprise, another man rose from the dead, his mouth shot to pieces. He said nothing. I don't think he could say anything in his condition, but he pitched a pair of revolvers at my Ben Rice's feet, and staggered over to his comrades, collapsing beside them, conscious, but dazed, his eyes showing shock.

"Oh, Jim, damn it, Jim," Bob said. "This

is all my fault. I'm sorry, Jim. I'm sorry, Cole."

"It's all right," Cole Younger repeated. "We're all right."

"Boys," I told the bandits, "this is horrible, but you see what lawlessness has brought to you."

I accepted an ivory-handled Smith & Wesson that Jim Severson offered me, my spoil of war, and found my bowler, which I placed on my head, then spied the last remaining outlaw. George Bradford and Charles Pomeroy stood over him.

"This one isn't another Lazarus," Mr. Pomeroy said, and kicked over the dead man.

He was a brutal-looking man, sightless eyes staring at the sky, a bullet through his heart and other buckshot and balls having penetrated his worthless, now lifeless body.

"Take him to the wagon," I said, then thought better of it, remembering my intention. "No, have Willis Bundy and one of those other shirkers do it when they reach us."

With that, I returned to the three surviving bandits, where Colonel Vought had knelt. Cole Younger looked at the Madelia hotel entrepreneur and, smiling, offered a bloody hand. "Hello, landlord," Cole

Younger said, and Vought shook the outlaw's hand, before rising, and removing his hat.

"You know him, Colonel?" I asked.

"I knew him as J.C. King," Vought replied softly. "The dead one over there called himself Ladd, Jack Ladd. They spent a night at my hotel a few days before the robbery. I became suspicious after learning of what had happened in Northfield. Now, I see my suspicions were not unfounded." Next, Colonel Vought pulled out his broken pipe, showing it to Cole Younger, and fingered the bent lead bullet that had lodged in his shell belt.

"The Lord works in mysterious ways, landlord," Cole Younger told him.

"I might desire to speak of this with you later, in private," Vought said, and I had no idea what they were talking about — none of my business — but I suspected that had been an interesting night at the Flanders Hotel.

"Certainly," Cole Younger said, "if we ain't hanged by then."

"That bastard has the right idea," someone said, revealing that the scavengers had joined us. "Let's string up all of them now, Cap. Let's get it done, Sheriff!"

"Yeah. Remember what they done in Northfield!"

"Hang the sons-of-bitches!"

It did not matter to me if we hanged them now, and I had no intention of stopping them, for I am not the sheriff, merely a volunteer citizen, but Sheriff Glispin whirled, and sent a round from his Henry rifle into the air.

"Next one of ye yellow bastards who I even think is considering a lynching, I'll tear ye faces apart with me fists. To Madelia we'll be taking these laddies, and taking them in alive. Now let us get them in the wagon."

I led the way out of Hanska Slough, my six brave comrades helping the badly wounded Younger brothers to the wagon, for Sheriff Glispin had countermanded my order, the one I had never verbally given, except to Rice and Pomeroy. So be it. Perhaps the Irishman was right. The Youngers were brave men and, though outlaws and vermin, deserved better treatment than being man-handled by shirkers and craven cowards. The rest of the sightseers, cowards, and gawkers scoured the earth for trinkets, shell casings and such. It disgusted me, disgusted Sheriff Glispin even more.

I figured we'd load the Youngers in my wagon, but a farmer had a larger one, so we selected it. Bob Younger asked for a chaw of tobacco, something to help him fight the pain, and the Sorbel boy borrowed one off Oke Wisty and took it to the broken-armed bandit. Wiry little fellow had a big mouth, or a bigger pain, I suspect, and he took about half of the ten-cent plug in one bite. When he offered it back to the Sorbel boy, the kid told him to keep it, and walked away.

As I returned to my buggy, something moved underneath the blankets in the back, and, to my horror, Ralph, my seven-year-old boy, poked his head out. Dropping my rifle in the mud, I raced to him, pulled him out of the wagon, demanding to know what he thought he was doing and why he wasn't at the Flanders Hotel back in town.

During all the commotion after hearing the Sorbel kid's sighting of the bandits, I had not laid eyes on Ralph. All that time, he had been hiding behind me. I had put him in harm's way, without my knowledge. His mother would tan both of our hides when he returned home.

"I wanted to watch, Papa," Ralph said, and I pulled him close to my chest, and felt myself trembling all over.

I don't think I stopped shaking till we reached the outskirts of town.

The Youngers were wretched creatures. Doc

Overholt counted five wounds in Jim Younger, the gravest being the wound through his mouth that had knocked out half his teeth and bled furiously. Their ruined boots were wrapped with foul linen, and, when Overholt unwrapped the layers over Cole Younger's feet, the bandit's toenails fell off.

Word spread like fire that we had captured the bandits, and farmers, friends, and townsmen came out to greet us as we rode to Madelia. Ladies gave handkerchiefs to the outlaws to cover their grisly wounds, and, as we rode into Madelia, a great cheer erupted from the lines of people, citizens and soldiers.

Despite eleven wounds, Cole Younger, ever the showman, pushed himself to his feet and tipped his hat to the crowd, then sank back down.

"What nerve," Charles Pomeroy's brother said in admiration. "That fellow can take it on the chin and still smile."

Nerve. Indeed. But how misplaced.

Not everyone agreed with Pomeroy. Once we stopped at Colonel Vought's hotel on Buck Street, and began escorting the wounded desperadoes inside, a Mankato banker — his name escapes me — rushed to Cole Younger, grabbed the man's bloody shirtfront, and spat out: "You and all these others are a despicable gang and a disgrace to our country!"

"Who the hell are you?" Cole Younger asked. Upon hearing the banker's answer, the outlaw grinned. "You know the difference between us?" he asked, but, before the angry townsman could reply, Younger added: "You rob the poor, and I rob the rich."

With that, Rice and Vought led the outlaw into the hotel.

We put them on the second floor, keeping many guards at the doors and windows, allowing our physicians to tend their wounds, while ladies after ladies brought the bad men clean clothes and blankets and food and milk, even brandy. Even Guri Sorbel, mother of the Sorbel kid who had alerted us, sent flowers to the killers. Other gawkers came to get a gander at the Younger brothers. Colonel Vought should have charged admission. I remember hearing that that photographer in Northfield who had taken photos of the two dead outlaws there was selling his photos at $2 a dozen. It wouldn't be long, I figured, till another photographer came to Madelia.

Ink-slingers had arrived, too, and, although I desired to go home as quickly as I could, Sheriff Glispin asked me if I would attend his interrogation of Cole Younger.

Dr. Cooley said he had removed buckshot from Cole Younger's left shoulder, arm, and armpit. One bullet had lodged in his jaw, although he had faired much better than his brother Jim, whose mouth wound had rendered his speech to little more than mumbles and groans. An older wound, one likely received at Northfield, had lodged in Cole Younger's left hip, and other bullets and shot had torn into his body.

"I've never seen a man with such a constitution," Cooley told us. "I'm not even sure a hangman's noose will kill him."

"We shall see, Doctor," I replied, and took a seat beside Cole Younger's bed. Sheriff Glispin remained standing.

"Special trains will be running, Mister Younger, on the Saint Paul and Sioux City Railroad, bringing all types of visitors, newspaper editors, and lawmen."

"I'm right popular," Younger said.

"When the doctors say ye can travel, sir, ye, too, shall find yeself on a train. And ye brothers."

"To Missouri, I hope."

"Nay. Faribault. Rice County seat. There ye shall face charges. It might go easy on ye, lad, if ye were to tell us of your comrades. The man killed at Hanska Slough, for starters?"

"Charlie Pitts. Other two men we lost at Northfield was called Chadwell and Miller. That's all there was."

"No, Mister Younger. Reports say eight or nine men took part in the raid. What happened to the others? They abandoned ye, left ye for dead."

Younger said nothing.

"They were the James brothers, we know. Jesse and Frank. Maybe another man. Come, now, lad, be a good man and ease ye conscience."

"I know Frank and Jesse. Frank has been a friend of mine, but Jesse and I ain't been on speaking terms for a spell now. And despite all you read in the papers, I never robbed no banks or trains with Frank and Jesse, and I'm right sure Frank and Jesse never robbed no trains, neither. We just get blamed for every crime across the country."

"Aye. No man ever hanged or imprisoned has ever been guilty."

"My brothers and me never robbed nothing, never tried to rob nothing, but the law kept hunting us so we decided, if we're gonna be branded outlaws, we might as well take up the profession. Northfield was our first go at it."

"A mighty poor performance," I said.

"Yeah. Well, that's the truth. We wanted Silver Spoons Butler's money, wanted to hurt Governor Ames. We joined up with two drifters. Not the James brothers."

" 'Twas the Jameses!" Sheriff Glispin yelled, slapping his black hat across his legs. "Admit it!"

"Don't believe all them blood and thunder stories you read, Sheriff. It was a fellow named of Wood and another man called Howard. Them was the two with us in Northfield."

The sheriff sighed. "And where might we find Mister Wood and Mister Howard? Where be ye pals?"

"Hell if I know, Sheriff."

Other than the identity of the three slain desperadoes, that might have been the only truthful statement Cole Younger made in my and Sheriff Glispin's presence.

CHAPTER
TWENTY-TWO:

DR. SIDNEY MOSHER

Your perspective changes when staring down the barrel of a Schofield revolver held by a man with murderous blue eyes.

Moments earlier, I had been dreading the task before me: a twenty-mile ride, one way, on a small bay mare I had rented from Mr. Broadbent to perform a goiter operation on Robert Mann's wife. The ride would leave my backside and thighs chaffed for a week, longer if I winded up getting lost on my way to the small Iowa settlement of Kingsley. Not only did I loathe removing goiters, which I had done several times since entering practice in Sioux City, but the Manns were opprobrious welshers and I would have to put up with the incessant chattering of their entire brood.

Now, I merely longed to live to see Mrs. Mann's goiter.

"Hands up!" the man instructed me, and fleetly I complied.

Moments earlier, I had espied the two men, riding sagging gray horses, and called out to the men's broad backs, asking if I were traveling the right way to reach Kingsley. They rode on ahead, as if they hadn't heard, so I urged the bay forward and hurriedly intercepted them. That is when they reined their horses around and the smallest one planted the Schofield barrel, unwavering, inches from my forehead.

"Well?" the gunman demanded.

Well . . . what? Oh, he wants to know my intentions. I wish I knew his.

"My name is Sidney Mosher," I said, attempting to effect a casual tone. "I am a physician residing in Sioux City on my way to see a patient in Kingsley. It is an emergency." A stretch, perhaps, but not for Bob Mann, hoping to hush the complaints of that ill-mannered witch he had wed.

"You are a damned liar," the man said. "You are one of those damned detectives from Saint Paul, chasing the robbers."

The robbers. Of course.

Of those bandits I knew. Why, just that morning outside Mr. Broadbent's, I had readily joined in on the gossip about the pursuit of those killers who had robbed the bank in Northfield, Minnesota earlier that month. *The Democrat* had reported the capture of three of the bad men near Madelia, but at least two were still eluding the law, and rumors had them having crossed the border into Dakota Territory. Maybe they'll come to Iowa on their return to those hide-outs in Missouri, we had said in jest, dreaming of how we would splurge on Minnesota Governor John Pillsbury's reward should those last bandits wander into our hands.

Well, here they are, Sid, how do you plan on spending that gold?

"I am no detective, gentlemen. Nor am I either robber or hunter of robbers. I am Sidney Mosher, doctor, from Sioux City."

"I think I shall kill this damned detective now," the killer said, and I caught my breath, trying to remain cool while fearing for my life.

"Listen, if you don't believe me," I said, my throat suddenly dry, my voice strained, "ride back to the farm a quarter of a mile toward town, ask that owner to describe Doctor Sidney Mosher. The farmer's name is Witherspoon, and I set his youngest son's broken leg last spring. Ask him. To a T he'll describe me."

"Maybe I'll do just that," the gunman said, but he didn't move, just stared, never lowering the Schofield one inch.

"Step down off that hoss, Doc," the taller, bearded man ordered, and we both dismounted, both stiffly. His filthy, rough hands turned my pockets inside and out, which I found bothersome as I had just spent $15 on this suit.

"I am unarmed," I informed them. "And carry less than five dollars in cash."

"Then what's this, Doc?" the taller man asked.

"A lancet," I answered at the surgical instrument he dangled under my nose. Don't tell me you fear that as a Bowie knife, as Mrs. Mann would certainly see it!

He pitched the lancet aside, thought better of it, and stepped back, bent over with a groan, and retrieved it. His mud-stained, ripped trousers leg had been wrapped tightly with strips from his shredded duster, and I surmised that a bullet wound troubled him. He resumed his search, finding my coin purse and medicine case in my inside coat pocket.

"Where's your bag, Doc?"

"I beg your pardon."

"Bag. Back home, doctors on an emergency call always brought along their black bag. Where is it . . . if you're a doctor?"

I nodded at the lancet and small case, which caused both men to break out in wild cackles, the likes of which I had never heard, except from coyotes. The shorter one spit out tobacco juice and, to my gratitude, holstered his revolver. He carried, I noticed, more than the Schofield belted around his waist, although one holster was empty.

"Just what kind of operation are you rushing off to perform, Doc?" the tall man asked, devilment in his blue eyes.

They laughed again. Well, I have been told in the past I am the worst poker player ever born.

"It's . . . a goiter."

Now, they howled, and spoke in unison, as if Thespians treading the boards: " 'Physician, heal thyself.' "

When the laughter had subsided, the shorter man dismounted, handing me his reins. "Cutting off a struma can wait, Doc. You'll join us for a spell, but take my horse. I like the looks of yours."

Certainly, for Mr. Broadbent's bay could catch this wheezing gray steed should I attempt an escape.

After they helped me back in the saddle, the tall man spoke. "We've be wont of company, Doc. So you'll ride along with us a ways, provide us with stimulating conversation. Don't worry, we sha'n't kill you . . . unless you make us."

Conversation. No, they just need a hostage. At least, I hope it's a hostage. If they seek a guide, then they are fools and we'll all be lost before sundown.

"Nice horse, Doc," the shorter one said when we had all mounted.

"Try not to jump any cañons," the other one said.

"You don't believe I did that, do you, Frank?"

"You said you done it, and you wound up on my side of the river somehow."

"You should have seen it." He laughed. "Hell, I wish I had seen it."

"Pretty soon, it'll be clear as a tintype, and that cañon in Dakota will be fifty feet wide 'stead of five."

"Fifteen. And these mounts got us to Iowa."

"Iowa ain't exactly Eden."

The banter ceased abruptly and we picked up the pace for a few miles in a bone-jarring trot.

"You know who we are?" the taller man said as the gray pounded my backbone and rattled my intestines.

Well, the killer called you, Frank, so I assume you are Frank James, and the other man your notorious brother. I am not a fool, sir. Everyone in America knows your names, and everyone in Dakota and Minnesota, and now Iowa, has been talking of you since September 7th.

"We haven't had formal introductions," I replied.

"True. My name is Woodson. This is Mister Huddleson. We live in Baltimore."

Liars. Poor ones, too. "What brings you to Iowa?"

"Heading up to the gold fields in the Black Hills."

You're traveling the wrong way.

"I see."

"I'm sure you do, Doc. No, we have no interest in joining Wild Bill in that bone yard. We just desire to see home. You can tell your grandchildren you rode with the outlaws that pulled the daring bank robbery in Northfield. What all did you hear about Northfield?"

I informed them of the stories I had picked up from the newspapers, including the capture of three assassins in arms a few days prior. That caused them to rein in their mounts, and I cursed my stupidity.

They'll kill you, Sid!

"Captured!" the man I presumed to be Jesse James roared. "The hell you say, Doc!"

"Alive?" the tall man inquired urgently.

Be honest. "Three were shot gravely, a

fourth killed. The last I heard is that the survivors were Cole Younger and his brethren."

"God have mercy on their souls," the shorter one said. "God spare them. I thought the laws might follow us, lead them away from Bob and. . . ." His head shook. "Well, at least they're alive."

"Yeah," Frank said in disgust. "Facing a rope."

I welcomed the silence, but it didn't last long for Mr. Huddleson — or should I say, Jesse James — started up another conversation, his mood surprisingly light.

"I rode with Bloody Bill in the war, Doc. Who did you ride with, or were you too yellow to serve?"

"I was a surgeon with the Army of the Cumberland."

"Reckon we never met up in battle, then. You hear tell of Bloody Bill?"

"I heard." I heard he was a monster, one of the biggest fiends America has ever fathered. I am glad they killed this murderer, glad they decapitated him.

I said nothing to offend Jesse — thought it, yes, but spoke not one inflammatory word — yet the killer reined in the bay, and snapped at me: "Damn you, Doc. I'll kill you yet."

"Temper, temper, temper," my mother used to scold. A violent, uncontrolled temper. Perhaps I should just remain silent.

"There's a code amongst bushwhackers, Doc," said the tall man, Frank James, alias Mr. Woodson. "Fight to the death. Fight for family and friend. You keep silent, even on the gallows, and you die game. You demand respect, and kill if your honor is slighted. Can you savvy all that?"

Your ethics are queer. "I suppose," I lied.

"Take no quarter," Frank James continued, "for you shall receive none. 'Nothing emboldens sin so much as mercy.'"

"Timon of Athens," I said, and quoted my own bit of Shakespeare:

The quality of mercy is not strain'd.
It droppeth as the gentle rain from heaven
Upon the place beneath: it is twice bless'd;
It blesseth him that gives and him that
    takes.

"The Merchant of Venice." Frank James smiled warmly. "I'm glad we didn't blow your head off, Doc."

"Yet," interjected Jesse, still sour.

A mile down the road, as Jesse stood in his stirrups to look at a puff of dust (from a dust devil, it turned out), his left stirrup strap broke, and he swore heavily.

"Damn, Doc, this is the worst dodd-dingus saddle I ever sat."

Fear not, Mister James. I shall take the matter up personally with Mister Broadbent upon my return to Sioux City.

Like a great Thespian, like Barnett or Booth, he turned his mood around as he rode to the next farm, switching our horses, putting me on the bay, leaving his brother in the road to watch for lawmen or errant travelers. The farmer exited his soddie as we eased our mounts toward his watering trough. Jesse did all the talking. Thinking of the armory this assassin carried about his waist, I prayed the farmer would not suspect anything.

"I'm on my way with Doctor Mosher to the Mann farm, and his stirrup strap busted on him," the outlaw lied. "It's an emergency, mister, and we need to borrow a saddle off you. So the doc can save poor Missus Mann's life."

The farmer studied me, then Jesse, and I held my breath. "There's a Morgan in my barn," he said. "Fetch it yourself and don't forget to bring it back."

Our next stop, around 6 o'clock for supper, proved a tad more hospitable, as we ate cornbread and soup before departing, paying 40¢ for the meal, making our way three more miles before reining in to bed down, I hoped, for the night.

"Doc," Frank James said wearily, "I must ask if you'd be kind enough to help me down off this horse."

I'm no horseman, sir. My legs are stiff as a fence post.

"Sure," I said, and coaxed the tall man out of his saddle, let him lean against me as we walked a few rods away and sat on the ground. Without a word, Frank James returned the lancet and medicine case, and I understood.

"Remove your pants, sir," I instructed him.

The bullet had carved a wicked gash a few inches above the knee joint, and how it had eluded infection might be an entry for the medical journals. As I examined the gash more closely, I found it amazing that this man had not bled to death. The wound, I was informed, had been received during the robbery. More than two weeks had passed, and I estimated the distance must be 250 miles, if not more, from Northfield to Sioux City — and they had fled west first, to Dakota Territory, and southeast, traveling hard, on horseback and ankle express, through the elements, fighting their way out of one scrap after another, covering much, much more than 250 miles.

What day is it? September 25th. Great Scott! And . . . what is this dark substance, remnants on the side of the wound and in the scabs?

I eyed Frank James with a mixture of curiosity and amazement.

"Gunpowder," he said. "Emptied it from the casings. Pounded it with the butt of my Remington, till it was fine as I could get it, then poured it over the gash, wrapped it with whatever I had handy. You learn to use what you have on hand, Doc, and, during the war, we figured how gunpowder can be a pretty good. . . ." He could not find the word.

"Styptic," I said.

"Well, I'm still kicking." Again he revealed an infectious smile. "Just not kicking so high lately."

You learn to use what you have on hand. How true. During the war, I stitched saber wounds with anything from thread and horsehair to fishing line and fiddle strings.

I cleaned Frank James's ugly gash as best I could, using the bandage I had intended for Mrs. Mann's neck on his thigh and offering him a tincture of opium to relieve the pain. Upon completion, I told him he could put his pants back on, only to find myself staring into his revolver.

"I reckon not, Doc. Mister Huddleson borrowed your horse. Now I'm going to swap my clothes for yours."

They won't fit, you fool. You have five inches on me.

The hammer of the .44 *clicked.*

I undressed.

Frank James's rags looked horrible on me, especially with the sleeves and pant legs rolled up, but the outlaw looked even more ridiculous in my ill-fitting $15 suit. The moon was rising by then, and a horse snorted behind me. To my surprise, during my examination of Frank James, his brother had sneaked off to a nearby farm and returned with a blue roan mare. The two grays were gone, but my bay — or should I say, Mr. Broadbent's, saddled still with the farmer's Morgan — stood ready at Jesse's side.

The Schofield had returned to Jesse's right hand, but first he pointed at a light perhaps a half mile away.

"See that farm, Doc?" he asked.

"Yes."

Now the .45 aimed at my head, again.

"You reckon you can run all that way and not turn around? Because I'll kill you if you turn around."

"So long, Doc," Frank James told me. "Your shoes don't fit worth a damn."

I did not wait to formulate a reply. I ran — Frank's worn, ruined boots, three sizes too large for my small feet, flapping in the night. At any instant, I expected to feel bullets tear into my back, and, as I stumbled, staggered, and loped in an awkward gait, the events of my kidnapping pulled taut my nerves. My legs buckled from the strain, fear enveloped me, and the light from the farmhouse did not appear to be drawing closer.

They'll kill me. They'll kill me. They'll kill me, shoot me in the back.

They didn't, though. Fancy that. I would survive the ordeal and remove Mrs. Mann's goiter in the afternoon, but not before sending a posse after my kidnappers. Jesse and Frank James would survive to reach Missouri, though, where they would rob and murder again.

But that was in the future. This was tonight.

I ran northeast. The James brothers galloped south.

CHAPTER
TWENTY-THREE:

SHERIFF ARA BARTON

The November morning brought a hint of snow, gray clouds blocking out the sun, and a crisp wind tried to cool the packed Rice County Courthouse room in Faribault. As my deputy escorted the defendants inside through the side door, their chains rattling, every man's head craned to get a glimpse at the three Younger brothers, and I read disappointment in almost every spectator's face.

Cole, Bob, and Jim Younger were freshly shaven, clean, wearing new clothes donated by various Faribault ladies. These men didn't look like killers, didn't resemble the ragged, wretched souls who had disembarked the train back on September 23rd. Cole was practically bald, and the only evidence of any grave wounds that could be detected were the small bandages plastered to Jim Younger's face. While my deputy removed their manacles, I stepped forward, took Mrs. Twyman, an aunt of the killers, by the arm and escorted her to the defense table. Retta Younger, sister of the brothers, walked behind us. I let them sit within the bar beside attorneys Batchelder, Buckham, and Rutledge.

The courtroom didn't stay cool, not as more and more people crammed inside, hugging the back walls. Mrs. Twyman began fanning herself with Jim Younger's hat, and, when the clock chimed ten, I stepped to the judge's bench and called court to order, the Honorable Judge Samuel Lord presiding.

"Thomas Coleman Younger," Judge Lord said in his stern baritone, "step forward." The big man looked nervous, placing his hands behind his back as he limped to the judge's bench, then dropping them at his side. He couldn't even look the judge in the eye. "You are charged with the crimes of accessory to the murder in the first degree of Joseph Lee Heywood on the Seventh of September in the year of our Lord Eighteen Hundred and Seventy-Six in the city of Northfield, state of Minnesota; with felonious assault with intent to kill one Alonzo Bunker on the Seventh of September in the year of our Lord Eighteen Hundred and Seventy-Six in the city of Northfield, state of Minnesota; with the armed robbery of the First National Bank on the Seventh of September in the year of our Lord Eighteen Hundred and Seventy-Six in the city of Northfield, state of Minnesota, and with the murder in the first degree of Nicolaus Gustavson on the Seventh of September in the year of our Lord Eighteen Hundred and Seventy-Six in the city of Northfield, state of Minnesota. How do you plead?"

My right hand slid into my coat pocket, and I fingered the note Cole Younger had written me the night before. I had visited him in his cell, told him it would go easier on him if he revealed the men who had gotten away, the men everyone knew to be the James brothers but could not prove. Younger wrote a note and handed it to me in silence. I knew what the note said. I knew how Younger would plead. I knew the sentence the judge would hand down, but still I found myself, like the rest of them in the courtroom that morning, holding my breath.

The prisoners hadn't been in my custody long before Adelbert Ames paid them a visit. Ames had charged Cole Younger with the murder of the Swede, Nicolaus Gustavson, during the robbery.

"How many men did you kill, Governor,"

Younger said at first, "down in Mississippi, you carpetbagging son-of-a-bitch?"

"I shot down no one, damn you. You killed the Swede. Murdered him!"

"That's a damn' lie!" the big man roared. "If anyone killed him, it was you, you and them city folks firing shots every which way. We kept shooting in the air, trying to keep innocent people from getting shot. It was you who killed that Swede."

"Liar! Liar and murderer!"

I had to pull Ames out of the cell, led him down the corridor. Tensions ran high back then, but now it was mid-November, and the trial had finally begun.

"Guilty." Cole Younger spoke so softly I heard a newspaper reporter on the first row ask a fellow journalist: "What did he say?"

"So be it," Judge Lord said, and called Jim Younger forward after ordering Cole back to his seat.

The charges were mostly the same, the exception being that Jim and Bob would only be charged with accessory to murder of the Swede. Relief swept over the faces of many in the crowd, but others looked disappointed, wanting to carry the fight on forever. At last, Cole Younger looked at ease, too. Jim tried to act a little more cocksure, but I've yet to see a man who could look a judge in the eye without his voice quaking. Jim did the best he could — his speech badly impaired from the bullet wound taken at Hanska Slough — and the judge instructed him to be seated after writing down the guilty plea. Bob Younger would plead guilty, as well.

Cole Younger would talk to anyone at first, although we both restricted visitors after Mr. Ames's visit, but Jim stayed in his room, his mood dangerously low. He wouldn't even speak to his sister and aunt when they visited, just laid on his cot and stared at the ceiling, crying sometimes, consumed by gloom.

Bob, the youngest, had been the most popular with the ladies. I had boxes and bouquets piled on my desk, sent by young women too shy to ask to visit the outlaw himself. So many presents came, I had to parcel them out, even tried to give some to Jim Younger, but he had remained morose, till that morning in the courtroom when he put on an act.

"The charges having been read, and the defendants having entered pleas of guilt to all charges, it is my duty to pass sentence on you," Judge Lord said.

My fingers still touched the note.

"Have you anything to say on your behalf?"

Retta Younger sobbed, dabbing her eyes with a handkerchief.

Some people in Rice County thought the Youngers should have been charged with another crime.

Back in October, Deputy Frank Glaser was guarding the outside of the jail, when another deputy, Henry Kapanick, started walking toward him on the night of the 2nd. You have to understand how things were then. Rumors kept spreading that the James brothers, or other bushwhackers, would sack Faribault the way they had almost wiped out Lawrence during the war. Maybe I should have asked for help from the Army instead of pinning badges on inexperienced civilians and giving them rifles and pistols.

Late that night Kapanick walked toward a fairly frightened Glaser. Turns out that Kapanick's pals had bet him $5 he could get to the jail without a problem. Perhaps we should have put those friends — friends, hell — on trial for what happened.

Glaser said, and I have no reason to doubt him, shaken up as he was after that incident,

317

he spotted the figure and called out to stop.

"Who are you?" Glaser said when the man kept walking.

"Don't you know I'm a policeman?" the man said, still walking.

"Stop!" Glaser cried. "I don't know you!" He brought up his rifle, and, when Kapanick reached inside his breast pocket, Glaser said he feared the man was pulling a revolver or knife. Scared for his life, Glaser pulled the trigger.

The buried Henry Kapanick the following afternoon, and an inquest found that Glaser had acted in self-defense.

I just wondered when this would all end.

As three Younger brothers shook their heads, Bob Younger answered: "No, Your Honor. Nothing to say."

The judge grunted. "It becomes my duty, then, to pass sentence upon you," he said. "I have no words of comfort for you or desire to reproach or deride you. While the law leaves you life, all its pleasures, all its hopes, all its joys are gone out from you, and all that is left is the empty shell."

" 'Leaves you life.' What does that mean?" someone in the gallery whispered. "Ain't they hangin' 'em?"

■ ■ ■ ■

It was the Madelia lawyer, Thomas Rutledge, who had first informed the prisoners of Minnesota law. Plead guilty to first degree murder, and the statutes demand life imprisonment, with the possibility of parole after ten years. Plead not guilty, and upon conviction — and no one doubted a jury would convict the Youngers — the death sentence could be meted out.

"Is that true, Sheriff?" Cole Younger asked me.

"It's the law," I conceded.

"Life or death, huh?"

"That's the game you've been playing all along, Cole."

"Silence in this courtroom!" Judge Lord roared, and the whisperer sank into his seat. "Thomas Coleman Younger, I hereby sentence you to spend the rest of your natural life in the state prison of Minnesota in Stillwater. May God have mercy on your soul."

The courtroom didn't remain silent for long. Bob and Jim Younger were also sentenced to life, and hurriedly we placed the manacles on them while their sister and

319

aunt bawled, chained the prisoners together as the judge pounded his gavel and bellowed for silence, then gave up and adjourned court. We led the Youngers through the side door, hurried them to the jail, and locked them in their cells.

"Thanks, Sheriff!" Cole Younger called out to me as I left the corridor. "Reckon I still thought they'd hang us."

"Perhaps you could have gotten a shorter sentence," I told him, "had you named your. . . ."

He was smiling, shaking his head, and I did not finish. Outside, I withdrew the note he had written.

It's finally over, I thought. Snow had started falling, Thanksgiving was right around the corner, and I always found the first snowfall to be cleansing, purifying, beautiful. A church choir had gathered around the outside of the jail and started singing "Are You Washed in the Blood of the Lamb?"

I unfolded the note.

> Be true to your friends
> if the heavens fall.
>
> Cole Younger

Folding the note again, sliding it into my

coat pocket, I pulled up my collar, and walked home.

Epilogue:

COLE YOUNGER

Seven minutes . . . seemed like seven lifetimes.

Maybe it was, too. Seven lifetimes. Seven
lives.

I think about that now, as this train carries me home, southward, at last back to
Missouri, after twenty-five years in the Stillwater prison and a couple more as a paroled
old fool.

Seven lives. Count 'em.

Joe Heywood, the fellow inside the Northfield bank. I've sworn that Charlie Pitts
killed the cashier, figuring how Charlie
wouldn't mind, being dead and all, and I've
sworn that the James boys was nowhere with
us in Minnesota, that we'd latched on to a
couple of no-accounts named Wood and
Howard, and that they're both dead now,
one killed in an act of violence down in
Arizona and the other claimed by fever. I've
sworn lots of things. Even placed my hand

on the Good Book and said that I had nothing to do with the killing of that Swede.

Hell, I killed the Swede. Don't even know why. Lost my temper, saw my brothers getting shot up. And my best friend, ol' Buck, he laid the banker low, and I'll never know why. Not sure even Buck knows why he done it. But he did. And it's over. Nothing can bring either one of 'em back.

Joe Heywood and the Swede, Gustavson. That's two lives.

Bill Stiles and those loyal boys — Clell Miller, smoking that pipe, and Charlie Pitts, telling me that he could die as game as us Youngers. Three more. That makes five.

Then there's my brothers.

When we pleaded guilty, avoiding the noose, they raised a ruction all over Minnesota. Figured we'd get maybe ten years, if we behaved ourselves, and that we done. But Yankees can be hard-pressed to forget. They never wanted us to set foot out of prison alive. Said they'd see us all dead.

Well, Brother Bob, he was the first to go. Just never did get over that chest wound he took at Hanska Slough. Come down with consumption, a death sentence after all. He was always asking us if we'd forgive him, if Jim and I would accept his apologies for getting us in this fix, that it was all his fault, on account he hadn't listened to us, but we told Bob he wasn't to blame. Jim and me, being older, should have made him listen. Besides, we didn't have to ride north with him. Family, like Jim used to say.

Stillwater ain't no place for a lunger, but Bob lasted longer than most give him. In the summer of '89, the old sawbones at the prison hospital told Bob and the rest of us that he was a goner, said he could go back to his cell or wait it out in the hospital. Bob said he'd just as soon stay in the hospital. We sent off a wire to Sister Retta, and she come up.

For the deathwatch.

In the early evening of September 16th, Bob asked Retta, Jim, and me to come be with him, that his time had come. A deputy warden sat in there with us. Bob . . . hell, I wouldn't have knowed it was him if you hadn't told me, if I hadn't seen him wasting away all them thirteen hard years in prison. His eyes was plumb yellow, nothing left of him much more'n skin and bones.

He heard this bird chirping at the window, and he turned to me and said: "Lift me up, Cole. I want to see the sky once more." For once, he didn't cough his words out, said them clear, if softly, hoarsely.

That caused Retta to start crying, but Bob

told her to hush, that he was going to a better place. He smiled. I hadn't seen him smile in ages.

"You know, Cole," he said, and this time he coughed some, but when he recovered, he went on: "I think when I die, maybe my soul. . . ." Another coughing spell, this one worse than the others. "I . . . think . . . maybe my soul will rest a while. . . ." More coughing. "On that hillside. . . . You . . . see . . . it?"

"I see it," I told him.

"Just a little while," he said. "Then I'll . . . go . . . on . . . to heaven."

He lasted three, four more hours, but didn't say much till he whispered in my ear to tell his girl, Maggie, that he was thinking of her. Finally Brother Bob just closed his eyes and went into that sleep we all must sleep.

He wasn't but thirty-four.

They shipped him back home, to Lee's Summit, and Retta wrote me that there must have been some 800 folks who came over to the Baptist Church that September 20th for Bob's funeral. So Robert Ewing Younger was laid to rest.

I figured that would be the same for Jim and me, but Fate took pity on us poor Southerners. I think Buck, my pard Frank

James, he was behind some of it. I'll get to that directly.

Well, the politicians got together in April of '01 and writ up this bill that said life convicts could be released after serving thirty-five years, lessen time off for good behavior. That was for me and Jim. The Northfield lawmakers didn't want no part of this, but the bill passed.

On July 14, 1901, Jim and me left Stillwater prison after twenty-five years. It was a Sunday morning. As I told the newspaper boys: "I ain't got a grudge against any human being alive or dead. Men, I'm happy." I meant it, too.

'Course, being a parole man means you ain't nothing in the eyes of the law. Can't do nothing. Can't marry. Can't leave the state of Minnesota. I got along fairly well, working these bum jobs, going to the theater, but Jim, he had a tough go of it.

He never could talk good after getting his mouth shot up so bad at Hanska Slough. Man just never could find no level place to be. I'm talking about his emotions. When he got up, he was way up. But when he got down on himself, he was lower than a snake's belly, and, since Northfield, he was mostly low.

Jim fell in love, you see, with this sweet-

326

heart of a newspaper reporter, and it was hard on 'em both. The girl's parents drove her out of the state, hounding her so for trying to love a murdering bushwhacker. Jim tried desperately hard to be with her, but he couldn't marry, on account of his status as a paroled convict, and he couldn't leave the state to be with his honey, couldn't do nothing.

"I'm a ghost," he once told me. "Ghost of Jim Younger, who was a man, not an extra good one, but a man. But now I'm nothing."

He tried for one of those conditional pardons, but the law wouldn't have none of that. Minnesota didn't want us here, but she didn't want us leaving, neither. Well, things got just worser and worser for my brother, and he sent off a telegraph to his honey. *Don't write* was all it said.

Early the next morning, October 19, 1902, Jim sat at his desk in his room and shot himself in the head.

I think Jim was insane, if only temporarily so. Pained me to see his casket loaded up and shipped south, where they buried him beside Brother Bob. Jim wasn't but fifty-four when he died at his own hand. 'Course, he had been dead long before that. Least, that's how he figured things.

They kept that service simple, Retta said. The choir sang "Rest, Weary, Rest" and "We Shall Know Each Other There", then took him to the cemetery, where some 150 people watched him pass.

Jim and Bob. Two more lives. That makes seven.

Seven lives . . . seven lifetimes.

Maybe even more. Y'all have all heard about the treacherous death of Jesse James. Dingus and Buck made it back safe, and I don't hold no anger toward them. They was honorable men. Dingus and me had our differences, and I can't say I liked him, but I respect a brave Southerner, and that he was. And nobody, ain't nobody, even that son-of-a-bitch who shot Brother Bob at Hanska after he had surrendered . . . ain't nobody deserving to die the way Dingus did.

Bob Ford, backed by his yellow brother Charlie, of them no-account Fords, shot him in the back of the head at his home in St. Joseph, Missouri, in 1882. His wife and young 'uns was there when they murdered him. Not that I shed no tears over Dingus's passing. Didn't shed no tears when I learned that Charlie Ford shot himself in '84 or when Bob Ford got blowed apart by a shotgun somewhere in Colorado in '92.

Buck, he surrendered after Dingus got

murdered, but Buck always was the lucky one. Got acquitted in a trial down in Missouri and another one over yonder in Alabama. Minnesota wanted to get him up here for a trial, but there just wasn't no evidence. They'd sure never get me to testify, so Frank James walked out of jail a free man and went home to be with his ma, be with his wife and strapping young son. And I think Buck had a hand in my getting out of prison. He knowed people, became a celebrity what with his trials and all, and folks started working mighty hard on getting me freed, getting me back home.

Maybe Buck figured he owed me something. I don't know. Reckon I'll ask him when I see him again.

I'm growing old. That's why the Board of Pardons awarded me this conditional pardon. Maybe they're just sick of me in Minnesota as I'm sick of being here.

It's February 16, 1903, and I'm heading home at last. Heading home to see my brothers' graves, to see Buck, see Retta and my other sisters, mostly, I hope, to live at peace.

Some folks say I'm a hero, but I'll tell you this, straight and true. I ain't no hero. Ain't no hero of nothing.

Seven minutes . . . seven lifetimes. Seven

lives: Gustavson and Heywood. Clell, Charlie, and Stiles. Bob and Jim. Almost twenty-seven years. I'm a fifty-nine-year-old bald, fat, old man. Age makes a man wiser, they say, and, looking back, I wonder if we ever knowed what we was doing when we rode north.

Hero? Not hardly. Have I been rehabilitated? I reckon so. Has prison taught me anything? Sure, and I don't just mean learning now to make tubs and buckets.

The train rocks its way south, and I wonder if it will take me through Northfield. Doubt it. Hope not.

Long before I ever set foot in prison I knowed one thing: I wish to hell I'd never laid eyes on that town called Northfield.

AUTHOR'S NOTE

Since George Huntington's *Robber and Hero: The Story of the Northfield Bank Raid,* first published in 1895, the James-Younger bloodbath of 1876 has been well-chronicled in the history book department. In addition to Huntington's book, my primary sources include *Jesse James, My Father* by Jesse Edwards James (1899), *The Story of Cole Younger by Himself* (1903), *Jesse James Was His Name* by William A. Settle Jr. (1966), *Youngers' Fatal Blunder: Northfield, Minnesota* by Dallas Cantrell (1973), *The Outlaw Youngers: A Confederate Brotherhood: A Biography* (1992), *Outlaws: The Illustrated History of the James-Younger Gang* (1997), and *Jesse James: The Man and the Myth* (1998), all by Marley Brant, *Frank and Jesse James: The Story Behind the Legend* by Ted P. Yeatman (2000), and *The Last Hurrah of the James-Younger Gang* by Robert

Barr Smith (2001).

Most importantly, I certainly could not have tackled this novel without poring over the works of Minnesota historian John J. Koblas: *The Jesse James Northfield Raid: Confessions of the Ninth Man* (1999), *Faithful Unto Death: The James-Younger Raid on the First National Bank* (2001), *Jesse James Ate Here: An Outlaw Tour and History of Minnesota at the Time of the Northfield Raid* (2001), and *Minnesota Grit: The Men Who Defeated the James-Younger Gang* (2005). I first met Jack Koblas at a Jesse James writers' conference in Liberty, Missouri, and he helped me through certain snags during the writing of *Northfield*.

All major characters in this novel were actual people, although interpretations of actions and character traits are my own inventions. Of course, you can find much debate on who killed Joseph Heywood, who and how many actually took part in the bank robbery (were Bill Stiles and Bill Chadwell two different people, or was Chadwell an alias Stiles used?) and why the outlaws chose Northfield. Likewise, the image of Jesse James leaping his horse across the Palisades in South Dakota may be folklore, and most likely is nothing more than myth, but I sure wouldn't put it past as brash an outlaw as Dingus, or leave it out of a Western novel.

When I visited Northfield and elsewhere in southern Minnesota, I found some tremendous allies in my project. I am deeply thankful to Chip DeMann of the James Gang for the beers, theories, and anecdotes shared at a Millersburg tavern. Likewise, Mark Fagerwick, then executive director of the Northfield Historical Society and Museum Store, offered much insight and other ideas, as well as access to the wonderful museum in the restored Scriver Building that housed the First National Bank in 1876. Kathy Feldbrugge of the Northfield Area Chamber of Commerce and Tara Mueller of the Madelia Area Chamber of Commerce and Visitors Bureau were gracious hosts, as were Wayne Eddy, Kurt Fishtorn, and Bob Abbott. On the Missouri side of the story, the Friends of the James Farm have always been supportive of my projects and provided valuable information and help. Much appreciation to Friends members Scott Cole, Howard Dellinger, Christie Kennard, and Phillip Steele.

Thanks also go to Bruce and Ruth Thorstad of Dresser, Wisconsin, Will Ghormley of Des Moines, Iowa, Jon Chandler of Westminster, Colorado, and the staffs at the Vista Grande Public Library in Santa Fé County, New Mexico, and Missouri Valley Special Collections at the Kansas City Public Library.

Other key sources include *Adelbert Ames: Broken Oaths and Reconstruction in Mississippi, 1835–1933* by Blanche Ames Ames (1964), *The Northfield Bank Raid, Sept. 7, 1876,* published by the Northfield News Inc. in 1933, *Before Their Identity* (1996), compiled by Ruth Rentz Yates, courtesy of the Madelia Chamber of Commerce, the September 14, 1876, edition of the Rice County Journal, and the 1991 University of Minnesota master's thesis by Paul Thomas Hetter, *The Last Raid of the Younger Brothers; or, Missouri, Outlawry and Minnesota, and How Their Histories Influenced the Outcome of the Great Northfield Raid,* courtesy of Missouri Valley Special Collections, Kansas City Public Library.

Among the main characters in this novel, Adelbert Ames lived to age ninety-seven, dying on April 13, 1933, the last full-rank general officer of the Civil War. Ara Barton continued on as sheriff of Rice County until 1885. He died in Morristown, Minnesota, on November 6, 1898.

Alonzo Bunker resigned from the First National Bank in 1878 and took a similar job at the Citizens Bank of Northfield. He later worked at banks in Kansas City, St. Paul, and Helena, Montana. He died in 1929 in Los Angeles. James Glispin wound up serving a fourth and final term as sheriff of Watowan County before leaving Madelia in 1880 for California. Later, he served as a lawman in and around Spokane, Washington, then became a realtor before going blind. He died in 1890.

Lizzie May Heywood left Northfield after her father's death, but returned at age thirteen and enrolled at a college preparatory school. She graduated from Carleton College with a degree in music, furthering her music studies in Indianapolis, and returned to Northfield again in 1897 to marry before moving to Scranton, Pennsylvania. She died in 1947.

Anselm Manning saw his two daughters, one born three years after the Northfield raid, graduate from Carleton College. At age seventy-five, he dropped dead of a heart attack in 1909 while walking through the snow to his barn. Farm hand Thomas Jefferson Dunning apparently continued farming until his death in Nicollet County, Minnesota in 1924. Joe Brown, Mollie Ellsworth, and Sidney Mosher (providing they aren't other bits of fictional folklore) seem to have faded from history after their alleged run-ins with the outlaws.

Two years after the raid, Captain William Murphy, one of the heroes at Hanska Slough, wound up in trouble with the law. After a man named Samuel Ash "exposed his person and made the most disgusting proposals" to two girls, including Murphy's daughter, Murphy went after Ash. He found Ash in the custody of the sheriff, but fatally shot Ash anyway. Murphy maintained his revolver went off accidentally, but was convicted of fourth degree manslaughter and served a one year sentence in the Blue Earth County Jail. He died at his home in 1904 at age sixty-five.

Asle Oscar Sorbel's father was killed in a wagon accident in 1879, and young Oscar moved to Dakota Territory in 1883 — some accounts say he feared reprisals from the James-Younger Gang, while other sources discount this — where he married in 1890. He worked as a veterinarian, dying in 1930 at age seventy-one.

Thomas Lee Vought left Madelia after the capture, living in New York and South Dakota before winding up in LaCrosse, Wisconsin, where he died in 1917. Henry Wheeler finished medical school and returned to Northfield to open a practice in

1877. He furthered his medical studies in New York City, married his childhood sweetheart in 1878, and hung his shingle in Grand Forks, North Dakota, in 1891. He died in 1930 at age seventy-six.

History tells us that the James brothers reformed their gang and continued their criminal careers in Missouri and elsewhere. On Monday, April 3, 1882, gang member Robert Ford shot and killed Jesse James at the outlaw's home in St. Joseph, Missouri, where he was living with his family under the name Howard. A short while later, Frank James negotiated a surrender to authorities and turned himself in at the Missouri governor's office. Acquitted in two trials (in Gallatin, Missouri, and Huntsville, Alabama), Frank James was never brought to trial for the Northfield bank raid. He never answered questions about his career as an outlaw. "If I admitted that these stories were true," he once said, "people would say: 'There's the greatest scoundrel unhung' and if I denied 'em they'd say: 'There's the greatest liar on earth,' so I just say nothing." On February 18, 1915, Frank James died at his home on the family farm, which he took over running after his mother's passing in 1911.

An ailing Cole Younger attended his old

friend's funeral.

Suffering from kidney and heart trouble, Cole Younger retired to Lee's Summit, Missouri, after an unsuccessful Wild West venture with Frank James, a series of lecture tours titled "What Life Has Taught Me", and his 1903 autobiography, *The Story of Cole Younger by Himself.* He joined the Christian Church of Lee's Summit, quietly living out his days. On March 19, 1916, Younger called friend Harry Hoffman and Jesse James's son, Jesse Edwards James, to his deathbed, where he told stories about the old days, and, if the story's true, swore James and Hoffman to secrecy before revealing that Frank James had killed Joe Heywood in Northfield.

Two days later, at 8:45 P.M., Thomas Coleman Younger, the last known surviving member of the gang of outlaws that raided Northfield, died. He was seventy-two.

"There is no heroism in outlawry," Younger wrote in his autobiography, "and the fate of each outlaw in his turn should be an everlasting lesson to the young of the land."

Johnny D. Boggs
Santa Fé, New Mexico

ABOUT THE AUTHOR

Johnny D. Boggs has worked cattle, shot rapids in a canoe, hiked across mountains and deserts, traipsed around ghost towns, and spent hours poring over microfilm in library archives — all in the name of finding a good story. He's also one of the few Western writers to have won two Spur Awards from Western Writers of America (for his novel, *Camp Ford,* in 2006, and his short story, "A Piano at Dead Man's Crossing," in 2002) and the Western Heritage Wrangler Award from the National Cowboy and Western Heritage Museum (for his novel, *Spark on the Prairie: The Trial of the Kiowa Chiefs,* in 2004). A native of South Carolina, Boggs spent almost fifteen years in Texas as a journalist at the *Dallas Times Herald* and *Fort Worth Star-Telegram* before moving to New Mexico in 1998 to concentrate full time on his novels. Author of twenty-seven published short stories, he has also written for more than fifty newspapers and magazines, and is a frequent contributor to *Boys' Life, New Mexico Magazine, Persimmon Hill,* and *True West.* His Western novels cover a wide range. *The Lonesome Chisholm Trail* (Five Star Westerns, 2000) is an authentic cattle-drive story, while *Lonely Trumpet* (Five Star Westerns, 2002) is an historical novel about the first black graduate of West Point. *The Despoilers* (Five Star Westerns, 2002) and *Ghost Legion* (Five Star Westerns, 2005) are set in the Carolina backcountry during the Revolutionary War. *The Big Fifty* (Five Star Westerns, 2003) chronicles the slaughter of buffalo on the southern plains in the 1870s, while *East of the Border* (Five Star Westerns, 2004) is a comedy about the theatrical offerings of Buffalo Bill Cody, Wild Bill Hickok, and Texas Jack Omohundro, and *Camp Ford* (Five Star Westerns, 2005) tells about a Civil War baseball game between Union prisoners of war and Confederate guards. "Boggs's narrative voice captures the old-fashioned style of the past," *Publishers Weekly* said, and *Booklist* called him "among the best Western writers at work today." Boggs lives with his wife Lisa and son Jack in Santa Fé. His website is www.johnnyd boggs.com.

The employees of Thorndike Press hope you have enjoyed this Large Print book. All our Thorndike and Wheeler Large Print titles are designed for easy reading, and all our books are made to last. Other Thorndike Press Large Print books are available at your library, through selected bookstores, or directly from us.

For information about titles, please call:
    (800) 223-1244

or visit our Web site at:
    www.gale.com/thorndike
    www.gale.com/wheeler

To share your comments, please write:
    Publisher
    Thorndike Press
    295 Kennedy Memorial Drive
    Waterville, ME 04901